A DEVIOUS DAME

CHRIS LAING

Editorial Consultant: Cat London
Author Photo: Michèle LaRose
Design and Typography: Julie McNeill, McNeill Design Arts
Hamilton Street Scene courtesy of Janet Forjan,
www.hamiltonpostcards.com

Published as an ebook in 2019 by Chris Laing
A Devious Dame 978-992-1062-6—3 (Kindle)
A Devious Dame 978-1-989670-00-2 (EPUB)

DEDICATION

This book is dedicated to Michèle LaRose, my love, my support and my bosom buddy. You may enjoy her art and poetry at www.michelelarose.ca

PROLOGUE

Intermission was Ida Lucas's time to go to work.

The Harry Waller orchestra finished its first set with a rousing version of Count Basie's "One O'clock Jump" and the musicians, on their feet now, placed their instruments on their chairs and took their bow. The energetic lindy-hoppers crowded in front of the bandstand, still clapping their hands in appreciation – some of them calling out, "One more time." Others shuffled back to their tables – their spirits lifted but their limbs complaining.

Ida schmoozed her way along the front row of tables here in the Circus Roof lounge. Tonight, she was wearing a fashionable, but low-cut, blue gown that matched the colour of her eyes. Holding her shoulder-length blond hair back from her face with a manicured hand, she leaned down to greet her customers, allowing them a glimpse of her wares – a peck on the cheek for Adam Simpson, Plant Manager at Westinghouse Canada who, she noted with interest, was on his own tonight – a pat on the back for Lorenzo Rizzo, a recently-elected alderman on Hamilton's city council – and a subtle squeeze for W.J. (Billy) Johnson, president of the Tuckett Tobacco Company and Hamilton, Ontario's 'Businessman of the Year' for 1947'. To the women who accompanied them, she offered a polite nod along with a sweet smile.

Her job as a hostess here at the swanky Royal Connaught Hotel allowed Ida the opportunity to mingle with the city's male elite and, on a good night, to offer them the special attention they might no longer receive at home. For a fair price, of course.

From an early age, Ida believed that her gift-wrapped, sinuous body was her pathway to success in life: money, adoring men, travel to exotic places, parties and to hell with tomorrow. So

4

what if that meant abandoning a family life in the straight world? Just look at what happened to her own mother – married at 16 to a work-weary, loveless husband who laboured on the assembly line at National Steel Car during the week and he also had a week-end job on the cleaning staff at Hamilton General Hospital. Even so, her mother still had to scrimp in order to pay the bills for rent, food, clothing and everything else. Not to mention the burden of raising her three kids almost single-handed; all of them under six years of age, plus another on the way. Just getting enough to eat was a daily struggle during the Depression years and Ida vowed that she'd never, ever endure such misery in her own life.

Her chance to escape from that women's world of drudgery came at age 13 when one of Ida's male teachers had kept her after school and showed her how to make some easy money. That event changed the course of her life by revealing the power within her own body to shape a better future for herself than her mother could ever imagine.

She'd made only one big mistake along the way but she managed to put that behind her – now she could no longer become pregnant. And she believed that her young son would learn to make his own way in life just as she had done.

Ida felt good about herself as she glided with confidence among these proud and powerful men at the Connaught: she had what they wanted and she knew what it was worth to them. When her good looks faded, she was determined to have saved enough money to avoid the wretched life that her mother had endured before her early death.

At the centre table, Ida whispered into the right ear of Vincenzo Belcastro, Hamilton's new Mob boss, "The Chedoke Room after midnight," she said. "Camille is here from Montreal with a couple of her friends." Belcastro now filled the shoes of Dominic Tedesco, who'd made an unscheduled departure from that position last Christmas when he dared to defy the big boss in Buffalo. At that time, a local wit began his 'About Town' column in *The Hamilton Spectator*: "True to his reputation, 1947 went out with a bang for Dominic Tedesco."

After the last of their guests had departed, taking the Montreal visitors with them, Ida and her friend, Trixie, flopped onto a sofa in the Chedoke Room, kicking off their high heels to rest their aching feet on the coffee table. "I think I'm getting too damn old for this stuff," Trixie said. "My face hurts from smiling and that's not all – that big guy with Mr. Belcastro was just too rough – I had to set him straight when we were in the other room."

Ida opened her purse, removed a small bottle of pills, and rattled it toward her. "Here, Trix, try one of these. It'll relax you."

Trixie shook her head. "No, thanks. I heard those things can be habit-forming. And I need my money for my kids. Tell you the truth – I've been thinking about retiring from this game."

Ida paused after she'd counted out the bills from the small basket on the table by the bar. "I'd think twice about that, Honey. Where else could you earn half of this $145 that the big boys left behind for the pleasure of our company? Especially when you consider that a labourer at the Steel Company is earning only 50 bucks a week. I'm tellin' you, Trix, 1948 could be our best year ever."

CHAPTER ONE

It was a mild spring morning when I entered the White Spot Grill on King Street, near my office. Spiro shot me a dark look from behind the counter as he grunted a tray-load of dirty cups and saucers into an industrial dishwasher with a loud clank. The sharp tang of burnt toast hung in the air and I guessed that Madge was late for her early shift.

The food here was nothing special and the coffee was so-so but this joint was close to my office. And don't get me started about Spiro Kostas, its owner. He was a short, stocky guy with a thick, black moustache, and an even thicker chip on his shoulder. Spiro had reluctantly taken over this café after his father's recent heart attack and subsequent retirement.

"Don't often see you in here, Max. Now that you're a big-shot private dick with a fancy-schmancy assistant and a secretary to fetch your coffee."

I'd met him last summer when I opened my private detective agency on King Street, across from the Royal Connaught, and right off the bat he'd taken a spikey kind of attitude toward me. But with the ladies, of course, he was always the perfect gent as he told them – "Yes, Ma'am. Right away, Ma'am. My, you're looking swell today."

I ignored his 'big shot' remark as I slid onto the end stool at the counter. "A large carafe to go. If it ain't too much trouble."

He bounced his hard look off me but I didn't react. Then he motioned with his head toward the rear of the café. "Bob said he wanted to see you if you came in."

"Okay. I'll be back in a minute."

At the end of the row of booths, Spiro had rigged up a small table that looked like a cut-down student's desk. It was low enough that my veteran friend, Bob, could use it while seated aboard his wheeled dolly that he used to scoot himself around downtown to sell his pencils at the busiest locations. Bob had lost both his legs during that disastrous raid on Dieppe on August 19, 1942 – a date engraved into the memory of every Hamiltonian when 197 soldiers of the Royal Hamilton Light Infantry had been killed and many others were wounded or taken prisoner by the Germans.

Bob was puzzling over a Daily Racing Form, scribbling something in the margin as I limped toward him. He looked up with a familiar gesture, flicking back a shock of brown hair from his forehead, then he parked his pencil behind his right ear. "Hi-de-ho, Max. How goes it?"

"Everything's jake with me." I bent down to kneel on my good knee beside him and I noticed that Bob had placed his display box of pencils on the floor alongside the table. I looked at it more closely when I noticed that the top had been inlaid with several different types of wood in a diamond-shaped pattern. "That's a beautiful piece of work, Bob. Where did you get it?"

"Made it myself."

"Get out of here. You're pullin' my leg."

"I kid you not. Before the war, I was a carpenter at the Evel Casket Company. You might remember that big casket sign painted on the side of the building – it's east of downtown, beside that church near Tisdale and King East. I've still got all my tools so I pick up a few bucks doing small woodworking jobs."

I shook my head, grinning at him. "Just when you think you know someone, you find out he's a master craftsman."

Then I pointed at his paper. "Trying to pick me a winner at the Woodbine track?"

He gave me a sheepish grin, shaking his head while he set the paper aside, taking care not to topple the plate on which the blackened crusts of his toast lay discarded. "Nah, I wanted to talk to you about, um … I guess you'd call it a situation."

He shifted toward me and I noticed that he wore a small silver shield in his lapel, issued to all veterans at demobilization – 3 maple leaves joined on a single stem, a crown on top; a scroll at the bottom with the words, *General Service*. He often joked that it was his 'General's badge'.

"Tell me about this situation," I said.

"Well, I met this kid a couple weeks ago – a real nice boy, about 12 or 13. He came to my rescue when a wheel on my dolly got stuck in a sewer grate while I was trying to cross Merrick Street near Eaton's there. When he saw I was in trouble, this kid rushed over, waving his arms to stop the traffic then he got me going again. Since then, he's been around to the apartment a couple of times to help me and Aggie."

He paused for a long swig of his coffee.

"Okay, but what's this 'situation', Bob?"

"It's the boy. His name's Danny; he told me he lives with his mother over on York Street near Caroline, above the Langley Cleaners shop. He said she works at Robinson's department store during the day, cosmetics or something, as well as having a part-time job in the evenings."

"How come she's got two jobs? Doesn't the dad work?"

"No dad – I don't know what happened to him and neither does the boy because he disappeared when Danny was just a little squirt. Now the kid has a tough life – almost living on his own, from the sound of it."

"So what's your plan? You're not thinking of having the kid live with you, are you?"

"Jeez, no … not enough room in our little apartment. We'd like to help him but he's clammed up – refuses to tell us anything more about his home life. So …" Then he began to fidget with his coffee cup, turning it round and round on the little tabletop while his big, sad, blood-hound eyes did their job on my heart-strings.

"All right … what would you like *me* to do?"

He puffed out the breath he was holding. "Well, I was thinking you might meet this kid, maybe find out what's going on with his mother. See if there's some way we could help him."

I shrugged. "But if he won't open up with you, what chance would *I* have? Do you think he's being harmed in some way?"

"Not physically, no. But it can't be good for a boy that age to be left to his own devices. He won't admit it but he needs some help. Then I remembered you told me that your own childhood was, ah – sorta similar to his … so I figured maybe you could meet him and, you know, we could go from there."

I gave him a good dose of my patented 'Max Dexter hard look' but he didn't even flinch. "You sure know how to push a guy's buttons, pal."

After I paid Spiro for the coffee, I stepped out onto King Street where I joined the folks bustling to their workplaces. Last Sunday was Easter and the weather had turned unseasonably warm with an early whiff of spring in the air. Judging by the energized pace of the downtown foot traffic, it was clear that Hamiltonians were anxious to erase the memory of the too-long winter of 1947-48. I read in *The Hamilton Spectator* that even the Skyway Drive-In theatre in Stoney Creek planned to re-open this week-end.

Tiny stopped the elevator on the second floor of my building, tipping his cap to a pair of chatty secretaries who thanked him for the lift. He was as skinny as a rake handle and about the same height, maybe a whisker over five feet with his boots on. He watched the women scurry down the hallway, toward the busy LoShiavo Insurance Agency, trailing a cloud of nose-wrinkling perfume. The shorter babe glanced back over her shoulder and blew him a kiss. He slid the door closed then winked at me; I was the only passenger as we continued upward.

He hoisted his rear-end onto the edge of his cut-down stool, a grin on his pixie face as he glanced at my pants. "Your fly's open."

I covered myself with my left hand in a reflex motion and looked down. It wasn't open. I turned back to him. "What the hell?"

"April Fool, Max." He laughed as he pointed to a 1948 calendar from the Gillies-Guy Coal Company that he'd taped to the wall near the elevator's control panel. "But at least I waited until those secretaries got off."

I grinned back at him. "Good one, Tiny. I guess that makes us even for my Hallowe'en prank last fall."

On the third floor, I carefully turned the doorknob at the Max Dexter Associates office, easing it open. It wasn't likely that my partner, Isabel, or Phyllis, our secretary, would have booby-trapped the door but these were heady times in post-war Hamilton so you couldn't be too careful.

But I met with no surprises – Phyllis was machine-gunning her typewriter and Isabel was on the phone, nodding her head, making notes while she listened. I parked the carafe on the coffee table for later.

Iz wiggled her fingers at me as I walked toward my office and she continued on the phone. Phyllis said, "Morning, Max. I have to finish this; it's rush-rush." She went on with her typing without looking up. She was wearing a light blue dress in a floral pattern and I thought it made her look a bit … well, frumpy. But I only knew what most guys know about women's-wear and you could fit that into a thimble with room left over. Maybe I'd mention it to Iz and she might offer Phyl some advice.

I opened the door to my own office a few inches – I didn't see anything on the floor to trip me up but when I swung the door open I was smothered in a blizzard of confetti from above.

"April Fool," came the chorus. God, it was hard being a good sport so early in the day. But I forced a smile and I even pitched in to sweep up some of the damn confetti.

Later, Isabel and I were seated at the long table by the window in my office where she pointed to a page on the ledger before us. "Our accounts receivable are lagging behind our payables again."

I couldn't keep the grin off my face and I edged my chair closer to hers, slipping my arm around her shoulders – she wore a pale green sweater this morning with a matching cardigan that complemented her shoulder-length, red hair. Not to mention the form-fitting black skirt that I couldn't stop admiring. I lowered my voice to whisper in her ear. "I love it when you use your accountant's lingo with me, Iz. It sends a tingle up my spine."

She gave me that special look women used instead of cuffing you behind the ear. Then she extended her left hand, waggling her ring finger, admiring for the umpteenth time the lustre of her mother's pearl engagement ring with the sparkle of diamonds that encircled it. This frequent performance, always in pantomime, was for the benefit of Yours Truly and carried with it the not-so-subtle message – 'when are you going to get off your duff, Buster, and finalize our wedding plans?' 'Soon' was no longer an acceptable response.

We'd gotten engaged at Christmastime and had been negotiating our wedding date ever since. I'd been dragging my feet because I still harboured some nagging doubts about my ability to become a good husband and father. When I considered the pitiful performance of my own parents, it scared the hell out of me that I might follow in their negligent foot-steps. I carried their genes, after all.

But it was clear that I couldn't go on dithering like this for much longer – genes or no genes. Isabel was eager to start a family. Recently, she'd taken to reminding me that we were both over 30 now and not getting any younger.

I inhaled a deep breath, counted to three and dived off the cliff. "Tonight, Iz. I promise we'll set the date." I reached for her hand, planting a loud smooch on it.

She flashed those green eyes at me. "Deal," she said. "Tonight's the night."

I reached over to my desk to nab the red file folder containing a proposal from the Nelligan and Nelligan law firm to undertake some surveillance work in a marital case. "I'm still not comfy with this divorce stuff. Sneaking around, spying on people who are tired of their spouses just ain't my cup of tea. Y'know, taking on these cases might even put off some potential customers – divorce is still a touchy subject for a lot of people."

Isabel straightened in her chair, shimmering a look at me that said, 'you're such an old fuddy-duddy' then she grasped my hand in a firm squeeze. "We're meeting with Jacqueline Nelligan this morning at her law office to review this proposal. She's adamant that we keep a low profile because she's concerned that even a hint of scandal might be picked up by the newspapers. So I don't think we need to worry about our reputation here."

I squirmed in my chair. "I don't know –"

"Don't forget, Max, this work pays the bills in addition to establishing our reputation with the other law firms in town as thorough investigators whose information stands up in court. So the next time they need some investigative work maybe they'll think of us."

She was right, as usual, but it still felt sleazy to me. "How about this – I'll agree to take these divorce cases if we can hire out the leg-work under our supervision."

When Iz leaned forward I recognized the devil, dancing in her eyes. "Like we contracted for the services of Robert Trépanier last summer?"

The very mention of that bugger's name still zapped a sizzle up my spine. Trépanier was a smooth character who'd served with the Vandoos during the war then relocated to Hamilton last year from Québec. He worked for Wentworth Security Services here in town and when we needed extra help last year on the Jake Benson murder case we'd hired him for a couple of weeks. But he took an immediate personal interest in Isabel and, *Boy,* did that test my patience. Which is a polite way of saying that I was jealous as hell when I observed Iz and Phyllis swooning over his suave, cosmopolitan manner – even letting his name roll off their tongues in their best high-school French, pronouncing Robert as *Row-Bear.* Then they would swoon like bobbysoxers at a Frank Sinatra concert.

But that was ancient history – Iz and I were engaged to be married now. So Trépanier would have to set his damn sights on somebody else.

"*Row-bear* would be an excellent choice," I said. "I'll call his boss to arrange it."

She gave me a sly smile that I couldn't decipher then she reached forward to pluck something from my jacket. "It won't be long now, Max."

"What won't be long?"

She had removed a few stray pieces of confetti from my lapel, fanning them on the table like a gambler showing a winning hand. "Confetti time."

CHAPTER TWO

Hamilton's legal eagles liked to flock together in the heart of the city – close enough to the court house on Main Street so they could walk. And handy enough to the big banks so they wouldn't have to tote their bulging money bags too far for deposit.

The Piggott Building on James Street South near Main stood tall in the very heart of this district where the Nelligan and Nelligan law offices were located on the 15th floor. Iz and I were right on time for our appointment with the managing partner.

When we boarded the elevator in the marbled lobby, I recognized the dark-haired operator in her smart, military-styled blue uniform from my last visit here. She glanced toward Isabel, giving her a quick once-over then turned back to me, raising her right eyebrow as though she approved of my choice in women.

"Floor please," she said.

I'd forgotten her name so I checked the small brass plate pinned to her trim-fitting, blue uniform. "We're heading to the 15th, Noretta. And don't take any detours."

She whisked us up near the top of the building and when she opened the doors she turned to my partner. "I've seen this Romeo in here before, Miss. You've got your hands full if you think you can train him."

Iz gave her a woman-to-woman smile and she lowered her voice. "You're tellin' me, Sister."

The Nelligan and Nelligan law firm occupied a large suite of offices along the south side of the building with an expansive view up James Street South toward the Mountain. The lawyers and the office manager occupied the private offices with the windows; the secretaries, stenographers and clerical staff were corralled in a large central area, alive with the clacking of typewriters that reminded me of small arms fire.

I approached the receptionist who operated a telephone switchboard near the entrance and passed her my business card, "To see Miss Nelligan," I said. She nodded her head, inserted a plug into the board and murmured a few words into the microphone hanging from her neck. Almost immediately a smartly-dressed secretary arrived to lead us to the corner office where we entered.

Jacqueline Nelligan walked from behind her half-acre of mahogany desk to shake our hands then led us to a conference table with a view up James Street South where the morning sun glinted off the windows at St. Joseph's Hospital.

Jackie was a handsome woman of a certain age – a few streaks of gray in her dark hair, slim and trim in a tailored beige suit, with a decisive air of authority about her. A lawyer friend had told me that she had one of the sharpest legal minds in Hamilton. Her elder brother was the other Nelligan in the firm's name.

We shook hands then settled at the table where she offered us coffee.

Iz wiggled her head. "Thanks, but we have another meeting right after this one."

"All right then, straight down to business." She opened a red folder in front of her. "Thanks for seeing me right away. You've had a chance to review the Peterson file I sent you?"

"We have," Iz said. "On the surface, it looks like a straightforward divorce matter."

"That's what I thought after my initial meeting with Mr. Peterson. But now, there's been a wrinkle in the case."

"Not usually a good sign," I said.

"No, it isn't. You see, I happened to meet his wife for the first time a couple of weeks ago at a fundraiser for a new Art Gallery of Hamilton building on land owned by the Royal Botanical Gardens near McMaster University, and she impressed me very much indeed. She's a fashion consultant in Toronto and has retained her maiden name for business purposes. I found her to be an intelligent, thoughtful woman and I liked her right away. So it surprised me when Mr. Peterson, a longtime client of mine, asked me to represent him in this divorce case. But I've been in this business long enough to know that appearances are often deceiving so I'm not dismissing the possibility that she may be the guilty party.

"Now, the file I sent you contained all the information I had at that time." She paused to pour a half-glass of water from a carafe on the table, took a few sips then set it aside.

"I've just received this report from a private investigator Mr. Peterson hired in Toronto to follow his wife and take some candid photographs to support his charge of infidelity.

"But the problem is – these photos are artfully shot: taken from a distance, they're somewhat grainy, so I became suspicious – you know how lawyers are. If it's a ruse, it's very well done. Even after meeting his wife I couldn't swear that the woman in these photos is not actually her."

She set aside the file folder containing the photos, then opened a small envelope to remove a single picture. "I asked Mr. Peterson if he had other photos of his wife and he provided me with this one." She slid it across the table and I angled it toward Isabel so we could both view it.

"A wedding picture," Iz said. "My, she's a beautiful woman. But he looks somewhat older than she. How long have they been married?"

"Five years," the lawyer said. "You'll see that she appears to be the same woman in the photos I've just received."

She passed us the folder and we flipped through those photos in silence: long shots of a couple at a cocktail party; to me, she looked like the same woman in the wedding photo. Her escort here was tall and thin – a good-looking guy but always in profile in these shots, appearing to be about her age. He could be mistaken for Mr. Peterson. Another photo showed the couple on the dance floor at some fancy-dress affair in a hotel ballroom.

Other photos showed the woman with the same man as they entered an apartment building together. The remaining pictures caught them as they attended a reception, obviously happy to be in each other's company.

I passed the folder back to the lawyer. "I presume you're suspicious about these because the man she's with won't be easy to identify – we see the back of his head or he's in profile and sometimes out of focus."

"That's correct," she said. "I looked up the name of the security company on the report, T.J. Martin Security Services, but it's not listed in the Toronto phone directory."

I made a note of the company's name. "I still have a few contacts in Toronto so I could check on that. But do you think Mr. Peterson is the type of man who'd hire someone to falsify evidence?"

She squinted, thinking about that. "I don't know but I'm counting on you two to find out.
I've met with the man a number of times over the past few years and he's been all business with me. He has an active portfolio of real estate investments and we've looked after transfers of deeds in addition to other business matters of that sort. I must say, he's quite impressed with his own success but many of these well-to-do businessmen are like that. "

Then she turned to Iz. "How about you, my dear, have you met him or his wife?"

"No, I haven't. But I can see why it's puzzling you. What would you like us to do, Miss Nelligan?"

"Oh, don't be so formal. Please – call me Jackie. I'd like you and Max to start from scratch on this case: dig into their lives to see if there are any grounds to support Mr. Peterson's claim."

When we stood to shake hands with her, Iz said, "Sorry we can't spend more time with you this morning but we have another meeting nearby in a few minutes."

Walking with us to the door, Jackie said, "This case smells fishy to me and I won't take it to court without knowing a lot more about this couple than I do now. I know you won't let me down."

CHAPTER THREE

Isabel had arranged a meeting with the assistant manager at the Bank of Montreal on the corner of Main and James Streets where I kept my business account. She'd attempted to explain to me why Max Dexter Associates would be better off using one type of account versus another but it was all Greek to me. "This is your specialty, Iz. Let's just see this manager guy and you can show me where we sign."

After our brief meeting we were leaving the bank through the side entrance onto James Street South when we were stopped short by two sharp explosions that I recognized as gunshots, echoing off the tall buildings nearby. For a spine-tingling moment we didn't move; a young mother with a baby carriage froze in her tracks, alert but confused as her child began to wail. An old duffer in a tired black suit was pointing in the direction of the YMCA across the road at the corner of Jackson Street, just a few doors away.

"I think it's a car backfiring," a young guy wearing a Hamilton Wildcats football jersey said, sounding more hopeful than certain. Then the blast of several more shots had folks scattering; some crouching low against the bank building while others rushed away in the opposite direction.

I grasped Isabel's arm, pointing toward St. Paul's Presbyterian Church beside the bank. We hunched down as we scuttled for cover in the tall bushes in front of the church but we stumbled when a bullet whizzed past us, whanging off the granite pedestal supporting the church's announcement board.

In that instant, the gun-fire transported me to the beach at Bernières-sur-Mer on D-Day in 1944. Crossing the Channel in the murky pre-dawn, six-foot seas crashing over us and the rain of German artillery shells splashing in the water as we neared the shore, many of us were still sea-sick, reeking of vomit and the stench of diesel fumes from the boats' engines as we stumbled onto Juno beach in the dark gloom. Charging toward the sea-wall, I was blown off my feet by a German mortar that slammed into a tank beside me; then my world went black.

That memory shattered when Isabel let out a sharp gasp as she staggered beside me. I managed to guide her further into the bushes where we hunched down on our knees. She was clutching her left arm, her eyes wide as she stared at me, gasping, "I've been shot, Max."

I eased her to a sitting position then peeled back her fingers from her coat where a ragged slash in the left sleeve was ringed with blood. She held her breath as I carefully removed the sleeve from her arm. "My God," she gasped through clenched teeth. "That stings like the devil."

Police sirens began to wail and I tried to block them out. I unfolded my clean handkerchief to wrap around the wound where a bullet had grazed a track along her forearm. Then I reached for her right hand and placed it over the bloody handkerchief.

"I doesn't look like a deep wound but keep some pressure on it to stop the bleeding." Then I slid her coat around her shoulders as she began to shiver. "How does it feel now – like a bee sting or an end-of-the-world pain?"

She looked up at me, her lips still pinched but her eyes a bit steadier now. "Not the end of the world but … I have to clench my teeth so I won't scream. We need to get to St. Joe's, Max. Right now."

I leaned down to plant a kiss her on the forehead. "You're a courageous woman, Iz. We could've used more soldiers like you overseas."

She gave me a brave smile but she winced as she turned to look across the street at the source of those gunshots. The shooting had stopped for the moment but the acrid smell of gunpowder still fouled the air and I heard more sirens whining in the distance. Pedestrians remained crouched against the buildings on James Street, afraid to move.

I nudged a branch aside for a better view eastward onto Jackson Street: a motorcycle cop had hopped off his bike, his gun extended in both hands as he was approaching two gunmen who stood with their hands in the air beside a black sedan abandoned in the centre of the roadway near the YMCA. An eerie hush gripped the wary by-standers as though everyone was holding his breath, eyes fixed on that cop as he moved slowly toward those shooters.

A police cruiser, its tires squealing, raced in from the opposite direction, blocking the car from that side. Two police officers, their guns drawn, joined the motorcycle cop and they cuffed the crooks – one of whom wore a blue baseball cap, pulled low over his eyes; the other guy had on a black fedora with a high crown that looked like a cowboy hat. Then they were muscled over to the police car and hauled away.

The motorcycle cop was speaking with a businessman on the sidewalk who was clutching his briefcase to his chest. A moment later, they turned to enter the large building behind the YMCA – its sign read, Canadian Porcelain Company Ltd.

You didn't need to be a private detective to know that we'd just witnessed an attempted robbery and the cop on the bike had arrived at the scene just in the nick of time.

I spotted a Veteran's Cab slowing down on James Street, its driver rubbernecking at the police activity until I stepped from behind the bushes to wave him down. I was glad to see my friend Dave behind the wheel.

"What's happening, Max? I thought I heard gunshots, then those police sirens."

"Take us to St. Joe's emergency; I'll tell you on the way."

Dave was fretting over Isabel as he fumbled with her good arm, trying to guide her into the cab's front seat but she pushed his arm away. "Stop being such a fussbudget, Dave. It's not as though I'm having a baby."

He gunned his cab the six blocks up James Street to St. Joseph's Hospital at the foot of the Mountain while I told him what little we knew about the attempted robbery.

"Wait here," he said as he jumped from the cab at the Emergency entrance and ran inside for a moment. Then he hurried back with a wheelchair. "If we rush in with Isabel in the chair, they're sure to examine her right away."

I guessed he'd done this before because a nurse met us at the admissions desk just as we hustled through the doorway.

"Chop-chop," she said, "We don't dawdle with gunshot wounds." She wheeled Iz into an examination cubicle with me in tow. Dave left to park his cab in the lot.

The nurse waved me over to the hospital bed where she was helping Isabel out of the wheelchair. The antiseptic hospital odour got my nose twitching and I stifled a sneeze. "Give me a hand here, Mister, we'll get the patient's coat off before she gets onto the bed." She turned back to Iz, "What's your name, Miss?"

"It's Isabel O'Brien," she said, sending the nurse a sharp look. "And I assure you that I'm not an invalid; it's only a superficial scratch on my arm."

The nurse stiffened and she stood a little taller, looking starchier than her white uniform and cap. "Oh, I see. I suppose you also know that a 'superficial' gunshot wound could cause internal bleeding, not to mention the risk of serious infection." Hands on her slim hips now, she sounded like a school principal, "And Lord knows how many dirty pockets that bullet was in before it was fired."

Iz appraised her for a moment then she glanced at the name tag pinned to her uniform. "You're right, Ann Sutherland. So let's get on with it."

I noted the flicker of a grin on the nurse's lips as she held Iz's good arm, helping her to stand. Then I slipped Iz's coat off her shoulders while the nurse guided her onto the bed. "Now just lie back on the pillow, Isabel, and we'll see what we've got here."

Nurse Sutherland took care removing the handkerchief that I'd placed over the wound and Iz's lips compressed as it was peeled off. "There's still some bleeding," the nurse said. "I'll clean that up before the doctor arrives. He won't be long now."

A long 10 minutes later, a brawny, young guy wearing a white coat and a stethoscope, jangled back the curtain to enter the cubicle. "Name's Darren Murphy," he said. "I hear we've got a gunshot wound."

I stared at him for a moment: he was as fresh-faced and eager as a guy who might've graduated from med school last Friday. "You heard right," I said then I stepped away from the bed. "This is Isabel, my fiancée. We witnessed an attempted robbery downtown when a stray bullet grazed her arm."

He nodded his head as though this were an everyday occurrence in post-war Hamilton as he moved to Isabel's bedside where he bent over to study the wound on the inside of her forearm. Then he pulled on a pair of rubber gloves and probed the area lightly with his fingers. When he'd finished his examination, he smiled at her. "You're a lucky lady, so you are. That bullet didn't go deep enough to reach the artery there. We'll treat it like a second-degree burn with one of the new antibiotic ointments then wrap it up. You should be right as rain in a week or so. But if it doesn't show some improvement in a few days you should see your family doctor."

Isabel asked him, "Will it leave a scar?"

"Just enough to remind you of your close call."

"Thank you, Doctor. Can I go back to work when we're finished here?"

He snapped off his gloves, a twinkle in his eye. "Depends upon the type of work you do. If you were working on the open hearth at Dofasco or the Steel Company I'd say give it a few days."

She grinned at him. "No open hearth. No heavy lifting – only my fountain pen."

"Well, your system has suffered a shock but if you feel well enough, go ahead. Now, Miss Sutherland will show you how to apply the medication and change the dressing."

As he hustled away, he called back over his shoulder, "And try to stay out of gun fights."

Dave dropped us off in front of our office on King Street and was out of the car, opening the door, reaching for Isabel's good arm before she could restrain him.

Her lips tightened for a fleeting moment but she surprised me when she said, "Thank you, Dave." His eyes were saucers when she pecked him on the cheek, "You've been a big help."

In the office, I was helping Iz remove her coat when Phyllis caught sight of the blood stains on her left sleeve and she was speechless for a moment. Then she gasped when Iz turned toward her and she saw the bandage on her arm.

"Oh my gosh, Isabel. What's happened to you? You weren't injured in all that shooting I heard, were you? Those gunshots sounded so loud that I thought the ruckus might be next door, but now …"

Iz walked steadily across the room to sit on the couch with Phyllis close beside her, still speaking, "If there's anything I can –"

Isabel held up her hand to quiet her, then described what we'd observed at the crime scene. "But I'm okay now, Phyl, so just calm down. One of those stray bullets grazed my arm then a doctor at St. Joe's patched me up. He said I'll be fine; there's no serious damage. So there's no need to worry."

"But –"

"No buts – here's my plan. I have to see Emma Rose after lunch to drop off some figures I've worked out for her – it won't take me long. Then I'm going home to rest up for this evening. Max is taking me out to dinner." Then she turned toward me, eyebrows raised.

"That was our intention. If you're feeling up to going out."

"Of course, I am. I'm not as fragile as you seem to think, Max. You heard the doctor – we just have to avoid gun-fights."

Phyllis sat dumbfounded, eyes wide, her mouth hanging open.

After lunch, young Rick, a copy boy in the newsroom at *The Hamilton Spectator* next door, plopped an early edition of the paper onto my desk, still reeking of printers' ink. I dug into my pants pocket, then flipped him a fifty-cent-piece for the week. The paper was only three cents a copy but when I was a youngster I delivered the old *Hamilton Herald* and I always appreciated a good tipper.

He snagged the coin out of the air one-handed, as if he played centre field for the Hamilton Cardinals. "Hey, thanks, Max. Guess you heard about that attempted robbery, eh? It happened too late for this edition. In fact, your Uncle Scotty's still at the scene now with a photographer."

Phyllis had followed him into my office, all ears for more news about that foiled hold-up.

I pointed at the kid, "What's the buzz in the newsroom?"

"They're saying the motorcycle cop is the big hero – I forget his name, Glen or Glebe – but after the shooting, he held the crooks at gunpoint until the reinforcements arrived. They were trying to rob the manager of that business behind the YMCA when he came back from the bank with the week's payroll. Must've been a lot of moolah, Max. But how would they know that he had a briefcase full of cash?"

I smiled at him: he was hopping from one foot to the other as though he had to go to the bathroom. "Maybe they had an informant inside the company," I said, watching the light bulb flash in his head.

"Yeah, maybe you're right." He made a dash for the door. "Gotta get back to the newsroom. Don't wanna miss anything."

Later, I called George Kemper at Wentworth Security Services. He was one of my instructors in Regina when I joined the RCMP before the war; since his retirement from the Mounties he operated his own security business here in his home town.

"Long time no see, Max. How's tricks?"

"I'm doin' all right. And Isabel sends her greetings."

I pictured him leaning back in his oversized leather chair, probably with a big, fat stogie clamped in his mug, looking more like that movie gangster, Edward G. Robinson, than a retired copper. "How *is* the little lady? I'm glad you haven't scared her off yet."

I was tempted to tell him about the shooting this morning but I changed my mind. He'd only badger me for every tiny detail and who needed that? "Nope, Isabel's still with me. In fact, we're now engaged to be married."

His breath come out in a whoosh, as though I'd punched him in his ample gut. "If that don't beat all. How'd you manage that? I wouldn't have bet a helluva lot on your chances with a classy woman like her."

When he stopped laughing, I said, "Love conquers all, George."

"Well, I guess it must. I wish you both the best of luck. Congratulations. Also –"

"Thanks, but can we get down to business now?"

He huffed out a Tallulah Bankhead sigh. "Okay, shoot."

"Remember when we borrowed the services of Trépanier last summer?"

He grunted.

"We'd like to do it again. Maybe a couple of weeks or so

on a surveillance job. We'd cover his salary, of course."

I waited while I listened to him riffling through some pages. "When would you need him?"

"The client wants us to start next week."

More page flipping. "Yeah, I think we can do that. I'll book him for next Monday. Now, gimme the low-down about your wedding plans …"

When I returned the Nelligan file to Phyllis, I said, "Did Isabel seem okay when she left?"

She picked up on the concern in my voice. "She says she's feeling fine, Max, but I'm worried about her, too. I guess you know better than I do that there's no point in arguing once her mind's made up."

I grinned at her. "Some people call it strength of character, but I'm learning to live with it."

"You're a lucky man, Max. I think she's the perfect woman for you."

I frowned, wondering what she meant by that.

"Isabel said that she'll pick you up at your apartment for dinner tonight." Then she shuffled through some papers on her desk, coming up with a scribbled note. "Seven o'clock sharp, Max and don't forget to wear your good suit."

"Okay, thanks." I tapped my fingers on the Peterson file. "Please make sure that Isabel sees this tomorrow. Trépanier will be joining us next week so Iz will look after the financial arrangements."

Her cheeks bloomed and her eyelids were fluttering in a little dance. "He's coming back?"

I was afraid she might faint. "You okay, Phyl?"

She reached across her desk, grasping my wrist. "Is it true, Max? Or is this an April fool's joke?"

"No joke. He'll be doing some surveillance work for us – maybe a couple of weeks."

Her face aglow, she was clutching the Nelligan file to her breast now as though it were the man himself. "I think he's just dreamy."

Back at my desk, I felt guilty that I wasn't with Iz, at least to provide some moral support. But I knew she'd think I was over-reacting and would tell me to stop fussing. I got back to work.

I referred to the notes I'd made while we visited the Nelligan law office this morning. T. J. Martin Security Services in Toronto wasn't much to go on and Jackie Nelligan said there was no listing in the Toronto phone book. I checked my copy of the Toronto edition of *Vernon's Street Directory* but couldn't find it – nothing in the Hamilton edition either. I began to wonder if this Martin outfit might be a cover for some shady photographer who provided his clients with photos that 'proved' whatever they wished.

I dialed RCMP headquarters in Toronto where I'd been stationed before the war. Then I had second thoughts about talking to the person I had in mind and quickly hung up – the receiver was sweaty in my palm. I took a couple of deep breaths to settle myself, then redialed and asked for Special Constable Wendy Crane.

Women had been employed in the Force as 'Specials' as far back as 1900 but they were still ineligible for appointment to full Constables, even though they often did the same damn work. Wendy had gained a degree of notoriety among the RCMP brass because she often pointed out the unfairness of that situation. When you're dealing with offenders, male or female, she would correctly say, there was always the risk of being injured or even killed – whatever your friggin' gender.

We'd become a hot item before I shipped overseas in '39 but our relationship had dried up and blown away like many other romances during wartime. I hadn't spoken with her since. As I was waiting, a vivid memory of Wendy and I flashed through my mind – we were jitterbugging to Lionel Hampton's orchestra at the Palace Pier in Toronto. Even the dance floor seemed to vibrate as Hamp drove the band through a dynamite rendition of his theme song, "Flyin' Home." Man, that was a night – we were really flyin' in that dance pavilion.

I heard a click in my ear, then, "Special Constable Crane here."

I lowered my voice to a raspy growl, "When is the RCMP going to come to its senses and appoint women as Constables, the same as men?"

Silence on the line, then, "Pardon me?"

I was about to respond when she said, "Wait-a-minute … it's that weasel, Max Dexter, isn't it? You're finally calling me after all these years?"

"Good to hear your voice, Wendy. I guess it has been a while."

"A while? Cripes, I haven't clapped eyes on you since you went off to war. A helluva long time for a gal to wait for a guy who said, 'I'll be sure to stay in touch, Honey'."

"I said that?"

"Damn right."

I could feel my face flush with guilt and I began to sweat. "I'm sorry, Wendy. I hope you'll accept my apology for the long absence. I know it's a feeble excuse, but when I arrived in Britain in 1940, I was swept away by the war and my former life back home just seemed to vanish. On my first night in London, I had to take shelter in a tube station during a bombing raid. Then life became more difficult after that."

"I didn't know if you were dead or alive, Max. No letter, no postcard – nothing at all. I thought you might've been killed in action or locked up in one of those POW camps in Germany. I even tried to get some information from the Army but I couldn't learn a thing about you."

I blinked, feeling another stab of remorse. "I'm truly sorry, Wendy. I was wounded overseas: almost lost a leg but I'm getting around well enough now. I didn't get back to Hamilton until '46; the RCMP wouldn't take me back because of my limp and the Hamilton police also gave me a pass. I was unsure about what to do because I wanted to stay in police work. Since that wasn't possible I'm now in business for myself as a private investigator. And I hope we might still be friends."

During the awkward pause that followed, even the hum on the line seemed to be thumbing its nose at me. I tried putting myself in her shoes – imagining how I might feel if the situation were reversed. It didn't feel good which gave me an inkling as to why she wasn't anxious to speak with me now. I was holding my breath while I awaited her reply.

"After years of no news from you, I decided to start dating again, Max. I learned that there's nothing better for a forgotten lover's broken heart than to find a swell guy and get married."

I felt a sudden wave of relief wash over me. "Good for you. That's great news. Congratulations."

"Thank you. But what about you, Max? I suppose you left a string of broken hearts overseas. Or maybe you even returned with a British war bride?"

"No, nothing like that," I said. "But I have met someone special since I've been back. In fact, she's my partner in our fledgling detective agency. And yes, we're engaged to be married."

"I see. But I don't suppose that's the reason for your call."

"Ah … no. I do have a small favour to ask. We're working on a divorce case and I'm trying to track down a security company in Toronto. I was hoping you might help me out."

She paused again while I fidgeted. She had every right to be angry about my failure to stay in touch so I understood why she might tell me now to take a hike. "While I was waiting for you to come on the line, I was thinking about the old days," I told her. "And I remembered what a great time we had when Lionel Hampton was playing at the Palace Pier. That was a night to remember."

It took her a moment to reply but the chill in her voice had warmed a little. "Yes, it was, Max. And I was hoping we'd have many more like that."

I apologized again. "I hope you might forgive me now." I could hear the bustle of her busy office in the background while I fidgeted, waiting for her reply.

She finally said, "All right, Max, for old time's sake. Now, tell me what you need."

I released the breath I was holding. "Thank you. I don't have much to go on but I do have a name. It's 'T.J. Martin Security Services' – apparently this guy's an investigator who did some work on a divorce case for a Hamilton man. But I suspect that he's not on the up-and-up. No listing for him in the phone book or the street directory in either Toronto or Hamilton so I'm hoping you might run a check on the guy for me. Perhaps you could ask around the office – see if anyone else might know about him."

"We're run off our feet here – you know the drill. And I can't let the Inspector catch me doing private work, so it might take me a few days."

"Zielinkski's still there?"

"Yep. And he's still a big pain in the you-know-where. In fact, we have an office pool on whether he'll retire before one of us shoots him."

I laughed along with her. "Thanks for your help, Wendy. I really appreciate it."

After I gave her my office number, I wondered if her hubby was a better man than Max Dexter. He was surely treating her better than I had.

CHAPTER FOUR

Bob lived with his sister, Aggie, in a small apartment at the rear of the Family Cleaners building on James Street North near the corner of Merrick Street, where I'd agreed to meet him later that afternoon. I limped up King William to James Street then crossed over to the City Hall side of the street where I noticed a one-armed vet wearing an army field-cap; he was stationed near the wide stairway at the front entrance of the weather-darkened, stone building.

The empty left sleeve of the guy's grungy suit jacket was tucked into the side pocket. He wore that sallow, hollowed-out look of a years-long prisoner of war and in his right hand he gripped a coffee cup with the red imprint, *Majestic Grill*. In the cup were a few coins that he rattled toward pedestrians, most of whom looked the other way as they passed him by.

His defeated grey eyes held mine as I limped over to stand beside him. "Where'd you serve, bud?" I said.

He remained silent for a moment then cleared his throat. "Overseas."

"I figured that much. Why don't we cross the street to Zeller's there – I'll buy you a cup of coffee at the lunch bar."

He shook his head. "Don't need your pity, Mister." Then he rattled his cup toward me. "But I could use a bit of change."

We stared at each other without speaking, then I took a peek in my wallet – only a $5 bill remained. I hesitated for a second, then folded the bill in half, stuck it in his cup and said, "Keep your pecker up, Pal."

He gave me a brief nod of his head, then slowly looked away. I could've felt disappointed by his lethargic response but I didn't know what horrors he might've endured.

I hiked down James North from City Hall, past Eaton's block-long department store and crossed Merrick Street to Bob's apartment. I knocked then entered through the door off the back alley behind the Family Cleaners shop that faced onto James Street.

"No need to roll out the red carpet," I called out; then I made my way down a dark hallway toward the living room where it was reeking of peanut butter.

I heard him speaking to someone inside before he raised his voice. "Come on through, Max. We just stopped for a snack."

Bob was seated on his low chair, waving me into the room. "I'd like you to meet my new pal, Danny Lucas. Then I could make you a sandwich."

"Thanks anyway on the sandwich; I had a big lunch." I liked peanut butter as well as I liked a kick in the rear end with a frozen boot.

When I turned to the kid, he stood up: he was short and skinny and I wondered if Bob might've been a bit generous when he'd told me this boy was about 12 or 13 years old. His tee shirt and pants were almost clean but rumpled as though he'd slept in them. And that blond hair curling over the back of his shirt collar told me he hadn't seen a barber for a while.

He swallowed what he was chewing, then croaked, "How do you do, Sir?"

I grinned at him then shook his hand, ignoring his embarrassment about his breaking voice. "Doin' just fine," I said. "But you can drop the 'Sir' – I was just an enlisted man."

Bob bellowed a laugh, then touched the kid's arm. "Don't mind Max. He was a military police sergeant during the war – and he thinks he's quite the joker."

I sat on a straight-back chair beside the kid. "Bob tells me you've been helping him with some chores. Sounds like you might be a member of the Eaton's Good Deed Radio Club."

His lips twitched in a near-smile. "Nope. But sometimes I listen to that program on Saturday mornings."

"So what's the good deed we're doing for Bob this afternoon?"

"He wants us to move the couch and chairs over to the far wall so we can clean this room."

"Aggie's got a bee in her bonnet about spring cleaning," Bob said. "So I told her to leave the living room to me and I'd get some help to do it today."

That sounded like his contrived way to have me meet young Danny but I figured the kid wouldn't give it a second thought. We spent the next hour or so pushing the furniture aside, waxing and polishing the floor, then dusting the furniture and washing the big window with the million-dollar view of the parking lot across from Eaton's.

Danny marvelled at Bob's ability to get around the apartment when he swung himself off his dolly. Aggie had bought a pair of elbow pads at Sam Manson's Sporting Goods store that she'd adapted to fit over his stumps. Then she'd shortened all his pants so they folded over the pads and that allowed him to propel himself around on the linoleum floors here while using his hands as paddles.

The tautness of his khaki army-surplus shirt told you that his upper body was as well-muscled as Whipper Billy Watson's. In fact, his chest and arms were so strong that he could balance on one hand while he propelled himself onto his chair. As a result, Bob was the very last guy you'd challenge to an arm-wrestling contest at the Dog and Gun pub on York Street.

When we'd finished cleaning, he directed us to replace the furniture in a new arrangement, following the plan drawn up by Aggie on the back of a paper place-mat from the lunch bar at Kresge's five-and-dime.

"I feel a lot better," Bob said when we sat on the couch beside his chair. "That was a good workout."

I caught the kid's eye and we grinned at each other.

"Don't think it hasn't been fun," I told Bob. "But I've got another appointment soon."

"Me too," Danny said as we both stood and headed for the door before Bob could dream up another chore.

Outside on Merrick Street I gave the kid a pat on his back. "Thanks for helping Bob and Aggie. They've taken quite a shine to you."

"I hope I can be like Bob when I grow up."

"You do?"

"Yeah. I think he's a brave man. He went to war for us and nearly died."

I looked more closely at this little runt. "Indeed he did."

"I see that you walk with a limp. Did that happen in the war too?"

"Yep."

"Is it rude to ask you about it?"

"Not rude. Some veterans might consider it too personal – but I'm not one of them. I was wounded in my leg when I was hit by shrapnel from a German shell in 1944. It took several operations plus lots of physical therapy before I made it back to Hamilton after the war. So you see I was one of the lucky ones."

"You think getting wounded was lucky?"

I clapped him on the back. "Sure I do – I'm still alive, right? I can't run as fast as Jesse Owens at the Olympics but I can help with the spring cleaning when I have to."

He gave me a long, searching look. "I was wondering about that cleaning … I think Bob just wanted you to meet me."

I levelled my eyes at the kid – raising my estimation of him by a couple of points. He seemed sharper than a 12 or 13 year old so I asked him, "How old are you, bub?

He didn't answer right away, maybe thinking I was a busybody. But after a moment, he said, "I'll be 13 on my next birthday."

I nodded my head. "When is that?"

"You sure ask a lot of questions, Mister."

I smiled at him. "Maybe Bob didn't tell you but I'm a private detective now – that's what we do."

He thought about that a moment. "Like Sam Spade and Philip Marlowe?"

I had to laugh. "Not that good yet, but maybe someday. Now, why do you think that Bob wanted me to meet you?"

"Because he's a nice man and I think he feels sorry for me."

"Maybe he does but what's that got to do with me?"

He shrugged his shoulders. "Dunno. But he's been asking me a lot of questions about my school and my mother. And I don't like to talk about that."

At that moment, a Belt Line streetcar began clanging its

bell on James Street where several pedestrians were attempting to cross in mid-block. When the ruckus died down, I asked him, "Do you think Bob's just a nosy guy?"

"Nope, he just wants to help me but I don't need any."

I shook my head. "That's what I said when I woke up in that hospital overseas."

His eyes widened but he kept his lip buttoned.

"Two hospital orderlies – big, burly guys were holding me down – one on each side. I was yelling at them that I was too busy to stay in bed; I had to get back to the war. And I didn't need any help."

"But that's a lot different than me."

"No it isn't. I was wounded but I didn't understand how severely – I guess I was in shock. But I needed help." When I leaned down so we were eye-to-eye, I noticed that his face was flushed. "I think you might be wounded too."

He drew back a step, eyes squinting. "No I'm not. Nobody shot me."

"No, but I think you might be wounded on the inside and I know about that, too." I placed my right hand on his shoulder. "Bob might have told you about my childhood and I think it's not much different than yours. I'd like you to tell me more about yourself – maybe there's some way I could help you."

That got him fidgeting; he shrugged my hand from his shoulder then began kicking the toe of his high-top running shoe at a tuft of hardy weeds trying to sprout from a crack in the sidewalk. Now he was looking up and down Merrick Street like a castaway hoping to be rescued. Finally, he turned back to me. "Don't think so, Mister. Gotta go now."

"Hang on a sec." I fished a business card from my jacket pocket, adding my home phone number beside the office number. "Here's my card. I want you to call me when you change your mind."

He retreated a step, as wary as a boxer back-pedalling from Sugar Ray Robinson.

"You're a smart kid and you know I'm on the level, Danny. So I'll be expecting your call." I narrowed the gap between us, stuck my card in his hand while I squeezed his shoulder. "Talk to you later, bud.".

CHAPTER FIVE

It was almost 1700 when I got back to my office. Phyllis was packing up for the day.

"Still warm out there, Max?"

"Feels like summer already. Did you hear from Isabel?"

She grunted an armload of folders onto the file cabinet then turned toward me. "She called 10 minutes ago, hoping to catch you. Told me she had a long snooze after her meeting with Emma and she's feeling a lot better now."

"Good news – I'm glad to hear it."

"She's a strong woman, Max. You shouldn't worry so much."

I received her advice in the spirit that she'd intended and I moved closer to the wall behind her desk to change the subject. A couple of months ago, she'd pinned up a few newspaper photos of Barbara Ann Scott and now they were curling at their edges – one showing her receiving the figure skating gold medal at the Winter Olympics in St. Moritz in February; the other picturing her triumphant return to Canada. There was also a cover from *Time* magazine that featured her smiling like a beauty queen. I leaned in for a closer look. "This cover was published just before the Olympics. Is there any more recent activity?"

"Coming soon," Phyl's eyes now glittering. "Barbara Ann and Dick Button, he's the men's Olympic champion, an American – they'll be skating an exhibition program at Maple Leaf Gardens next month. They're both so young, Max – only 19."

Her excitement was almost contagious but I managed to hold myself in check. "I'm betting you'll be front and centre at the Gardens, eh?"

"Gee, I don't know about that. They say that tickets will be as scarce as hens' teeth."

After Phyllis left, I riffled quickly through the afternoon mail that she'd placed on Isabel's desk. Bills and more bills. Here was an advertising flyer from Lou Davidson's Men's Wear. If Isabel were here she might have pinned it to my coat – a not-so-subtle suggestion about my wardrobe. I popped it into the round file then dialed her home number. She picked up after five rings.

"This is your lover-man who worries too much about you, according to Phyllis. She also tells me that you've had a miraculous recovery."

"My lover-man, eh? I like the sound of that." Her voice was perky, hardly a trace of the trauma from this morning's shooting. "There's been no miracle but the throbbing in my arm is much less and I had a good, sound sleep this afternoon. So I'll pick you up as planned."

I knew it wasn't bravado. Just last Christmas, Isabel had to shoot a man when she was taken hostage by a couple of mobsters. That's when I learned that she had Courage with a capital C.

I sat at my desk, staring out the window, my mind wandering as I thought again about Wendy Crane's disappointment because I hadn't kept in touch with her during the war. I was wondering how long she'd waited before she began dating again. I still felt like a heel for my neglect and the disappointment it caused her. In that moment of clarity, I determined not to risk the same result with Isabel. I'd promised her that we'd set our wedding date tonight and I resolved to keep that promise.

It was almost an hour later when I hung the calendar back on the wall and tucked away the notes that I'd taken while making my inquiries on the phone.

I had a plan.

When I returned to my apartment, I showered, shaved, and changed into my good suit as ordered. I had some time so I retrieved the Home edition of *The Hamilton Spectator* from under the prickly bush beside my front door. Since I'd barked at the newspaper kid about his helter-skelter delivery method, he was challenging me with a new hiding place every few days.

I brushed off the paper before spreading it open on the

kitchen table. The headline shouted at me: DARING PAYROLL ROBBERY FOILED. A four-column photo above the fold showed the felons' vehicle, a pre-war DeSoto sedan, its front doors open, marooned in the middle of Jackson Street beside the Canadian Porcelain Company. On an inside page, a diagram outlined the route taken by Mr. C.A. Vivian, the company's treasurer, when he'd walked from the Bank of Montreal with $11,000 in cash in his briefcase for the company's payroll to his office on Jackson Street, only a block away. A large X marked the spot where he'd been accosted by two thieves. Beneath the diagram was a small photo of the Hamilton police officer who'd been returning to the station on his motorcycle for lunch at the time of the holdup attempt.

According to *The Spec*:

"The officer was attracted by the gleam of the sun off one of the bandit's nickel-plated gun while he was struggling with Mr. Vivian to take his briefcase containing the money. Officer Gleave quickly radioed the station for backup. They exchanged gunfire then several police cars raced to the scene in response to the officer's call.

"Two men were taken into custody, one of whom wore a false mustache and sideburns of burned cork; his face was made up with grease paint. Mr. Vivian was unhurt but he later discovered that a bullet had been fired through his hat. After a search of the area, two women who were parked in a nearby car were also transported to the station for questioning. Police believe the women were waiting in the intended getaway car. Names of the suspects have not been released pending their appearance in Magistrate's Court tomorrow."

I looked blankly through the window, thinking about the danger to the general public caused by those criminals; even the damn streets were becoming unsafe. Isabel could've been killed by that wild gunshot. It made me wonder if this might be a preview of life in post-war Hamilton; the hometown we fought for overseas.

My thoughts were interrupted by the tap-tap of Isabel's car horn. I folded the paper before shrugging into my light-weight topcoat. This navy blue coat was a newcomer to my hall closet, courtesy of my bride-to-be who was gradually replacing my old duds with spiffier clothing. I could barely recognize the fashionable reflection of the guy in my mirror these days.

Isabel leaned across the front seat of her '47 Studebaker when I slid in beside her and she pecked me on the cheek. "Handsome guy in his smart new topcoat," she said, wiggling her eyebrows.

"Thanks. It was a gift from one of my admirers."

She pinched my arm – hard – then put the car in gear, heading uptown.

I scooted closer to her, so we were touching. "Tell me how you're really feeling, Iz. Is your arm still sore?"

She shot me a dark look. "That's enough about my arm, Max. I don't want to hear another word about it. I AM FINE."

We didn't speak as she drove down to King Street then turned left at the Canadian Tire store on the corner of West Avenue. I chose a neutral subject. "I read an item in the paper about that big new Studebaker plant on Victoria Avenue. The 1948 models will be rolling off the line this summer."

"Yes, I read about that." Her icy tone had melted.

"I guess you'll be trading in this car for a made-in-Hamilton model, eh?"

She shot me a glance that I couldn't decipher. "No, I won't. I just got this four-door model last fall. My motto is: if you like what you've got – hang onto it." Then she batted her eyes at me.

"Funny thing – that's my motto too. Now what's the big occasion tonight?"

"Don't be a smarty-pants, Max. We're going to a nice, private spot where we can finally set the date for our wedding – just as you suggested." She straightened in her seat. "And we're not leaving until we do."

I smiled to myself, looking forward to the right moment when I'd reveal my plan. "A promise is a promise, Iz. I even brought my calendar."

CHAPTER SIX

Isabel must've made a special arrangement with the maître d' at the Royal Connaught: after we'd checked our coats, the head waiter guided us to a table set for two in a secluded alcove off the main dining room. I admired Iz's smart, green silk dress, long-sleeved to cover the bandage on her arm.

The head waiter stood tall behind her chair and slid it forward as she sat down. I knew he was the head waiter because the shiny brass nameplate pinned above the pocket of his tuxedo jacket said, *Paolo Medaglia - Head Waiter*. I seated myself quickly at the table before he could come over to hold my chair.

"It's my pleasure to welcome you both this evening," he said with a bow, then he lit a pair of tall candles in silver holders. He removed a wine bottle from an ice bucket beside the table, wrapped it in a linen cloth then showed the yellow label with some French words on it to Isabel for her approval. He popped the cork then poured the fizzy stuff into tall, slender glasses at our place settings. He replaced the bottle then bowed his head saying, "*Buon Appetito*." Then he left.

I raised my glass to my partner. "Here's to a long and fun-filled life together, Iz. You've made me the happiest man in Hamilton."

She reached across the table to clink glasses. "I love you too, Max. Now, let's see your calendar."

I grinned at her. "Later for that."

After we'd eaten our tiny roasted chickens in some kind of sauce that tasted of oranges, I excused myself to go to the washroom. I took the long way around to give my bum leg some exercise and that brought me through a dimly lit bar area where a musician wearing a shiny tux was tickling the ivories, singing quietly, "A Nightingale Sang in Berkeley Square." I recalled hearing that soulful tune in a smoky London club when I was stationed in England early in the war.

I spotted a couple of love-birds, their heads together in a corner booth, maybe lulled by the sentimental music. When I stopped beside a pillar to observe them for moment, I recognized the man right away – he was in profile: greying red hair, thinning on top, in his early sixties but with a robust look about him as though he still had a tankful of gas. The woman in the lacy blue dress whose arm was draped around his shoulder shifted in her seat and I had the quick impression that she was half the age of this old goat. With her left hand she held back her long, blonde hair as she whispered in his right ear.

A voice startled me from behind. "Can't break the surveillance habit, eh Sarge?"

I snapped my head around. It was Longo - a waiter here whom I'd arrested in England for liberating government property while I was a sergeant in the Provost Corps during the war. These days, he kept an eye on certain of the Connaught's guests for me from time to time. Of course, I had to cross his out-stretched palm with silver for his intel.

I shook his hand. "Man, you almost scared the pants off me. Didn't see you in the dining room so I figured it was your night off."

"No rest for the wicked, Sarge. I'm serving a private party upstairs; had to come down to the kitchen for more Vichyssoises so I'm in a hurry – can't talk now."

"Just a sec. What the hell is Vishy – whatever you said?"

"It's a puréed soup made with leeks and potatoes. It's served cold."

"Well then, there's no need to rush, is there?" I nodded my noodle toward the bar. "I'm looking at J.B. O'Brien."

Longo turned in that direction. "So am I."

"Who's the babe?"

"You don't know her? Name's Ida Lucas."

That perked my ears up. "Do you happen to know if she has a son?"

He shook his head. "I haven't any idea. But why d'you want to know?"

I waved his question away, "Doesn't matter. Does she come here often?"

"Three or four nights a week."

I gaped at him. "What?"

"She's a hostess upstairs. In the Circus Roof lounge."

"Oh. What d'you think she sees in an old geezer like that?"

"Well … she's resourceful."

"Meaning?"

"Ida's the type of dish who's more interested in your bankroll than your bedroll but she enjoys both."

I grinned at him. "That rascal Cupid knows no bounds, does he?" I could feel my feet begin to shuffle. "Better pick up your cold soup, Pal. You don't want it to warm up."

By now, I was more than a little anxious as I made a bee-line for the washroom.

I was still thinking about Iz's father on my way back to our table. He was a widower, after all, so he wasn't cheating on a wife whom he'd left at home alone. I supposed he had every right to a little romance in his life. But that honey nuzzling his ear didn't look a day over 35 and I'd bet that when she told J.B. to jump, he'd ask, 'Over which tall building?' And I wondered about her possible connection to young Danny.

When I took my seat, Isabel wrinkled her brow, squinting at me in a way that said, 'What took you so long?'

"Sorry for the delay, Iz. I ran into my pal, Longo, and we had a little chin-wag."

She lowered her voice. "Our waiter's been hovering nearby; he'll bring our dessert as soon as he spots you. So stay put, for Pete's sake."

I gave her a mock salute. "Yes, Ma'am." Then I passed her one of our business cards along with a wide grin on my mug.

She glanced at the card then squinted at me.

I made a flipping motion with my hand.

She turned the card over, then frowned. "What's this mean? *September 17.*"

"It's our wedding date."

I couldn't decipher the look on her face but I kept my smile in place.

"Why this date? Why wait so long?"

I reached for her hand then squeezed it. "Because we'll need plenty of time to prepare, won't we? I called someone at City Hall today and you wouldn't believe the rigamarole we have to go through to get a license; then we'll have to plan our reception, maybe right here at the Connaught, and invite our guests. No doubt, you'll want a new outfit for the occasion and it wouldn't surprise me if you wanted me to do the same. Then, it'll take some time to wrap up our current contracts at the office. By then, it'll be the hottest part of the summer.

"So I figure, the weather will be more suitable for travel in September – not too hot, not too cold. I understand it's lovely in Québec City at that time of year so we'll need to book ahead for a suite at the Château Frontenac. We'll visit the Lower Town, the Plains of Abraham – all the highlights. Of course, we'll also need to reserve a sleeper on the train for the round trip."

I scooted my chair closer to hers and whispered, "How's that sound, Sweetheart?"

Her eyes had widened as I was rhyming off my itinerary and now she was blinking. "You've really thought this through, haven't you, Max? I can hardly believe it."

I caught sight of the waiter hovering nearby and I signalled him to bring our dessert.

Isabel didn't have much to say on the way home. She was paying attention to her driving, the trace of a Cheshire-smile on her serene face. I was surprised when she didn't head east to Emerald Street to drop me at my apartment. Instead, she drove west to James Street where she turned left to take us to her home on Ravenscliffe Avenue at the foot of the Mountain.

When we entered she kicked off her shoes then waved toward the living room. "Get some nice music on the radio, Max, and put your tootsies up. I'll get us a *digestif*, as they say in Québec City."

"I'm guessing that's a drink to help us digest the news of our wedding date."

"Smart boy."

One *digestif* led to another as we snuggled on the living

room couch; Artie Shaw serenading us now with *Begin the Beguine*.

"I'm crazy about our wedding plans, Max. Everything you said makes perfect sense to me. There's only one thing missing."

"What's that?"

She shifted closer, locking her eyes onto mine. "Why should we wait until September to move in together? There's nothing to stop us from doing it right now."

I drew back from her, a mock scowl on my mug. "You mean we'd live in sin?"

"Do you think our love for each other is a sin?"

"Certainly not. But what would people say?"

"If they're friends of ours, they'll be happy for us. If they're not, then what does it matter? Look at this way, you'll be freeing up a hard-to-get apartment for someone who needs it more than you do – doing your bit to solve the housing shortage. It's not as though you have a van-load of stuff to move."

I mulled that over. "Maybe you're right … but what will your father say?"

"Oh, I gave up worrying about him years ago. This is about us. Do you want to move in now or not? I'm counting to three, Max. One … Two …"

I tightened my arms around her, covering her lips with mine before she could finish counting.

In the morning, I was awakened by the cooing of a pair of mourning doves. They were perched on a low railing surrounding a patio I didn't recognize at first. Jeez Louise, I was in Isabel's bedroom – and in her bed!

I sneaked a peek at my fiancée – she was facing toward me, still asleep, her red hair fanned across her pillow. I breathed a sigh of relief when I saw the fresh bandage she'd placed on her arm last night had remained intact, showing no sign of bleeding. I noticed that the freckles on her nose and the tops of her cheeks were more prominent now without her light makeup. I wondered which lucky star had brought me here to share a bed – to share a life – with the most beautiful woman I'd ever met. On a scale from one to 10, she was an 11.

I pinched myself – I wasn't dreaming.

Her left eye popped open, studying me. "Do you still love me in the morning, Max?"

I snuggled closer to whisper, "More than I believed possible."

"I hope this means you've decided to move in."

"I'm here for good, Iz. But –"

She drew her head back, both eyes opened wide now, "There's a *but*?"

"Well, we don't have to place an announcement in *The Spectator* or anything like that, do we?

CHAPTER SEVEN

Isabel stopped at my apartment on our way to the office. I held the door for her to come inside while I changed my clothes.

When I emerged from my bedroom she was walking from room to room inspecting the furniture. "Is there anything here you want to take with you? Your special chair, something of sentimental value?"

"It's a furnished flat, Iz. Besides, all the sentiment had been wrung out of this old stuff long before I moved in."

"When's the lease up?"

"It's already up. I'm month to month now."

"Well then, we can move you out anytime." Arms around my neck now, her springtime scent invading my senses, she whispered, "I'm ready when you're ready."

When we arrived at the office Phyllis had the phone to her ear, rolling her eyes with feigned patience, "Okay, Mum. Listen, I'll call you later. Max and Isabel just arrived … yeah … me too, bye."

She hung up the receiver with a sigh. "Morning, Max. It was just my mother."

Then she turned toward Iz as she stood up. "Oh, Isabel. How's your …" Hand to her mouth now, she stopped herself before she said the forbidden words then switched gears in a hurry. "What a beautiful spring jacket – it's one of those new shortie coats, isn't it?"

I watched Iz as she spun around, the light-green coat flaring out at her hipline while Phyllis gawked: then she slipped it off, holding it open for Phyllis to try on. I beat a hasty retreat to my office, wondering– what the hell was it about dames and their clothes?

45

I sorted through my in-basket to retrieve a summary of the Nelligan file for the Peterson divorce case then made a few notes in advance of my meeting with Trépanier this afternoon. Then I read it again, mindful of Jackie Nelligan's suspicion about what might be doctored evidence. I still thought these divorce cases were sleazy but Isabel was correct – they did pay the bills as well as enhance our reputation with the other law firms in town because our work held up in court.

Before lunch, Isabel and I walked through Gore Park on our way to Robinson's department store on James Street South near the corner of King. Bob had told me that Danny's mother worked there and I wanted to look her over, to get some sense of her. But I couldn't make a direct approach without causing her to wonder why I might be interested in her son. So I asked Iz to accompany me while I played the part of her reluctant husband, dragged along on a boring shopping trip – not a difficult role for me.

The park benches here in the Gore were crowded with old-timers enjoying the warmer weather: they were like early mushrooms, popping into view overnight. Many of these guys were WW I veterans: enjoying the antics of the pre-school children with their mothers. A large squadron of pigeons had invaded the park, pecking along the sidewalks which made me wonder where they'd spent the winter – they weren't here a week ago.

We paused near the ornamental fountain, not yet in operation for the season, to watch the little kids playing tag, jumping and squealing when they were touched to be 'it'.

"Oh, aren't they cute, Max? How many would you like?"

"How many what?"

"Children. How many?"

"Hang on a minute, I haven't even thought about that yet. Do we have to decide right now?"

She gave my arm a tight squeeze. "No, but we should talk about it soon. We're both over 30 so if we're going to have a family, we need to get cracking."

Holy mackerel, everything was happening way too fast now. My life had become a whirlwind since meeting Isabel last summer. We'd had our adventures with some of Hamilton's gangsters and that included my own mother. She'd abandoned me after my father, a Hamilton copper, was killed during a raid on a bootlegger's operation on the Beach strip when I was just a kid. Shortly after that, my mother, now an accountant, moved to Miami where she handled the finances for the Florida mob.

Now I was on the doorstep of marrying the woman of my dreams and raising a family with her. But that old bug-bear was still lurking at the back of my mind – what kind of parent would I be? I worried that I might be as lousy at parenting as mine were with their only child. But with Isabel at my side, maybe I could …

"You okay, Max? You look like you're in a trance."

I wrapped her in my arms, squeezing her tight against me. "I'm all right as long as you're with me."

She kissed me on the lips which caused the old boys on their park benches to give us a hearty round of applause along with a few shouts of, "*Encore*."

One saucy old character called out, "I'm next."

Walking past him as we were leaving the park, I leaned toward him, lowering my voice. "Sorry, Jack, but I'm all kissed out."

When we passed through the revolving doors at Robinson's I stood aside from the customers crowding in behind us. "Bob told me the kid's mother worked at the cosmetics counter," I said. "But I don't know which floor that's on."

Iz tipped her head forward. "Ten feet that way. It's always front and center in a big department store."

As we approached, a tall blonde woman behind the counter was chatting with a customer in the perfume section, their backs to us. The intense aroma of the competing scents here had my nose twitching in protest. I took Iz by the arm to move her along to the end of the counter beside a display case of lipsticks, a large Max Factor sign above it. She picked one out, popped the top off and applied a dab to the back of her hand. "Do you think it's my colour, Max?"

I was puzzling over what a proper answer might be when the clerk finished with her customer and moved along the counter toward us. She plucked the lipstick from Iz's fingers, returning it to the display. "That shade won't do a thing for you, honey. Not with your colouring." She ran a long, crimson fingernail over the row of tubes before she selected another. "Peach Passion," she said with a sly wink. "Suggestive, but not too bold."

Iz shook her head. "Maybe something with a little more blush in it, to complement my hair."

The saleswoman turned toward me, pointing to a nearby chair. "Why don't you park it over there, Handsome? You might find this girl-talk a little too rich for you." Then she flicked her spikey red fingernails toward me.

I stepped away and slumped on the chair. But not before I'd read the silver name plate pinned to the clerk's tailored suit jacket. *Ida Lucas.* That embossed name hit me like a punch in the gut. According to Longo, it was the name of the babe I'd seen with Isabel's father in the bar at the Royal Connaught. I hadn't seen her features clearly then, so I wasn't positive that this was the same woman, but …

Isabel chatted with her for a couple of minutes then waved toward me. "Ready, Max? We don't want to be late for our appointment."

Out on James Street, I asked her about that 'appointment.'

"I had to escape somehow. She was trying to sell me some facial products. She told me I had nice bone structure as well as wonderful skin tone. Then she said that all I needed was Ida's loving care."

"That's all you got out of her?"

"Well …" she tilted her head back and forth in a teasing motion. "I did casually mention how difficult it must be to work full time if you're raising a family too."

"You vixen – what did she say to that?"

Iz raised her right eyebrow, "She agreed that it would be." She paused a beat. "Then she said her life was far too busy to have any children."

What the hell? It would be a world-class coincidence if there were two women named Ida Lucas who both worked at Robinson's as well as the Connaught. So why would she have lied to Isabel?

We returned to Gore Park to sit near the fountain again. An

old guy on the next bench waved at us, calling over, "Welcome back, folks."

Iz blew him a kiss, then turned to me, still smiling. "Did we get the information you wanted at Robinson's, Max?"

"I'm not sure what we got. Bob told me that Danny's last name is Lucas and his mother works at Robinson's at the cosmetics counter. She must be his mother, but why would she deny having a child? It makes me wonder what else she doesn't want to admit."

CHAPTER EIGHT

Trépanier was right on time for his appointment at 1400. I knew he'd arrived when I heard the hubbub in the outer office. Isabel and Phyllis were peppering him with questions and I heard him responding in that baritone voice with the debonair accent.

Phyllis ushered him into my office – he was about my height, five foot 10 or so. And a pungent cloud of Old Spice after-shave was trailing in his wake. I came around my desk to shake his hand. "*Bonjour, Row-bear*," my non-accent on sorry display. "Good to have you back with us."

Phyl remained in the open doorway, seeming to float a few inches off the floor. Then I noticed she was wearing a slim black skirt with a pink silk blouse – a smart outfit that I hadn't seen before. I wondered if Iz might've taken her on a shopping trip.

"Thanks, Phyl." I nudged my head toward the door, "See you later."

Her face was flushed as she backed out of my office, closing the door behind her.

We sat at the long table beside the window. "George told me you've had more surveillance experience since you worked for us on the Benson case last summer," I said. "Could you tell me a bit about that?"

"Yes. We had some clients during the past year who suspected their employees to be stealing from them. I worked on three cases like that. One time I pretended to be a new employee and I was able to hear about plans to make false deliveries. I also got better at watching people so they didn't see me. Sometime I'm able to get information by saying I am a visitor from Québec."

I nodded my approval. I knew he'd be good at that. "Were you ever caught by someone you were watching?"

"Only one time so far. He was a driver for a delivery

company who caught me watching when he removed some boxes from his truck then placed them in his car."

I nodded – I'd had a similar experience. "What did you do then?"

"I took his picture then ran like the hell."

I laughed out loud. "Did he catch you?"

"No. I run fast."

The smile was still on my face when I opened the Nelligan file, placing it on the table in front of him. "Okay, down to business – this is a confidential file from a law firm we often work for. You can take notes but the file can't leave this office. It's a divorce case that requires gathering information that can be used in court. I'll leave you alone now to read it, then we'll discuss it when I return. *Ça va?*" Isabel told me that meant 'okay' so I threw that in.

He gave me a wide grin. "*Oui. Ça va.*"

When I returned I resumed my seat by the window. "How did it go, Rob?" I'd switched to using that diminutive of his name – he'd suggested earlier that it might be simpler for me, but it was probably easier on his ears. "Do you understand what's required in this case?"

"Yes, I believe so."

"Good. Now, tell me what you think we should do."

He opened the file, arranging the pages on the table in a certain order. "Mr. Peterson is vice-president at the Steel Company of Canada. It says his wife is a fashion consultant…" He turned toward me. "I don't know what that is."

"I wasn't sure either so I asked Isabel. This lady's business involves advising clothing manufacturers, exclusive women's wear shops and sometimes wealthy individuals about fashion trends, wardrobes … all that folderol. So it's a service catering to ritzy women. She uses her maiden name for business purposes, what was it?"

He glanced at his notes. "It's Gauthier. Carole Gauthier," he said with a grin in his voice. "Another French name for you, Max."

"Maybe she uses that name because it sounds classier for someone in the fashion business."

He pointed to a glossy photo clipped to the inside of the file folder. "She is certainly *très belle*. The file says she works mostly in Toronto, where she has an apartment. In Hamilton, she lives with her husband in the Westdale district and they have no children. Mr. Peterson says his wife is having adultery in her Toronto apartment so he is making a legal case against her for divorce. It will be necessary for us to get evidence that shows she is guilty."

Now he glanced toward me, a pleased look on his movie-star puss.

"That's good," I said. "And how do you think we should proceed?"

He shifted in his chair, scooting it closer to the table. "I believe most of the investigation will be in Toronto. I will watch her apartment, see who comes and goes, if a visitor stays overnight. Or perhaps she stays over somewhere else. I could also talk with some of the people in her building, also some neighbours or people she works with. I don't know if she goes to an office to work but if she does, I can watch there also."

He sat back in his chair. "*Ça va,* Max?"

"I think we're off to a good start here. But what about her life before she moved to Hamilton?"

"There isn't much in the file about that. It says she came from Montreal ... 10 years ago but that's all."

"So it wouldn't hurt to contact the Montreal police to make inquiries would it? You could say you're a private investigator, now living in Hamilton after your service in the Van Doos, and you're doing a background check on Madame Gauthier."

"Good idea, Max. One of my army friends works for the *service de la police* there."

"Okay. Now what about Mr. Peterson, the husband."

"What about him?"

"Do you think he might be the guilty party?"

He shook his head, squinting at me. "There's nothing in the file about that."

"No, there's not much about him at all – just that tiny photo from some business journal. But these cases are never all one-sided so it's good practice to also take a look at the person who's suing for divorce. The Nelligan lawyers will want to know if there's something in their client's background that's going to rebound in court and bite them in the ass."

He gave me an ear-to-ear grin. "You have a special way of speaking, Max, but I understand. I can watch him after I learn about his wife then make a report to you."

"Good. Now, we'll need photographs. Do you have a camera?"

"*Oui*. This is my pastime – *non* – my hobby. I bought a good used Leica in England after the war."

"All right. We'll need photos of the woman, maybe her husband too, if you learn anything suspicious about him. You can pick up your film and have it developed at Hamilton Photo Supply on King Street across from the Bus Terminal. I'll call the owner so you can charge it to my account. You'll have some out-of-pocket expenses, too – gas for your car, meals and, if you have to stay overnight in Toronto you'll need a hotel – as long as it isn't the Royal York. Keep a record of what you spend then I'll reimburse you. I'll need receipts for anything over $10."

"I don't think a hotel will be necessary. I live on the north side of Burlington so it's close to Toronto on the big highway. Is there anything else I must know?"

"Not right now. I'm guessing we might have gathered enough information in a week or so, but it could take longer. Make sure your notes are as detailed as possible; times, places, names of contacts, phone numbers whenever possible and, of course, good clear photos. Remember that your information may be used in court and the outcome of the case may depend upon it. Finally, I'd like you to call me every day with a brief report. If there's a big problem, we'll meet here. I want you to start Monday morning. If you need extra help or anything else then let me know at once."

"I have one more question, Max."

"Go ahead."

"What if I can't get the information that shows Madame Gauthier to be guilty?"

"Then that's a problem for the lawyers. We would discuss it with them; they'd have your detailed records and photos: we could show them your interview notes. But if there's no case against Peterson's wife, well, there's no case. So it's no longer our problem. But we still charge them the same price, of course."

He smiled at that. Then we stood and shook hands. "About that after-shave you're using," I said, "it has a powerful aroma …"

He looked away then back to me, his face flushed. "I know it's strong now but you should smell my bathroom. I receive it for Christmas and this was the first day I'm using it. It comes fast out of the bottle then it slipped to the floor this morning. I had another shower but it didn't stop the smell. So I put the bottle in the garbage."

I grinned at his story, shaking my head as we walked to the door.

"*Merci*, Max. I am happy for this opportunity."

"You're welcome, Rob. Break a leg."

"*Pardon*?"

After he left, I phoned Ronnie at Hamilton Photo Supply. He was one of my pals from the old neighbourhood.

"Ronnie, my good chum, it's Max calling. How's tricks?"

"Oh, oh. I don't like the sound of this. Whenever you call me your 'chum', never mind 'good chum', I can feel your hand in my pocket."

"Hey, be nice. I send customers your way, don't I?"

He grunted. "What d'you need now, Max?"

"Working on a case that requires some photos of the people involved and I'm trying out a new guy on the job. He's got his own camera but I told him to get his film and processing from you. Need any extra business?"

"Always. What's the guy's name?"

"Robert Trépanier. He's about my height, not as good-looking as I am, mid-twenties –"

"Hang on, Max. He's already a customer of mine. He's a better-than-average shutterbug with a good camera. I'll look after him and send you the bill."

"Thanks, bud. One last thing – this is a sensitive case. Meaning, if any of those photos got into the wrong hands then the brown stuff would really hit the fan."

I heard him bark out a laugh. "Gotcha, Max. Not to worry on that score."

Later, I phoned the office that looked after my apartment building in order to terminate my rental. I was transferred to a woman who took down my information then asked, "Do you have a date when you'll be moving out, Mr. Dexter?"

I hadn't finalized anything with Iz yet but I knew she wanted me to move right away. "I was thinking about next week, maybe Saturday. Is that any problem?"

"Not for us, Sir, but you're on our monthly plan so you'll have to pay for the balance of this month. And we'll need to inspect the premises with you on your last day."

I had second thoughts about paying for the time that I wouldn't be there, then stopped myself. What the hell did it matter? I'd be moving into a far better place that had the added advantage of being rent-free – well, in a manner of speaking.

We agreed to meet for the inspection on the following Saturday at 10:00. My hand began to quiver as I was hanging up the receiver, and I could feel the sweat dampening my armpits. I'd had my share of bad luck during my lifetime so when Isabel O'Brien, the smartest, most beautiful woman in Hamilton says that she loves me – that she wants me to share her life and her home with me – Holy mackinaw, was it any damn wonder that I thought I must be hallucinating?

CHAPTER NINE

"I'm ready to leave, Max."
Phyllis had entered my office at closing time, wearing a light-weight, tan coat with a sporty green hat, a red Robin-Hood feather tucked in the hatband. "Is there anything you need before I go?"

"Don't think so. I'm still finishing up this Neatby report and I'll lock it up later. You're looking pretty chirpy, Phyl, got a big date tonight?"

"Well," her voice a sing-song drawl, "not exactly. *Robert* asked me for my phone number, so … maybe."

I shook my head, giving her a smile. That dog, Trépanier, didn't waste any time with my staff – last year he was sniffing around Isabel and now the bugger's got his eye on Phyllis. But I couldn't disagree with his taste in women.

"Enjoy the weekend, Phyl. Weatherman says it might even be in the seventies."

Later, I locked up my files, ready to leave when the phone rang.

"Is that Mr. Dexter?" a kid's voice.

"Yeah. I'm guessing this must be Danny – right?"

"Yes sir. You said I could call you, so –"

"You sound as though you have a cold. Are you feeling all right?"

"It might be a cold but there's something else."

I waited but he'd dried up. "C'mon, Danny. What is it?"

"Umm …" a long pause while he coughed, then cleared his throat. "Bob said that you're a detective, right?"

"Yes, I am. What's happened?"

"I haven't seen my mother for a while."

According to Bob, the kid was often left on his own so I

wondered what was different now. "How long has she been gone?"

"This is the third day, but, ah … um…" He stammered to a halt. "Maybe I shouldn't bother you…"

"Hang on, I'll help you if I can. Why don't I come over to your place? Give me your address and I'll be on my way."

"But you don't know me –"

"Listen, Danny. Something's got you worried or you wouldn't be calling me. So tell me the address."

I dialed Isabel's number: after five or six rings I was about to hang up when she answered, out of breath. "Is that you, Max? I was just coming into the house. Sorry I took so long to answer."

I briefed her about the situation with Danny. "There's probably a simple explanation but he didn't sound well to me so I'd like to check on him. Would you mind picking me up? I'm still at the office so we could see him together."

Isabel found a parking spot on Caroline Street then we walked back the short distance to York Street where I'd spotted the Langley Cleaners shop near the corner. I peered through the storefront window. "No customers right now – why don't we stop in for a minute to speak with the clerk?"

A well-fed, middle-aged woman greeted us when we approached the counter, racks of clothing behind her and a strong whiff of dry-cleaning chemicals tainted the air. I noted her nametag. "Hello, Mrs. Macaluso. I'd like a bit of help if you don't mind. A good friend of mine met a boy who lives in an apartment in this block. My friend is a wounded veteran and this boy, Danny's his name, was able to help him with some chores. Do you happen to know the lad?"

She was nodding her head before I'd finished speaking, giving me a broad smile. "You bet I do. He's a sweet little guy – he often helps me around the shop. He lives in one of the apartments upstairs here. Is there a problem?"

"I hope not. But I gave him my phone number and he called me today. You see, he's worried about his mother."

"Well, I can't blame him for that. I hate to say it but she's not much of a mother. She works days in one of those downtown stores, plus she's got another job at night. But, my Lord, you should see some of the men who drop her off here from time to time – they look like some of those gangsters whose photos you see in the newspaper when they've been arrested or their bodies were found floating in the Bay. I help the boy when I can and once or twice a week I bring him a good Italian dinner when his mother's not home."

"That's kind of you Ma'am. I'm sure he appreciates it."

"Oh, he does, he does." She glanced at Isabel with a smile. "It's good that you and your wife are taking an interest in him. God bless you both."

Back on York Street we located the entry to the upstairs apartments through an unmarked door beside the cleaner's shop. Inside the cramped foyer, there were three buzzers beside an interior door: Apt. 1 – Rule; Apt. 2 – Ippolito; Apt. 3 – no name – it had been erased but I jabbed that button.

I heard a click when the inner door unlocked and we walked up a steep flight to the second floor where the kid's head was sticking out of a doorway, watching us walk toward him from the far end of a shadowy hall, the stale odour of boiled cabbage wrinkling our noses. In Apt. 1, we could hear a music lover listening to Fats Waller singing on the radio, "Your Feet's Too Big."

"This is Isabel," I told the boy at the end of the hallway. "She's my partner at the detective agency. Can we come in, maybe sit down for a minute?"

His dark eyes darted between us. "Um … ah … I guess so." I got the feeling that I'd somehow betrayed his trust by bringing this stranger with me.

We followed him through the living room where I noted a sagging sofa that also served as a bed – a folded sheet, a faded red blanket and a lumpy pillow now piled neatly at one end. In the kitchen, Danny flicked on the overhead light where we sat on red chrome-legged chairs around a green arborite table.

Iz scooted her chair closer to him. "Max told me you think your mother might be missing and we want to help you. When was the last time you saw her?"

He was staring at Iz while she spoke but he remained buttoned up.

"Max and I are in the investigation business, Danny. Sometime it's part of our job to find people. Whatever you tell us remains private between us. Now, how long has she been away? You told Max it was about three days. But has it been longer than that?"

I knew better than anyone that Isabel had a certain manner about her – when she asked you a question you couldn't stop yourself from spilling the beans. Somehow, you felt compelled to please this woman and this kid was no exception.

"If she's not back tonight it'll be four days, Miss," his voice a mousy squeak, then he coughed.

"Is that unusual? Has she been away that long before?"

He was nodding his head while he cleared his throat again. "She's usually gone two or three nights a week, sometimes more."

"But what about your meals, looking after the apartment?"

"Oh, I can do all that stuff. She has an account at that little grocery store near the corner of Park Street so I just charge what I need then she pays Mr. Agro at the end of the month. Same with the laundry – I take it to Mrs. Macaluso downstairs."

Iz turned toward me, her eyes widened, and I motioned with my head for her to continue. Bob was right to suspect this kid was almost living on his own.

"Then why are you worried about her now? Was is it something she told you?"

He began scratching his chest through his Hamilton Tigers hockey shirt while he shook his head. "Nope. When she stays away overnight she always takes her makeup case and her small red suitcase but they're both still here."

"Ah … now I see why you're concerned," Iz said. "Would you mind showing me her bedroom? I won't touch anything."

The kid stared at her for a long moment before he made up his mind then got up from his chair. He opened a cupboard door under the sink, removed a canister marked GREEN TEA, popped the lid off and fished out a key. Then he walked along a short hallway, Iz and I close behind him.

"That's an odd place for your mother to keep her key," Iz said.

"It's where she always hides it."

59

Her bedroom was frilly and pink, in sharp contrast to the small living room that was an ugly, dull colour – what we used to call brindle-shit brown in the army. A large bed dominated her room; a narrow, full-length mirror beside it. I spotted a tiny photo, the type you got from one of those photo booths on the midway at the Canadian National Exhibition in Toronto. It was wedged into the top corner of the mirror and I had to step in much closer to make it out – two smiling faces cheek-to-cheek, a poster of Niagara Falls roaring in the background. The woman's face wasn't quite in focus but I presumed it must be Ida or it wouldn't be here in her bedroom. But the sport with the ear-to-ear grin on his puss who'd squeezed into the booth beside her was Isabel's old man.

While Danny moved with Iz to a closet, their backs to me, I nicked the photo from the mirror then slipped it into my shirt pocket where it seemed to sizzle against my skin. Isabel would be disappointed to learn that her father was lovey-dovey with this boy's mother. I hoped that I wouldn't have to upset her with that info.

Danny opened the closet door, the small space crammed with silky dresses. He pointed to the floor, "There's her makeup case and overnight bag."

A second, larger closet contained several women's suits, some skirts and blouses. A hat shop on the upper shelf – an army of shoes standing at ease on the floor. Iz was about to close the door when I reached for her arm. "Hang on a sec."

I'd noted a pencil sketch of a woman's face on a page torn from a notebook, thumbtacked to the inside of the door. I moved in for a closer look then turned to Danny. "Say, this is a pretty good drawing. Is it your mother?"

"Yep."

"Who drew it? Does she have an artist friend?"

The kid's face bloomed in a caught-in-the-act shade of crimson. "Ah … I did."

Then Isabel examined it. "This is really good, Danny. Do you take drawing lessons?"

He was staring at his running shoes now. "No, Ma'am."

"Well, good for you. This is a wonderful sketch – would you like to become an artist someday?"

"I don't think so … Umm, maybe."

"Do you have any more drawings?"

"Well … I have a notebook."

Iz bent down so she was eye to eye with the boy. "I'd love to have a look at it."

He shook his head, stalling for time, then finally said, "I can't find it right now. I think I might've lost it."

Isabel gave him a sweet smile, patting his shoulder. "Okay. Maybe we could see it some other time – when you find it."

Then she stood and glanced around the bedroom again. Two dressers along the opposite wall were no doubt filled with the rest of Ida's clothes but we didn't snoop further.

"Quite a wardrobe," Iz said.

Danny looked up at her. "She has to dress up for her job - she works at Robinson's."

"But I don't see a dressing table and mirror."

"Oh, she does her make-up stuff in the bathroom."

We followed him across the hallway where we gaped into the tight little room – an array of creams, bottles of lotions and a Gillette safety razor were displayed on two narrow glass shelves mounted on the longer wall above the bath tub. On a small shelf beneath the medicine cabinet, there was a tin of Dr. Lyon's Toothpowder, a couple of toothbrushes in a red plastic cup, and a bottle of Alka-Seltzer tablets with the top off.

I was leaving the bathroom with Danny when I glanced over my shoulder to see Iz closing the small door to the medicine cabinet then slipping something into her pocket.

We resumed our seats at the kitchen table after the boy returned the key to its 'hiding place' beneath the sink.

"When your mother is away overnight where does she stay?" I said.

"At the hotel or sometimes with friends."

"Which hotel is that, bud?"

He coughed again. "The Royal Connaught. She works there two or three nights a week, sometimes more. But the hotel stays open very late – that's why she has to stay overnight so much."

By now, I was sure that we were on the right track here but I made it a habit of dotting my i's and crossing my t's. "What's your mother's name?"

"Ida Lucas."

Even though I'd caught a glimpse of her at the hotel as well as seeing her in Robinson's, it still annoyed me to hear her name confirmed by her neglected son. I felt a sudden urge to plunk this woman down in a chair and talk some sense into her. She was a mother in name only – a department store cosmetician by day; and a lady of the evening at the Connaught and god-knows-where else. I was getting hot under the collar because I couldn't dismiss the comparison to my own mother – like her, Ida was too caught up in her own life to give a damn about her young son.

I also wondered about Isabel's father, J.B. O'Brien – did he bother to learn anything about Ida or her home life, if you could call it that? Or was he simply blinded by his infatuation with a beautiful younger woman and didn't give a damn about the rest of her life?

Iz was kneeling on one knee beside the boy, feeling his forehead with the back of her hand. "I see that you have a rash on your face. How long have you had this cough?"

"Few days."

"Maybe a bit longer?"

His darted his eyes toward me until I motioned with my hand for him to continue.

"Maybe," he said.

"Does it hurt to swallow? A sore throat?"

"A bit."

"Could you lift up your shirt so I can see your back?"

"Why? What's the matter?"

She smiled at him. "Just let me have a quick look."

He shifted in his chair to hoist his shirt while Iz looked him over. "Okay. Now lift it in front."

He shot me a pleading look, maybe hoping I'd save him from this crazy lady. I gave him an encouraging smile to follow orders.

When she finished her inspection, Iz said, "Have you ever had measles?"

He shook his head. "Don't think so. But some of the kids at school have them."

"I think you might have them, too. Do you have a family doctor?"

Another head-shake. "Nope. But last year Mrs. Macaluso

took me to the Hamilton General Hospital."

"What was the problem?"

"Chicken pox."

Iz stood up, her lips pursed while she walked a circle around the kitchen table. "I've got an idea. But first I have to make a call and I see your phone's on the wall there, beside the door."

She paused behind Danny, placing her hands on his shoulders as he stared at me. "Why don't you talk to Max in the living room while I'm on the phone?"

I jumped to my feet. "Good idea. Have you got a collection of hockey cards, Danny?"

"Yeah, I do. But I've put them away."

"Well, dig them out. I'd love to see them."

His eyes scoured my face, as if he were determining my sincerity. Then he bobbed his head and we entered the living room where he knelt down to pull out a Cut-Rate Shoe box from under the couch.

I removed his blanket and pillow from the couch, then set them on the floor. He sat beside me and opened the box containing his cards.

"Who's your favourite player? Wait-a-minute, let me guess. I'll bet it's Syl Apps."

"Yep." Then he removed a thick pack held together with a fat, red elastic band. "I've got six packs of cards, one for each of the NHL teams, but Toronto's my favourite."

He passed me the Maple Leafs pack – there was the Syl Apps card right on top. I flipped it over to read the back.

"That's not my best Apps card." Then he covered his mouth while he coughed.

"Show me your best one."

From the bottom of the shoe box he removed a cellophane sleeve containing a single card then passed it to me. "Leave it covered up, so you won't get your fingerprints all over it." He paused. "Please."

On one side it showed Apps in the usual face-off pose, his printed signature scrawled beneath it. On the reverse was a brief history in both English and French. I had to hold the card near the lamp on the end table to read the small type. "Let's see … it says, 'he was born in Paris, Ontario where he played hockey for the

Paris Juniors, then played for McMaster University and the Hamilton Tigers of the Senior O.H.A'." I pointed at the black and gold Tigers shirt Danny was wearing, then continued. "He represented Canada at the Berlin Olympics as a pole-vaulter. He also plays football and baseball. Then he joined the Toronto Maple Leafs in 1936." I handed it back to him and he tucked it away.

"I bet that card'll be worth a lot of money someday," I said then I noticed the hint of a grin on his face.

"It's worth a lot right now. I showed it to the father of a kid at school who offered me $5 for it."

"That much? Let me see it again."

This time I took a closer look. "It's from the 1937-38 season so you're right to hang on to it."

When Isabel entered the room he gathered up his cards then closed the shoe box.

"We'd like to take you over to a friend of ours who's a nurse in training," she told him. "If you do have measles she'll tell us how to treat them. So let's get an overnight bag packed for you, just in case."

He turned quickly to me, grabbing my arm. "I can't just leave, Mister. What if my mother comes home when I'm not here? What about my school? We have an English test tomorrow."

"Let's see if you have measles first," Iz said. "Then we can decide what to do about your school and all the rest. I'm leaving a note for your mother on the kitchen table with the telephone number she can call."

He hung back a moment longer, glancing around the dismal, shabby room as though he were etching it into his memory in case he might not see it again.

CHAPTER TEN

We stood on the spacious veranda of a two-storey brick home on Bold Street, kitty-corner from Central Public School, and I rang the doorbell. We had met Grace Clark last summer when our artist friend, Roger Bruce, was arrested for the murder of Grace's wealthy employer for whom she worked as his live-in housekeeper.

At the conclusion of that case, Roger was released from jail when Hamilton mobsters were found to be responsible for the crime. Fortunately for Grace, she had inherited the bulk of her wealthy employer's estate which allowed her to buy this home where she was raising her young son, Vincent. We'd become close friends since that time.

Grace's story had a true-to-life 'rags to riches' aura about it. She'd emigrated from Jamaica some years ago and originally she worked as a live-in maid for a wealthy family in Toronto. Later, she married Owen Clark, also from Jamaica; they'd moved to Hamilton in the mid-1930s when Owen got a better-paying job at the Steel Company. But sadly, he was one of the RHLI soldiers who gave his life for his country at Dieppe in '42.

Since that time Grace was raising her young son on her own and we'd kept in contact with them.

As we waited, I could feel Danny's grasp tightening on my arm as he huddled closer beside me.

Grace welcomed us in her usual effusive manner, kissing Isabel on both cheeks, clutching my hand in hers. She leaned down to shake Danny's hand as he stared up at her. "Don't be afraid," she said. "I have a son about your age and I'll bet you'll be great friends."

We followed her along a wide hallway hung with a profusion of colourful pictures then entered a sitting room with comfy chairs, a long sofa and a view of the treed backyard through a picture window. A floor model Crosley radio console in a gleaming mahogany cabinet stood tall in the corner – Bing Crosby was crooning "Now is the Hour" until Grace gave him a rest.

"I thought you might not have eaten so you can join us for supper," she said.

The 'us' she referred to included her son, Vincent, who was a year or two younger than Danny, as well as a beautiful young woman.

"This is my younger sister, Samantha," Grace said. "We call her Sam. She just moved here from Jamaica a couple of weeks ago."

Then she placed her left arm around her son's shoulder, scooting him closer to Danny. "And this is my boy, Vincent. He's in grade five at Central Public School. How about you, Danny? What grade are you in?"

He opened his mouth to speak but his voice cracked. He coughed into his fist then tried again. "Grade seven, Ma'am. At Hess Street Public."

Grace took Danny's arm, heading toward the hallway. He glanced back at me, his eyes jittery, maybe hoping I'd rescue him from this stranger – this *black* stranger.

"You folks can chat with Sam while I have a look at this boy," Grace said. "If he does have measles, we won't get them because we've had them already." She stopped, glancing back at Isabel. "How about you and Max?"

"We've both had our turns," Iz said.

We settled ourselves on the couch where I said to Vincent, "Stanley Cup finals start tonight?"

He grinned back at me. "Leafs against those Red Wings, I can hardly wait."

"I know you'll pick Toronto to win but how many games will it take?"

He answered right away, "Four straight," sounding just like Foster Hewitt.

"Enough of that hockey talk, boys," Iz said then she turned to Samantha, "How about you, Sam? What made you decide to move to Hamilton?"

"Well, Grace has been after me to move in with her ever since our parents died last year. She finally wore me down."

"Makes sense," Iz said. "What are you planning to do in Hamilton?"

"I worked in an accountant's office back home and I enjoyed it a lot. So I was thinking of getting more training in that area." She spoke with a warm West Indian lilt in her voice. Then she glanced over at Vincent, giving him a wink. "But my big sister is urging me toward the nursing profession."

Isabel raised her eyebrows. "Well, for what it's worth, I think you should stick to your guns. I'm a chartered accountant so if you wish to talk more about it, just give me a call." She withdrew a business card from her purse and passed it to her.

Grace joined us a few minutes later. "The patient has a thermometer in his mouth, so I'll give you a quick report. He definitely has measles and he'll probably remain contagious for the next week or so."

She turned to Isabel. "When you told me on the phone that his mother's left him on his own, I knew right away that he should stay here with us. Sam will be around when she's not out job-hunting and I've got a light schedule right now, so –"

I stopped her there. "It's kind of you to offer but this is far too big an imposition for someone you've never met before."

"He's a child, Max, and he needs some help. So he's welcome here – that's all there is to it."

During supper Grace was telling us that she'd enrolled in McMaster University's School of Nursing last September when the school began to offer a five-year program for a Bachelor of Science degree in Nursing.

"It's a difficult course of study but the instructors are top-notch and best of all, they're very patient with me because I've been out of school for longer than I care to remember."

"You're already a terrific nurse," I said. "You looked after your former employer for years; I think that counts for a lot."

"Nice of you to say, Max, but I have a lot more to learn. Right now we're getting a crash course in infectious diseases because of this measles outbreak here in town. Hundreds of new cases were reported in Hamilton during the past couple of weeks, bringing the total to nearly 2,000 since January. A number of people have already died from it but the scientists say that a vaccine won't be developed for at least another five or 10 years."

Before we left, I went upstairs to check on Danny. Grace had settled him in one of the twin beds in Vincent's room. An array of Toronto Maple Leaf players' photos was thumb-tacked to the wall beneath a blue and white pennant. Danny looked up as I approached his bed, giving me a weak smile while his head resting against a couple of pillows.

On the bedside table I noticed half a glass of milk and a sandwich with a couple of bites out of it. I pointed to his plate, "You must be pretty sick, bud, if you can't gobble down a peanut butter and jam sandwich."

"Maybe I'll finish it later."

"Grace says you've got a good dose of measles so you need to lie low for a little while." I sat on the side of the bed. "If not, you might give it to others and you don't want that, right?"

A slow shake of his head, "Guess not. But I'm still worried about my mother and I don't know these people here." Then he clutched my sleeve as he whispered, "And they're Negroes."

I bent down so we were eye to eye. "These are good people, Danny. They're kind and they're generous. They'll help you get well – you'll even have your own private nurse. Don't forget that Jackie Robinson's a Negro – last year's rookie of the year with the Brooklyn Dodgers. And the Brown Bomber is the heavyweight boxing champion of the whole world."

"Joe Louis," he whispered. He opened his mouth to speak again, then closed it. After a moment he nodded his head, maybe deciding to make the best of his circumstances.

I pointed to the Westinghouse mantel radio on the night table between the beds. "Sick or not, I bet you'll be listening to the first game of the playoffs tonight."

"Yep. I don't wanna miss hearing the Leafs beat those Detroit bums."

"Vincent's a loyal Toronto fan too so I know you fellas will become friends in no time."

I stood up, ready to leave when he grabbed my arm again. "I don't know what'll happen to me now. Maybe you should take me back to the apartment."

"No can do, bud – you're a sick boy. Isabel and I will try our best to find your mother. Tomorrow we'll notify your school that you're sick. Believe me, they don't want a guy with measles in the classroom. In the meantime, your main job is to get better – your other job is to cheer the Leafs onto victory."

His mouth squidged down at the corners, a frown on his rosy face. "Okay Mr. … sorry, I don't remember your last name."

"It's Dexter. But you can call me Max."

When I got back downstairs, Sam had her arm around Vincent's shoulder. "Come on now, give your mother a kiss good-night and I'll take you up to bed."

He pecked Grace on the cheek while she hugged him. "Good night, Honey. Now, get up there and listen to the game with our new friend."

We watched them leave and I turned to Grace. "We're really grateful that you've taken Danny into your home. You've got a generous heart."

"I'm happy to help out for now – we'll see how it goes."

Isabel was driving east along Hunter Street to my apartment at the corner of Emerald Street and I turned toward her. "I noticed you taking a peek into Ida's medicine cabinet earlier. Find anything interesting?"

"Maybe." Then she pushed her purse along the seat toward me. "Open it, Max. There's a pill bottle on top."

I hesitated. "Isn't it taboo or bad manners to open a ladies' purse?"

She flicked her eyes toward me, shaking her head. "Just open the darn thing."

"Yes, Ma'am."

I snapped it open and removed a small brown bottle, no label. I heard the rattle of pills inside it, "Any ideas?"

"While you were upstairs with Danny, I had a chance to speak privately with Grace in the kitchen, then I showed her those pills. There's no label on the bottle so she offered to take them into the chemistry lab at McMaster. She has a friend there, also from Jamaica, who would analyse them if she asked him nicely. I thanked her then she shook a few of them into a small envelope that she stashed in her purse."

I scooted myself closer beside her, pecking her on the cheek. "Aren't you the clever detective, Miss O'Brien."

CHAPTER ELEVEN

I called Grace Clark from my office the following morning to check on Danny. "Morning, Grace, I hope the hockey fans didn't keep you up too late."

"It's Sam, Max. People say we sound alike on the phone."

"Well, people are right about that. I'm calling about the patient. Did he wake the house during the night?"

"No, no, nothing like that. But he's still glum about staying off school."

"Does he talk about his mother?"

"Not a word about her. But on the bright side, the boys seem to get along just like brothers. I listened to some of that game; it was the first one for me. It sounded like that announcer was speaking in a foreign language – quite confusing. But the boys cheered whenever Toronto made a score, especially when they won the game."

"I'm grateful that you and Grace are looking after him for now. Is she there? I'd like to thank her too."

"No, she's at school this morning. We decided to spell each other off while Danny's with us – she has her university classes in the mornings then I'll do my job-hunting in the afternoons."

I gave her my numbers at the office and home. "If you need anything, just give me a call."

I was opening the Peterson file on my desk when it dawned on me that I hadn't informed Mrs. Macaluso at the Langley Cleaners shop that we'd taken Danny to Grace's home.

"It's Max Dexter," I said when she picked up her phone. "I wanted to tell you about young Danny – in the apartment upstairs?"

"Yes, I was wondering about him. Is he alright?"

"He's got a good dose of measles so we took him to a friend's home who's in a nursing program at McMaster. She has a boy a little younger than Danny and she volunteered to keep him at her place until he recovers. The two boys seemed to get along well so we're hoping he'll be fine there for now."

"Thanks for letting me know. I've been worried about him. Maybe you could call me when he comes back so I can keep an eye on the boy."

I'd just hung up the phone when Phyllis buzzed me. "I've got *Row-bear* on the other line, Max. Can you take it now?"

"Thanks, Phyl. I'll talk to him."

I hit the button on the phone for the second line – this new feature was a recent addition to the office; one that Isabel said we couldn't do without. What the hell's next, I wondered – maybe a real-life version of Dick Tracy's two-way wrist radio? I shook my head, banishing that impossible thought.

"How're you doing, Rob? Just get out of bed?"

He finished his yawn before he spoke. "Yes, I did. I got home late so I sleep longer today. But I don't have much to report about Madame Gauthier."

"Tell me."

"On my way to Toronto yesterday, I drove by their big house in Westdale. A beautiful place – near the end of Forsyth Avenue North, close to some woods beside McMaster University – some big flower gardens out there."

"The Sunken Gardens."

"That's it – a *très chic* area, Max."

"If that means ritzy, you're right. Did you see anyone around the house?"

"No cars in the driveway, but a garage big enough for two cars, maybe three. Two gardeners are working in the yard but they don't know if anyone was home so I drive on to Toronto."

"All right. Did the gardeners have a truck parked nearby?"

"Yes. An old red Ford with rusty fenders."

"A company name painted on the doors?"

"Mohawk Landscaping. In case you are going to ask, the licence plate is also rusty but the last three numbers are 662."

"Very good, Rob. You've got the makings of a good snooper. Now tell me about Toronto."

"Madame Gauthier, you remember that's her family name?"

"Sure. First name Carolyn, I think."

"That's close, but no cigarette. Her name is Carole."

He paused when he heard me chuckling. "Why do you laugh, Max? Did I speak wrong?"

"Yeah, sort of. The usual expression is 'close, but no cigar'. But a cigarette is smaller than a cigar so it might even be better. Now, what were you saying?"

"I was telling you that Madame lives in a big old house divided into five apartments. It's on Prince Arthur Street at the address I get from the file – close to the Women's Art Association building. This is also a *chic* area, like some places in Montréal."

"Did you see her there, Rob?"

"No, but I talked to the ... *concierge* - the guy who looks after the place ..."

"The caretaker or building manager."

"Yes. He sees me looking around then he asks me, am I lost?"

"Oh-oh. You got caught?"

"Yes, but when I see that he wears a 48th Highlanders badge on his cap, I say I'm looking for a friend I met during the war. So we talk about that, you know how army guys do, 'Where did you serve', et cetera. Then I learn that we were both fighting in Italy and later in the Netherlands."

"The old soldier's connection."

"That's it. Then I say that I have a civilian job now as investigator and I have some interest in Madame Gauthier. He said, 'Me too – she's a real dish.' After that he was friendly with me.

"He told me she leaves her apartment every morning about 0830 then she returns around 1800. He said she often goes out in the evening during the week but she's not usually there on weekends –"

"Wait a minute now, how could he know all that about her?"

"He has a small apartment in the basement and he says it's his job to know about the people who live there. I laughed when he

73

said their private affairs were not his business. He said, 'I get paid the same whatever the tenants do in their apartments'."

"A wise guy."

"Yes, but I liked him right away. He walks like you, Max – he told me he was wounded in his leg when they were fighting the last of the Germans in Holland in 1945.

"Then he shows me the long, open garage building behind the house where Madame Gauthier and the others park their cars. She has a new Nash coupé, a green colour. The tires have those white rings around them."

"White walls."

"Yes. After that, we walked slow to Bloor Street at the corner where I buy him a beer."

"That's good work, Rob. I think you're off to a fine start. Did you learn anything else from your new friend?"

"He told me Madame has an office downtown on Adelaide Street West. So I'm going there tomorrow."

"Maybe you could get that caretaker guy to keep an eye on her at the apartment then you could concentrate on what she does when she goes out."

"I'm thinking the same thing, Max. Oh, I almost forgot – I talked to my friend from the Montreal police – he told me Madame has a clean record there. She has a rich family who live in Westmount."

"Good work, Rob. I'll hear from you again tomorrow."

I hung up the phone in slow motion, deciding that I was pretty damn smart to think of hiring Trépanier for this job.

CHAPTER TWELVE

Later, I called Phyllis's mother, Vera, who provided Max Dexter Associates with credit and other background information that she learned from her contacts throughout the city. She was formerly the manager of the Hamilton Credit Bureau until a near-fatal automobile accident in 1940 had left her paralyzed in both legs. But a couple of years after that, she was able to set up her one-woman 'Confidential Information' business in her wheelchair-friendly home office, using a telephone operator's rig so she could speak hands-free. Her business catered to Hamilton lawyers and their staff but she made an exception for me.

"How's Vera doing?" I said. "Still keeping those phone lines humming?"

"Humming and then some, Max. What can I *do* you for?"

I smiled at her trademark, wise-guy patter. "I'm wondering if you've got any info on a Mr. J.A. Peterson. He's one of the big wheels at the Steel Company and he's suing his wife for divorce – infidelity."

"Aha. Is she guilty?"

"Remains to be seen. We're looking into it."

"Okay, hang on a sec…"

I listened to her wheeling around the room, then a file drawer sliding open. And after a moment, "Yep, here he is. Peterson – he certainly is a bigwig; a V.P. at Stelco is no small potatoes." A pause while I heard her riffling more pages. "What're you after, Max? I've got some info here but this guy doesn't appear to be the type to interest a small-time gumshoe who likes to play footsies with the Hamilton Mob."

"But you never know, do you? You might have something iffy."

A longer delay, then, "Okay, both he and his wife must be

rollin' in dough. They live on Forsyth Avenue North, that swanky area in Westdale, married in '43 – no kids. Mr. P. is a member of the Hamilton Jockey Club and he belongs to the Hamilton Club – that's a private men's club for bigshots at the corner of Main and James Streets. He belongs to the Scottish Rite Masonic Lodge here in town. A Progressive Conservative party member – no surprise there – and he's also a member of the Hamilton Golf and Country Club in Ancaster as well as a private health club out in Aldershot where the high rollers do whatever they do there." She paused a moment, then said, "That's a men's club too, Max – makes you wonder if he prefers male-only company, if you catch my drift."

I thought about that. "Mmm – that might be a possibility, I suppose. But listen, I need a good photo of him – think you could rustle one up?"

"Sure, I'll dig around. These rich guys just love to have their pictures taken. Now, what else … Mrs. P. works as a fashion consultant – self-employed. She goes by her maiden name, Carole Gauthier, must be French … and I guess she's the artsy-fartsy type 'cause she's on some kind of committee at the Art Gallery of Toronto.

She paused and I heard more page flipping. "Oh, this is interesting – I guess she doesn't commute to Toronto because I have an address for her there. Now, that might be worth looking into. You know what they say, Max, 'when the cat's away, the mice will play'."

"Thanks, Vera. I'm always surprised that you're able to locate all this info – almost like you had a team of spies working undercover for you."

I heard her sigh. "I wish I did. But during my 20 years at the Credit Bureau I made a lot of contacts in this town. In Peterson's case I simply looked up his profile in the Hamilton Businessmen's Association annual report, where he's on the board. And a couple of other sources, too. You just hafta know where to look, Mister."

"Thanks for this. If you come up with anything else about either one of them I'd appreciate hearing about it. It's always a treat to shoot the breeze with you."

"You're welcome, Sherlock, but hang on a minute – how's my Phyllis doing? I've been getting quite an earful lately about this *Row-Bear* character. I think she's going gaga over him but she says, 'Oh no, we're just friends'."

"I keep my nose out of that stuff. All I know is that she's a hard worker and she's personable with the customers – now, who do you suppose she learned that from?"

"Aw, you're a real sweetheart, Max. Abyssinia."

I spent the rest of the morning working through some employment applications for the big Westinghouse plant in Hamilton's west end. Management there was concerned about the reliability of potential employees who were hired to handle personal data, money or proprietary information. In order to protect their interests, the company engaged investigators to conduct background checks on those candidates. Vera handled much of this work for me by verifying educational backgrounds, former employment records and other references.

But in some cases, I sent the pertinent info to one of the lawyers at the Nelligan and Nelligan Law Office to check for criminal or other convictions. While some of this information might be available to the public from provincial and county courts, I found it was a helluva lot quicker to have the folks at a legal office obtain that info on my behalf. Of course, I passed that cost along to my clients.

Much of this work could be done by phone but sometime it required personal visits to the agencies or companies involved. And once in a while, surveillance of the applicant was necessary. While some of this work could become tedious, it was the bread and butter of many small agencies like ours. And contrary to the public's romantic notion, a private investigator's life usually bore little resemblance to Humphrey Bogart's escapades in that Sam Spade movie. But often enough it got interesting and I had an inkling that this Peterson affair might be just such a case.

Vera called me back later.

"Sorry, Max, I've had no joy in finding a good photo of Peterson. Seems odd, doesn't it? Makes me wonder if he might be avoiding the camera for some reason. But I did come across a reference in a *Spectator* article to a photo of Mayor Lawrence presenting him with a trophy that one of his horses won last year at the Hamilton Jockey Club."

"That's good – did you get the date of that article?"

"Ixnay – it just says 'last summer'. You could probably have your Uncle Scotty get you a copy from the *Spectator's* files."

"Thanks for the tip, Vera. I'll follow it up."

After lunch, I stepped out onto King Street and joined the small knot of passersby next door who'd paused to read the headline stories posted in the large front window at *The Hamilton Spectator*:

Toronto ices Detroit 5-3 in exciting Stanley Cup opener. I imagined Vincent and Danny cheering their team on to victory.

Soviet blockade in Berlin 'to keep western spies out of the Russian zone'. That bit of news made me think the Russkies might someday become an even bigger pain in the ass than the Nazis had been.

I boarded the new-fangled elevator at the *Spectator* building and pressed the button for the second floor – this was another example of what was called *automation*, squeezing another citizen out of a job.

And I wondered what would happen to all those elevator operators at Eaton's and Robinson's and the other big buildings. It just didn't seem right that my veteran friend, Tiny, could be replaced by a button. Too damn bad in my view but I didn't see an end to this trend.

Upstairs, I spotted my Uncle Scotty in a corner of the City room, banging away with two fingers at his old Underwood typewriter that was mounted on a small wheeled table beside his desk. His top coat lay in a heap on the floor beside him, his battered black fedora askew on his head.

I stood close to him but he continued typing for a moment before he paused and looked up. "Well, shit! If it ain't my favourite nephew. Whaddya want?"

"Nice greeting, Unc. Makes me feel as welcome as a boil on my behind."

He grinned up at me now. "Couldn't have said it better myself." He pointed to the wooden chair beside his desk. "You've got two minutes. I'm on deadline."

I removed a stack of newspapers from the chair and set them on the floor before sitting down. Then I told him I was looking for a photo from a past issue that might be helpful in a civil case I was working on. "You could have somebody dig it out of the morgue for me – don't even have to leave your desk. What do you say?"

He squinted his eyes at me. "What kind of civil case? What's your angle?"

I shook my head. "C'mon, Unc. It's no big deal – I just need a photo."

His dark, doubting eyes held mine for a moment. "You're lying. But I'm too busy to think about it right now. Just remember – if anything newsworthy comes of it, I get first dibs."

Then he scribbled a note and passed it to me. "Give that to the librarian, she'll look it up for you – a new girl but I forget her name."

At the end of a hallway away from the hubbub in the newsroom I tapped on the door marked Library and entered.

Three walls of this room were lined with filing cabinets – many of them were metal but some were of the old-fashioned wooden type. Recent issues of *The Spectator* hung like drying laundry on wooden racks in the centre of the room.

In one corner a good-looking blonde woman was down on one knee, riffling through a file drawer.

She swivelled her head, looking me over. I returned her gaze, then a wide smile brought her face to life. "Max Dexter … as I live and breathe."

I extended my hand to help her stand and she gripped it in both of hers as I searched my memory for her name. "Marjorie …"

"Scott. I was Thomas Sherman's secretary."

"Of course you were. I remember you now, Marge, you were a big help when we were investigating the murder of Thomas's father."

I watched the glow fade from her sunny face, "That was a sad business."

We didn't speak for a moment. "But now you're at *The Spectator*. Do you enjoy the work?"

"Not much, but it was all I could get when I left the Sherman company. Now, with the men back from the war, we women are expected to go back to that so-called 'women's work' of typing, filing or flogging dresses and corsets in the retail shops.

"Don't get me wrong, Max, I like the gals who work on the Women's page here, especially the Women's Editor, Leslie Johnson – she's a peach. But the male reporters are such wolves. You've gotta be on your guard all the time, that's for sure. Most of these guys have Roman hands and Russian fingers, if you know what I mean."

I smiled, imagining her setting those reporters straight, then I got down to business. "Scotty Lyle's my uncle – a reporter here."

She gave me a puzzled look; then shook her head.

"A grumpy little fat guy with a red face?"

"Oh, him. He's such a sourpuss – not at all like you, Max."

"He does take some getting used to, but I'm able to squeeze a little information out of him from time to time." I passed her Scotty's note. "And he authorizes me to speak to you."

She gave me a bright smile, balled up the note and tossed it into a waste paper basket. "No note required. Tell me what you need."

I explained what I was after and it took Marge only a few minutes to track down the article with Peterson's photo receiving a trophy from Mayor Lawrence.

"I'll write up an order and take it to the Photo department right away. For you, it'll cost $1 for an 8x10 print."

"All right. How much is it for other people?"

"The same – but folks like to think they're getting a bargain."

"You're a peach, Marge. Could you put a rush on it?"

"Sure. I'm sorta … friendly with one of the photographers. He'll do it for me lickety-split."

I paid for the print and she gave me a receipt. "Should be ready in a day or so, Max. Gimme your number and I'll call you."

CHAPTER THIRTEEN

When Isabel and I arrived at the office the following morning we could hear Phyllis speaking with someone inside. I swung the door open and was surprised to see Trépanier jump to his feet from the couch where he'd been snuggled close beside her.

His cheeks reddened as he stepped toward me to shake my hand. "Morning, Max. We were just … waiting for you."

I glanced at Phyl – she stood tall, smoothing her skirt and – holy cow, I think her lipstick was smudged.

"*Row-bear* has invited me to that Barbara Ann ice show I was telling you about, Max. Remember? It's next month – at Maple Leaf Gardens."

I vaguely recalled her gabbing to me about an ice show but with Trépanier now on board for a while, I was glad that she was directing her Barbara Ann enthusiasm his way and letting me off the hook.

He stepped toward me, looking anxious to change the subject. "I have some news about Madame Gauthier and I was waiting to see you before I drive to Toronto."

We took our usual seats in my office and I behaved myself by not asking him embarrassing questions about his intentions toward our secretary. "Good news or bad news?" I said.

"I don't know yet. I was watching at Madame's office late yesterday afternoon, a little after 1700, and I see her leaving with a man – he looks a bit younger than she is. They are very friendly, laughing and talking so I follow them. They walked to a *chic* restaurant called Winston's near King Street and Spadina Avenue so I went back to get my car then I drive to the restaurant to wait for them. A long wait, Max, more than one hour.

"When they came out, they got into a taxi and I followed in

81

my car to the Art Gallery of Toronto where they entered. So I bought myself a ticket to the opening of an exhibit by somebody called …"

He flipped a page in his note book and read, "*Lawren Harris – abstract paintings from 1910-45*". A lot of people there, Max – women in fancy dresses, some men in those tuxedo suits. I watched Madame and the young man laughing and talking with many of them, like they are all friends. So I walked around and pretend to like these paintings, then I left and waited in my car.

"When I saw them coming out, some newspaper photographers were taking pictures so I join them and take some too."

I reached over and delivered a light punch to his arm. "Nice work, Rob. Now, let's get your film over to Ronnie's shop right away –"

"Already did that. I put the film in his mailbox after I return from Toronto last night and I left him a note to please rush. I hope he has them ready later this morning."

"Okay – anything else?"

"Yes. After the art show, I follow Madame and the young man in their taxi; they stopped at her apartment and they both go inside. I parked my car and watched the lights come on in her windows and I wait for 15 minutes but he doesn't come out. Then I look for my caretaker friend but he was not at home. So I wait there longer – almost one hour more and then all the lights go off but the man stays in her apartment."

"Aha. Sounds like the pot's beginning to boil."

He paused, giving me a quizzical look, then said, "Yes, I think so. When I get the photos printed I will show them to the caretaker to see if he knows this man. And maybe this is the proof we need for the divorce case, Max."

I watched him lean back in his chair, a slight twitching at the corners of his mouth, his body language telling me, 'There you go, buster. Case closed.'

"This is good news, Rob. But let's not get ahead of ourselves. Call me after the caretaker looks at those photos and we'll go from there."

Mid-afternoon, Marjorie Scott called me from *The Spec* to

say the photo of Peterson and Mayor Jackson at the Jockey Club was ready.

When I got to the newsroom, I paused near the entranceway, glancing around, hoping to avoid my Uncle Scotty. I breathed a sigh of relief when I didn't spot him. I rounded the corner toward the library, and dammit, there he was in the hallway, speaking with a tanned, muscular character toting one of those Speed Graphic flash cameras favoured by news photographers.

As soon as Scotty noticed me he gave the guy's hand a quick shake. "Catch you later, Steve. Gotta run now."

He shuffled over beside me and draped a beefy arm around my shoulder. "Back so soon, laddie? This photo must be important so I'd better go along with you, if you don't mind."

"Of course, I mind. It's none of your damn business – but I suppose you'll try to butt in anyway."

"Fine way to talk to your dear old uncle. Now, let's get on with it."

He followed me into the library and when Marge was passing me the envelope imprinted, *Photo Do Not Bend*, he moved quickly to snatch it from her hand. "I'll look after that, little lady."

Her left hand shot forward as though it were spring-loaded and she clamped his wrist while his eyes bugged out. "No you won't." She plucked the envelope from his chubby fingers. "It's my job to give it to my customer. And I'm certainly not your 'little lady'."

Then she handed me the envelope along with a sweet smile.

I said, "Thank you, Miss," and walked out of the room.

He caught up with me in the hallway, grasping my arm. "Hang on, my boy, maybe I was a bit hasty in there."

"More than hasty. You were damn well rude. And I think you owe that woman an apology."

He scowled, then looked away for a moment. "What's that photo about, if you don't mind me asking?"

"What if I do mind?"

"Then I'll have the supervisor of the Photo section check the records and make me a copy."

I shook my head. "You can be such a horse's ass sometimes."

"I know. But it's part of being an ace reporter. Now, let's

have a wee peek, laddie."

I removed the photo from the envelope and he nudged me out of the way to scan it. "Hmmm. A guy at the Jockey Club shaking the mayor's hand while he receives a trophy."

He glanced up at me. "This guy looks familiar – his name's Peters … or something like that."

I let him hang for a moment – "Peterson."

He squinted as he zeroed in on some of the other folks crowded around the mayor in the winner's circle. Then he surprised the hell out of me when he looked up and said, "It's an interesting photo – why don't we step down the street, grab a quick one at Duffy's – my treat."

I couldn't believe my ears when Scotty had said "my treat" – it was the first time I'd heard those generous words slip from those stingy lips. And that set my antenna quivering about the contents of this racetrack photo.

CHAPTER FOURTEEN

We entered Duffy's and sat on a pair of red leatherette stools at the far end of the long bar, away from a small knot of noisy regulars. The jukebox was mercifully quiet – it wasn't often when you were in here that some chowder-head wasn't playing *The Woody Woodpecker Song* or some other so-called 'novelty' tune now popular on the Hit Parade.

Scotty withdrew a pouch of Player's Fine-Cut tobacco from his jacket pocket and a tiny packet of Vogue papers and proceeded to roll a cigarette. After he'd massaged the cigarette between his thumb and his fingers, he licked the edge of the paper and offered me his 'makings.'

I shook my head and he fired up his smoke with a wooden kitchen match that he snapped to life with a yellowed thumb-nail.

Liam made his way toward us, a grin on his flat, Irish mug. "You guys antisocial or somethin'? What's your problem, sittin' way down here?"

"My famous uncle is buying today and he doesn't want anyone to witness this historic event."

Liam guffawed as he delivered a light punch to Scotty's arm. "Say it ain't so, my friend. There goes your reputation – shot all to hell."

"I don't want to talk about it. Just bring us a couple of Peller's Ale – and a bowl of nuts."

As we waited for our beer, he was poring over that photo and I asked him, "What's so interesting about these guys?"

He slid it toward me and pointed to a short, swarthy guy standing near Peterson and the mayor. On his mug he wore a pencil moustache and a wide smile. "Looks like he might've placed a bet on Peterson's winning horse," I said. "D'you know him?"

He raised his eyebrows. "You haven't met him yet? I'm surprised, my boy, – a guy with your reputation for mixing it up with the Mob."

"Only when I can't avoid it,"

He tapped his finger on the photo and I paid close attention – despite, or maybe because of, his often-invasive manner, Scotty had earned a respected reputation as a top-notch crime reporter. "That's Vincenzo Belcastro. He's the new boss in Hamilton since your bosom buddy Tedesco left for a permanent vacation in Dante's Inferno."

I looked at it more closely. "Short, dark and handsome," I said. "Looks like a Latin lover in one of those steamy Greta Garbo movies."

"Don't let appearances fool you. He began his career as a soldier in Buffalo with the Maggadino crime family where he rose quickly through the ranks. As I understand it, the Don has taken a special interest in him – has him working on the Canadian end of an underground network to import heroin from the Middle East, via some family connections in Italy, then into the U.S. and Canada. And for the last several years he was Tedesco's underboss, strategically located in Niagara Falls – a foot in both countries, so to speak."

Tedesco had disappeared last December but I missed the news that Belcastro was now in the boss's chair. Of course, I wasn't on the Mob's Christmas card list.

Liam returned with a couple of bottles of Pellers in one hand and a small wooden bowl of Spanish peanuts in the other. He plunked them down in front of us and squinted his eyes at me, "So, Max – there's a rumour goin' around that you're engaged to be married. I hope the lucky lady is that assistant of yours – the lovely Isabel."

Scotty swivelled toward me and clamped my wrist. "What's this? Engaged? I didn't hear a damn thing about it."

I peeled his fingers off me. "I guess I forgot to ask your permission, Unc. So now you know."

His face drooped like a British bulldog in a bad mood. I felt a tiny pang of guilt but it didn't last long. If he knew what Isabel and I were actually planning, he'd be poking his nose in, trying to run the show – and to hell with that.

"We're talking about a fall or maybe winter wedding – just a small civil affair but we haven't settled on any details yet."

"You're one lucky dog," Liam said as he shook my hand like a pump handle. "Congratulations, Max."

Several of the professional drinkers down the bar were clinking their empty bottles together in unison, signalling for service. Liam bustled away, saying, "Duty calls."

Scotty pulled a long face, then he grumped, "Fall or winter, eh?"

"We're still in negotiations, Unc."

"Your Aunt Flo would be disappointed if she wasn't invited to your wedding. You wouldn't want that, would you?"

I stared at him but didn't reply. Scotty had always hoped that Flo and I might become friendly some day – after all, she was my only aunt. In fact, she and Scotty were the only relatives I knew. But Flo had never gotten along with my head-strong mother and had nothing to do with her since she'd left town years ago. And since then, Flo had transferred her anger and disappointment with her sister to me.

Scotty always hoped that Flo might come around and 'forgive' me but that hadn't happened. She was always stiffly polite whenever we met, but my mere presence seemed to rekindle her hostility toward her sister. Some wise man once said, 'You don't get to choose your family – dammit!'

We clinked bottles and took a long swig of Peller's Ale. "We're not in a rush to tie the knot, Unc. I'll keep you posted."

Setting my beer aside, I took a closer look at that photo, concentrating on the animated features of the trackside punters surrounding the Mayor – Peterson, the proud winner with his self-satisfied smile and this natty Belcastro character behind him. But that mobster's smile was more like an alligator's grin.

I tapped the photo. "This Peterson guy, do you know him?"

"Never met him. But I do like to follow the ponies, so I know he's a local businessman and he races several very nice nags that he keeps at a horse farm near Whitby, I think. I've seen him here at the Hamilton Jockey Club and at the Woodbine track in Toronto." He glanced up from the photo, sending me a sharp look. "So he's the reason you ordered this photo? C'mon, Max, open up – what's the story here?"

I didn't respond because someone else in that photo had caught my eye – I'd just noticed the image of a woman half-hidden behind Peterson's shoulder and an electric jolt zapped though me.

Scotty noted my reaction. "Someone you know, Max?"

"Not sure. I'll have to take a closer look when I get back to the office."

I watched his eyes when he snatched the photo from my hand, trying to see what might've attracted my attention. Then he shook his head, slid it back into its envelope and passed it to me. "You'll let me know if there's any funny business going on here, eh?"

"You can bet on it, Unc. Scout's honour."

"Sure, sure – you told me the same damn thing a couple of months ago and I'm still waiting to hear from you."

CHAPTER FIFTEEN

I was surprised to see Trépanier pacing in the hallway in front of our office when we arrived the following morning. He got my full attention when he bent forward to take Iz's hand in his and brush it lightly with his lips. "You look *très belle* this morning, *mademoiselle*," he said in that Maurice Chevalier accent.

She glanced toward me, lifting one eyebrow, enjoying the frown on my mug.

I clapped him on the shoulder, maybe a bit harder than I'd intended – maybe letting him know who was boss here. "Morning, Rob. You're the early bird today."

We sat in my office while we listened to his report.

"When I arrive in Toronto early, I watch Madame Gauthier go to her office. The man I saw her with yesterday was not around and she works downtown all day. It is hard to watch when nothing is happening, Max."

"Don't I know it."

"After I follow her back to her apartment, I showed my caretaker friend the photographs I took at the Art Gallery of Toronto."

He paused a moment and I sat forward in my chair. "C'mon, Rob. Who is this guy in the photo?"

Isabel was shuffling her feet.

He lowered his voice to an almost-whisper. "He says the man is Madame Gauthier's brother."

"No," Iz said, at the same time that I said, "Dammit."

"It's true. The caretaker says he visits his sister several times a year –" He paused while he glanced at his notebook. "He stays a few days so he can meet with curators at some art galleries in Toronto. He has a job at a big art place in the United States. Then my new friend shows me the brother's business card and I copy it in my note book."

He flipped back a page and read, "Marc Gauthier - Assistant Curator, Painting and Prints Department, Museum of Modern Art, New York, N.Y."

I leaned back in my chair. "I'll be damned."

"That's an important job," Iz said. "He may be a young man, but he's no lightweight in the art world with a position like that."

Rob flipped another page and continued, "The caretaker said he met the brother last summer when Madame asked him if he could find a parking spot in the garage for his car. He told me her brother always gives him a couple of dollars for parking there before he goes back home. But when the weather is bad, he travels by train.

"I ask him if they act like brother and sister. He said, yes, when they meet they just give a small kiss on both cheeks. I believe him, Max. I don't think Madame is the guilty one in this case. But I will continue to watch her if you say so."

I agreed with Trépanier that this lead now appeared to be a blind alley and I turned to my partner.

"What do you say, Iz? Think we should switch our focus here?"

She didn't respond right away, appearing to examine the palm of her left hand as though she might read the future in the crisscrossing lines there. Then she raised her head, "I think we should go back to Jackie Nelligan. If it can't be proven in court that Peterson's wife is committing adultery, then the family assets would be divided equally – not what he might be counting on."

"You're right about that," I said.

"But do you really believe that Mr. Peterson might've paid his investigator to rig his report to make it look like his wife had committed adultery?" She was shaking her head at me; "It would ruin the man's reputation if that became public knowledge."

I shrugged my shoulders. Isabel had been raised in a sheltered world of wealth – she was schooled by the nuns at Loretto Academy before attending university. She'd had little opportunity to see what a lot of folks did to survive in a world that favoured that fortunate flock who perched on the upper rungs of society.

"You can hire someone to do anything you wish, Iz. All you need is the moolah to do it."

No-one spoke for a moment as we sat as silent as mourners at a grave site in the Holy Sepulchre Cemetery across the bay.

Then Isabel stood up. "I'll call the Nelligan office right now to see if Jackie has time for us today." Then she bustled out of my office.

"I think you are correct about Mr. Peterson," Trépanier said. "But I don't know why he would make such a risk. He is already a rich man with a beautiful wife."

"I don't know either. Could be jealousy or greed or god-knows-what."

We remained silent for another moment. "What do you wish me to do now, Max? Maybe I should return to my regular job."

"Hell, no! I agree that Madame doesn't look like the guilty party. It looks like her husband is lying – maybe to cover up something he's doing. But let's keep that caretaker on tap; you can stay in touch with him – ask him to keep his eyes open and if he sees someone other than her brother there, he could let you know. When this investigation is over maybe we'll give him a case of beer or a bottle of hooch for his help."

"Good idea, Max."

"In the meantime, Isabel and I will see Peterson's lawyer and we'll explain what we have so far. If we're still on the job then I've got a few ideas."

I flipped through some papers on my desk and withdrew the photo of Peterson and the Mayor. I tapped an image with the eraser end of my pencil. "Here's our man at the Hamilton Jockey Club accepting a trophy from Mayor Jackson. And this guy in the background is Hamilton's new Mob boss; his name's Belcastro. But I'm also interested in the woman who's just behind him."

I was pretty damn sure it was Ida Lucas and I planned to show this photo to Longo at the Connaught to get his opinion – too bad this wasn't a clearer image of her …

"You're the photographer here, Rob." I kept my pencil on the woman's picture. "Is it possible to enlarge this section of the photo?"

"I could take a photo of this one and have it enlarged but it wouldn't be any better. We need the negative to get a clear image."

I gave him an ear-to-ear grin, picked up the phone and dialed Ronnie's number at the photo shop. "It's your best friend calling," I said. "And I need a small favour – does that buddy of yours, Gordie White, still work in the photo department at the *Spectator*?"

He paused, making me squirm before he answered. "He might. But why should I use up a favour from him on your behalf?"

I took a deep breath and puffed it out. "Because I saved your life in grade five when Kevin O'Neill was beating the crap out of you in that vacant lot behind St. Mary's School."

"You sure it wasn't the other way around, Max?"

"Positive. And I recall you promising me that you'd do anything for me for as long as I lived."

"Oh boy, you've gotta fanciful memory. Now, what d'ya need this time?"

I explained what I wanted and added, "Trépanier is still working with us and he'll bring the photo right away. So when you talk to Whitey –"

"All right, already. Send him over – I'll see what I can do."

"I'm really grateful, pal, I owe you …" I hung up the receiver when I heard the dial tone in my ear.

Rob was shaking his head while he listened to my malarkey. "You're not like anyone I've met before, Max."

I slipped the photo back into its envelope and passed it to him. "Take this to Ronnie and show him the woman we're interested in. I guess he'll outline that area or –"

"I know how to do all that, Max. After he calls his friend, I'll take it to the *Spectator* office. And if I stay in the photo department they might work faster so I will leave."

"Good man." And I waved him out the door.

Isabel entered my office a few seconds later. "I almost ran into *Row-Bear* hurrying out. You didn't let him go already, did you?"

I shook my head. "He's gone to have a photograph enlarged and he'll be back later. Were you able get a hold of the lawyer?"

"She's tied up in court all day but she can see us first thing tomorrow morning."

"Okay, thanks." I stood up as she approached and I wrapped my arms around her, squeezing her tight against me. "In that case we have time to slip over to the Wentworth Arms for a nice, romantic lunch."

"That's sweet of you, Max," and she took a half-step back to straighten my tie. "But I'm meeting Emma Rose at her office for what she calls a 'working lunch.' She'll have something sent up from that Chinese restaurant on the main floor of her building so we can eat while we discuss the fraud case she has me working on. I won't bore you with the details."

"It's not that I'm bored …"

Her eyes held mine in a wrestler's grip. "Okay, what would you call it?"

"Um … you know. Accounting fraud, cooking the books, well – that guff's just not up my alley."

"But it helps to pay the bills."

"Of course …" I could feel the corner I'd backed myself into getting tighter by the second. "Please don't think I'm ungrateful for your contribution to the business, Isabel …"

When I began to fidget she moved forward, planting a kiss on my cheek. "I'm just teasing you, Max. You respect what I'm able to do and I admire your spirit – your strength of character when we're in a difficult situation."

I let out the breath I was holding, tightened my arms around her and whispered, *"You're the cream in my coffee*, Iz."

She crooned in my ear, *"And you will always be my necessity."*

It was just before noon when Phyllis poked her head into my office. "I was going to have lunch with *Row-Bear*, but he's not back yet. You want me to bring you a meatball sandwich from Spiro's?"

"Okay, thanks. But with an extra meatball this time and maybe on one of those Kaiser thingees for a change."

She rolled her eyes. "It's your stomach, Boss."

CHAPTER SIXTEEN

After lunch, I called Grace to check on Danny.

"He's feeling a little better, Max. On my way back from McMaster today, I dropped in to see his teacher at Hess Street School. I told her Danny's mother was away for a while and I was helping out – and that his measles should run their course in a week or so. She's a sympathetic woman and appreciated my visit. Turns out that Danny's one of her best pupils, especially in art class but you and Isabel already suspected that. And he tries hard to get along with his classmates – 'eager to fit in' was how she put it. Have you learned anything more about his mother?"

"We're still working on that. In addition to her jobs at Robinson's and the Royal Connaught she leads a busy, after-hours life, if you know what I mean. And she might even be involved with some members of the Hamilton Mob. So that doesn't leave her much time to look after her son."

Grace remained silent for a moment. "That's a shame – but I suspected it might be something like that. You must've seen that his clothes are quite worn and they're a bit too small for him. When he's over the measles, I'm planning to take him and Vincent over to Eaton's boys' wear department. He'll probably object at first but I'm learning that when he sees I'm serious about something, then he toes the line."

"Hang on a minute. I certainly didn't intend that you'd have to clothe the boy –"

"Let's not argue about it. Danny needs help and I'm going to see that he gets it. I don't want to hear another word about it."

"Okay, Grace." I knew her well enough to know that once she'd set her mind to something it would take a small army to change it. "I'm glad he's in such good hands," I said. "I'm thinking about approaching his mother but I'm not quite ready to do that yet."

"Well, don't rush on my account. I'm enjoying having another boy in the house. You should have heard them during that hockey game on the radio last night – Toronto won the second game of that series and, my goodness, I've never heard such cheering. Their voices were still hoarse this morning."

"One more thing, Grace: is it too early to ask if you'd learned anything about Ida's pills that Isabel gave you for analysis?"

"'Fraid so. I dropped by the lab this morning and my friend hasn't had a chance to check them. I'll let you know as soon as I hear, Max."

Trépanier returned to my office later in the afternoon. "You'll be pleased with the results, Max. This enlargement of the woman at the racetrack is better than I expected."

He slid the envelope across my desktop and I withdrew the photo. "Yowza - this is pretty damn good."

The photo showed Ida turning toward the camera as she was moving between Peterson and Belcastro, the mob boss. It made me wonder which one she'd actually accompanied.

"Nice work, Rob. It's just what the doctor ordered."

I slipped the photo back into its envelope and I added one of Trépanier's shots of Peterson's wife. Then I pushed my chair back and stood up. "Let's take a hike across the street. There's someone I'd like you to meet – I'll fill you in on the way."

When we walked past Phyllis's desk, I watched her look up at Trépanier and her eyes fluttered as though she were about to swoon. 'Ain't love grand,' I said to myself.

We entered the Royal Connaught's main dining room where the staff was busy preparing the tables for dinner. I saw Longo chatting with another waiter and gave him the high sign. He joined us right away.

I cocked my thumb toward Trépanier. "This bum served with the Vandoos. You remember they were on vacation in Belgium and Holland near the end of the war? Meet Rob Trépanier."

Longo nodded in his direction. "Max thinks he's a comedian so try to ignore him – that's what I do." As they shook hands, he said, "Everyone calls me Longo, you might as well, too."

Then he turned back to me. "So what are you after now, Max?"

"I brought a couple of photos I'd like to show you. Can we go somewhere private?"

He checked his watch. "I'm free now so let's slip down to the Men's beverage room. I've got time for a quickie."

We followed him down a flight of back stairs to the street level where the beverage room was located along the John Street side of the hotel beside the coffee shop.

Inside it was dark, smoky and surprisingly busy for so early in the afternoon. We sat at a table away from some loud-mouth characters and within seconds a skinny waiter balancing a tray-load of draft beer glasses plunked down a filled-to-the-brim, 10-ounce glass in front of each of us. "That'll be 10 cents apiece, gents."

I took a dollar bill from my wallet and slapped it on the table. "Bring us another round in 10 minutes and it's yours."

He reached for the bill but I kept my hand on it. "I said 10 minutes, bub."

He shrugged then hurried away.

Longo grinned at my antics. "You really work at being a hard-ass, Max. Now what about this photo?"

I removed it from the envelope and tapped a finger near Peterson's image. "We're interested in this woman. D'you know her?"

He angled it to catch the light from the glass entrance door. "Of course I do – it's Ida Lucas. The same dame who was with J.B. O'Brien when you were here for dinner last week."

"You'd swear to it on a stack of bibles?"

"Damn right. She often stays here overnight so I see a lot of her – well, you know what I mean."

I pointed to the man just ahead of her. "How about this guy?"

"Name's Peterson – a big gun at the Steel Company. I see him here quite often but he's snooty when he's sober; you have to call him, 'Mr. Peterson, Sir'."

"What about when he's not?"

"He's got a skin full, he says, 'call me Pete'."

"Does he come here with other businessmen or with some babe on his arm?"

Shaking his head now, giving me the hard eye. "That'll cost ya, bub."

I checked my wallet – a lonely bill inside. I slid it across the table, careful to avoid the beer spills.

He snorted, "Two bucks? That's the best you can do?"

"Sorry pal, but the cupboard's bare." From the corner of my eye I spotted Trépanier reaching into his jacket pocket and I placed my hand on his arm.

"Take it or leave it," I told Longo. "But if you leave it, I'll have to beat you to a pulp."

He shook his head as though he were pitying a beggar on the street corner. But not before snicking the deuce off the table and stashing it in his pants pocket. Then he reached for the photo and pointed to the image of Ida. "She's his favourite."

I sat back, taking a long pull on my beer as Trépanier turned toward him. "Do you see Peterson during the week or just on the weekends?" he said.

Longo eased back in his chair, not about to play ball with some slick-looking guy he'd just met. He reached for his beer, swallowed a healthy gulp, set the glass down precisely in the centre of its condensation ring, then zeroed in on him. "Vandoos, eh? You guys still dragging around that flea-bitten, shaggy-assed goat you keep as a mascot?"

I caught the faintest trace of a grin on Trépanier's mug as he shifted in his chair, now closer to Longo. "We're looking for a new goat." He paused a beat. "Had to eat the old one when Nazi storm troopers trapped us inside a bombed-out church for five days without food or water."

Longo didn't speak for a moment, squinting at him. "Oh, yeah? How'd you cook it then?"

His face close to Longo's now, Trépanier lowered his voice. "Didn't cook it. We ate it raw."

Longo gaped at him, his mouth hanging open.

"Now let's get back to business." Some steel in Trépanier's voice now, taking the reins. "Does Peterson come here just on the weekends?"

Longo's eyes were wary, maybe revising his first impression of this varsity-type, clean-cut war veteran with the foo-foo accent. "Just during the week," he said. "Never on the weekend."

"Okay. But if Ida's his favourite – does that mean he also sees other women?"

My head swivelled from Longo to Trépanier and back, as though I were watching a ping-pong match.

Longo said, "Yeah, that's right. He's also sweet on Trixie – she's one of the other hostesses here and Ida's best friend. They often go on double dates."

Trépanier sat back in his chair and flicked his eyes toward me, passing me the ball.

"These … dates," I said. "Does another guy join them or do both women go with him?"

He frowned at me and shrugged. "I've just seen two men and two women."

"Do they stay here in the hotel – book a room?"

He shook his head. "Sometime, but they usually go to his place. In fact, he slips me a few bucks to drive them when he's flyin' high."

"To his home in Westdale, eh? On Forsyth Avenue?"

"Nope. He's got a swanky place on the top floor of the Pasadena Apartments – over on Bold Street, near James South."

That rang a bell – Grace Clark lived on Bold Street, just a block west of there. "What do you do with his car?"

"Park it in the lot there and I leave the keys with Ida. Then I walk back to the hotel – it's not that far."

I thought about that for a moment, then asked him, "Sounds like you're pretty chummy with this guy."

"He's my best customer, Max, and I rely on him for a good part of my income these days. So I need to keep him sweet."

When he handed the photo back to me it jarred my memory. "Almost forgot – this guy beside Peterson, you probably know him, eh?"

He glanced at the photo again. "Sure. That's the Mob boss, Belcastro. Everybody in the night life knows him. And I've seen him at Peterson's apartment too. I heard on the grapevine that he sometimes uses party photos to blackmail some of the bigshots in town. He squeezes them for a sweet deal or some other favour."

I shook my head and filed that away in my memory bank. "One last thing," I withdrew the photo of Carole Gauthier from the envelope and passed it to Longo.

"Do you know this woman? You might've seen her with Peterson."

He made a close inspection of the image and passed it back it to me. "Nice lookin' babe, but I've never seen her before – with Peterson or anyone else. Who is she?"

I waved his question away. "Doesn't matter."

The waiter returned with a full load, shuffling his feet while I drained my beer glass; then he doled out three filled glasses and clinked the empties onto his tray. The dollar bill had disappeared and he said, "Come again, gents."

CHAPTER SEVENTEEN

Early that evening, Iz parked in front of Frank Russo's small home on Mulberry Street in the north end of town. She'd instructed me to buy a bouquet of posies at the outdoor Farmers' Market for Angela and she'd picked up a bottle of vino for dinner.

Frank ushered us in at the front door and Angie bustled toward us from the kitchen, drying her hands on a tea-towel. "Welcome, good friends." She kissed Isabel on both cheeks and hugged me. "Haven't seen you folks for weeks and we've missed you." She inhaled the fresh-cut aroma of the technicolour tulips and smiled. "They're lovely, Max, thank you. I'll put them in a vase."

Isabel linked arms with her and said, "Let me help." They chattered their way into the kitchen.

Frank held up the wine bottle we'd brought and read the label with a flourish, "*Montepulciano d'Abruzzo*" then he smacked his lips. "Now, this is a wine with some hair on its chest, Maxie." He draped one arm around my shoulder, holding the bottle up to the light. "Betcha anything that Isabel picked this out. You don't know your ass from your elbow when it comes to wines. Or a few other things that I could mention."

"Thanks, bud. Is this how you greet all your guests? No bloody wonder you have so few friends."

A big grin on his mug now as he walked me to the sofa where we sat. I pointed with my chin toward his leg, "Still got a bit of a limp, I see. We make a fine pair of bookends."

"But mine's getting better," he said. "You'll probably be stuck with yours forever. That takes some grit, man."

Frank had been shot high up on his left leg last Christmas when we were ambushed by some mobsters in the basement of a vacant house only a few blocks from here. For him, the sawbones at St. Joe's was able to patch up his wounds and his mobility was almost back to normal. I couldn't say the same for my leg; the army medics had said I'd been damn lucky not to lose it. But walking with a limp beat the hell out of not walking at all.

"Like me to put on a little music, Max? I got a couple of classic records today."

"Thanks but I think I'll pass on that." Frank wasn't what you'd call a music connoisseur – his idea of classical music was Slim and Slam's version of *The Flat-Foot Floogie with the Floy Floy."*

"Okay, what'll you have to drink? A Peller's ale or a Peller's ale?"

I grinned at him. "Lemme think about it a minute."

He returned from the kitchen with a couple of Peller's and two beer mugs. As he sat down, he said, "You're company. And Angie doesn't like me drinking from the bottle when we have people visiting – she says it's not couth."

"Yeah, I'm learning about that." We clinked our bottles together, drank a couple of big glugs, then poured the remainder into the mugs.

I set mine down on a cardboard coaster that someone had pocketed from the Flamingo lounge on MacNab Street. "Where are the twins, Frank? You hiding them upstairs?"

"They're with their grandmother – she'll bring them back after dinner."

"I guess they're walking now, eh?"

He gave me a dark scowl. "Of course, they're walking – they're a year old now. And they're Russo boys: walkin' wherever they damn well please."

I lowered my voice. "I guess you'll be thinking about another one now – maybe a sister for the boys."

He placed his beer mug on the coaster just so, taking his time, his voice an almost-whisper. "How did you know? Did Angie tell you?"

I shook my head. "She didn't tell me a damn thing. But is it true?"

"Yeah, but the Doc says she might have some kind of pregnancy-related thing with one of those long medical names. Don't worry, he says, we'll monitor her condition closely – as if that might set our minds at ease."

"Is there some medication for whatever it is?"

"He's prescribed some pills for her blood pressure, but we're not sure what's really going on. Just the thought of losing this baby, or God forbid, losing Angie, well, I've gotta admit that it scares the shit out of me, Max. I don't know what I'd do without her. I'm tellin' ya, we're so damn worried that we're even talking about going back to church again."

I stared at him a moment, his features contorted, but he didn't continue – I could only imagine the depth of his distress. "If there's anything we can do, Frank, just let me know."

I watched Angela carefully during dinner – she chatted and laughed and appeared to be as happy as usual. It made me wonder if Frank was just another worried father – more concerned than he needed to be over some common pregnancy condition. But I only knew what most men knew about the female reproductive system – and that was Sweet Fanny Adams.

"We're hoping for a girl this time," Angie said. "We've agreed that three children is the perfect size for our family."

Frank was quick to respond. "Yeah. I wanted a big Italian family, maybe six or seven, but Angie was happy with two so we sawed off in the middle."

I looked him in the eye, a serious look on my mug. "But how can you know in advance how many children God will send you?"

He scowled at me. "Not at the table, Max." Then he pointed at the large serving dish of lasagna and I passed it to him.

When the coffee was served, I tapped my cup with a spoon. "Isabel and I have a little announcement to make."

Frank stretched way back in his chair at the head of the table, puffing out his chest, looking like a proud papa whose foot-dragging, unmarried son had finally decided to get off his duff and pop the question. He hadn't been promoted to detective sergeant for being slow on the draw.

"We're planning to get married later this year and we're just working out the details –"

"Hang on, Max." Isabel was holding up her hand and I put

on the brakes.

"Angie and I settled all the details in the kitchen. She and Frank will be our witnesses at City Hall on September 10 – that's a Friday. Then we'll have a small evening reception at the Connaught and leave for Québec City the following day."

Then she was quick to add, "Just as you suggested, Max."

I thought I'd proposed a later date and I hadn't mentioned the Connaught, but what the hell.

Frank was out of his chair, leaning over Isabel, kissing her on both cheeks. Then he pulled me to my feet and wrapped me in a bear-hug. "You've finally come to your senses, Maxie. I've been telling Angie for years that you weren't as dumb as you looked. We couldn't be more pleased for you both."

Now, the four of us were on our feet, forming a circle like a football huddle, laughing like loons.

Frank broke the spell. "This calls for a special toast." He made a dash for the kitchen and returned with a bottle of wine. "Nino Franco Prosecco," he said. "The perfect toast for this handsome couple – Angie and I hope you'll be as happy together as we are."

While we were sipping a second glass of the bubbly wine, Frank's mother returned with the twins. As soon as they entered, the boys wriggled away from their grandmother and ran toward their dad. When she noticed me, she opened her arms wide and I kissed her on both cheeks as I hugged her. "It's good to see you, Mama. It's been too long." She'd taken me in when I was just seven years old and raised me as her own son when my mother had skipped town back in the 1920s.

The boys wrapped their arms around Frank's legs – one on each side – while he pretended to escape their grasp, lifting his feet in slow motion. They clung to his legs like magnets to a steel pole.

"This is their 'catch the giant' game," Angie told us. "When the giant falls down the boys climb all over him."

Isabel poked me in the ribs. "Cute, aren't they Max? I hope it won't be too long before you can play 'giant.'"

Frank's mother turned toward me, her eyes wide. "I hope that means what I think it does."

She left her seat and wrapped her arms around me, kissing me on both cheeks. Then I told her about our wedding plans.

"Congratulations, my son. You deserve a family of your own."

"Thank you, *Mama*," I brushed the tear-drops from her eyes with my fingertips. "My family will always be your family too."

When the women trooped upstairs to get the twins ready for bed, Frank and I sat in the living room where he poured us another Peller's. "Married life," he said, his feet propped up on a well-worn leather ottoman. "It takes some getting used to, Max. You have to be prepared to forget what you always thought you knew about women."

I stared at him. "What's this? A father to son talk about the birds and the bees?"

He shook his head. "You're just like I was – I thought I knew the score too. But I've learned that women are a helluva lot smarter and tougher than we are. Men like to bluster about, barge into a situation that we know nothing about, believing we can solve any problem because we're big and strong and that we can fix any damn thing. But when we find out we can't, we just hit it harder or shout louder." He moved toward me. "Sound familiar?"

I shrugged. "Yeah. I've known some guys like that, especially during the war."

"It's in our natures, bud. We're stubborn louts – we elbow our way through life looking for sex and an easy way out. And when we're unsuccessful we blame someone else. Or punch a hole in the wall."

We stared at each other for another moment while I considered his little speech. "You've got a dark view of life, Frank. Not all men are like that."

He shook his head. "Of course not. But I believe it's at the core of our natures – something we have to overcome."

"And I suppose you'll say that women are the opposite – thoughtful, understanding and in control of their emotions."

"Not always, but a helluva lot more so than we are. I was beside Angie all the way through the birth of the twins: I couldn't believe her courage and determination – it was something I'd only seen on the battlefield in France."

We didn't speak right away, his words of wisdom still bouncing around in my mind. Then I reached forward and tapped my fist on his knee. "Thanks. I'll take that to heart."

Our beers had sat neglected while he was delivering his big-brother advice and we made up for it for now. When he set his beer mug down, he let out a loud burp. "Better out than in," he said.

I shook my head – since our childhood Frank was always the champion burper.

"Did you see the big race on the weekend, Maxie?"

"What race was that?"

"Around the Bay Road Race, you dummy. Happens every spring – don't you remember it when we were kids; watching them running down Burlington Street toward the canal?"

"Oh, sure. They're still doing it?"

"Damn right! They've been doing it since the 1890s."

"That long? Who won this year?"

He rolled his eyes. "Where've you been, pal? Scotty Rankine won again. You know, that guy from Galt? This was his seventh win, for Pete's sake."

"Okay, I remember him now. Yeah … Scotty. And there was also that famous guy from the Six Nations Reserve years and years ago."

He was nodding his head. "Tommy Longboat. He won the Hamilton race in 1906. And the following year he won the Boston friggin' Marathon."

"That's right. He was quite the runner – *and* a veteran of WWI."

Frank took another long taste then gave me a sly look. "Place a little wager on next year's Round the Bay? I'll take Scotty Rankine and give you 10-1 on anyone else."

"The hell you will. I wouldn't bet against that guy."

When the women came downstairs, Frank's mother pointed to him. "The boys want to say good-night to their Papa. Up you go."

I watched him leave the room, his left leg still dragging a little – it might've been painful but he was the type of guy who'd never let on.

Then his mother led Angie to the sofa. "Lie on your back, *cara mia*, knees up and try to relax."

I was on my feet now and I whispered to Iz, "What's going on? Angie's not feeling well?"

She squeezed my arm. "It's nothing to worry about. Frank's mother knows how to find out the gender of the new baby."

Angie grinned up at her mother-in-law. "Does this method come with a guarantee, *Mama*?"

"Money back if you're not satisfied." She asked Angie for her wedding ring and tied it to a piece of string about a foot or two in length; then she dangled the ring above Angie's belly. "If the ring moves back and forth in a straight line, you're having a boy. And if it swings in a circle, it will be a girl."

At that moment, the man of the house clumped down the stairs and into the room. "Oh, no, *Mama*, you're not practicing your hocus-pocus again. That ring on a string trick is just an old wives' tale."

She held up her hand like a traffic cop. "I'm not listening, Frankie. Old ways are still the best ways. Just you wait and see."

We stared at the ring for a long beat then it slowly began to rotate. "Thank God," Angie said. "I was really hoping for a girl."

Frank's mother looked up and sent him a self-satisfied grin but she didn't say a word. He shrugged his shoulders but kept his trap shut.

Later, Frank and I sat on the top step of the front porch where he fired up a Buckingham cigarette. "Angie doesn't like me to smoke in the house. She read an article in *The Spec* saying that smoking might be bad for your health and just in case it's correct, she doesn't want the kids to breathe my smoke."

"Yeah, I read something about that. Think it might be true?"

"Prob'ly not. But smokin' outside's a small price to pay for a happy wife."

An older couple ambled by arm-in-arm on the sidewalk and Frank returned their wave. After they'd passed by, he said, "Heather and Larry Johnson. I used to date their daughter in high school."

"You dated everyone's daughter in high school."

He punched my arm, grinning.

I cleared my throat and changed the subject. "I've got a small favour to ask, Frank."

"Nertz, not another one."

I ignored his remark. "Know anything about a character called Peterson? He's a vice-president at Stelco – rich guy, big house in Westdale, beautiful wife and all the trappings."

"Never heard of him."

I filled him in on the background of what appeared to be his trumped-up case for divorce and our suspicions about Peterson's Toronto investigator. "I'm hoping you might check your old files at the cop shop – see if there's anything that's not kosher in this guy's past. You know – gambling, driving offences – that type of thing. He owns some race-horses so that might be an angle. And I'm learning that he has an eye for a certain type of woman-about-town. What do you say?"

"Shee-it, Maxie. Here we go again. I don't know what the hell gave you the idea that my files are also your files. You want me to break the law?"

"What law?"

"The law that says I can't feed Max Dexter any of the confidential bad shit held in the strictest confidence by the City of Hamilton's finest – *that* law."

CHAPTER EIGHTEEN

I hurried into my office the following morning when I heard the phone ringing off the hook. Phyllis hadn't yet arrived and Isabel had gone into the florist's shop at the Connaught after she parked the car. But as I grabbed for the phone, the cord got tangled around my desk lamp and they both thumped to the floor. It took me a moment to get everything back upright.

"Is that you, Max?" Frank's voice loud in my ear. "What the hell's goin' on there?"

"Sorry, but the phone's got a life of its own this morning."

"I called a half-hour ago and got no answer. You keeping bankers' hours now?"

"What's on your mind, pal?"

He paused before answering and I pictured his dark features as he puffed out an exaggerated sigh.

"I was a bit early this morning, so I checked the files for this Peterson guy you asked me about. You said he was a big-shot in the business world and you're right on that score. After his first wife died, he remarried in '42. And he's had a couple of traffic violations – once for impaired driving, the other was a small fender-bender –"

"Wait-a-sec. If they were only minor offences why would the record show anything about his marriage?"

"I wondered about that too. It's because the car he was driving was still registered in his first wife's name. I guess he hadn't bother to have it changed."

"Oh."

"Other than that, there's nothing that jumped out at me in the file, so I don't know what's making you suspicious about him. This guy is what some people call 'a pillar of the community.'"

"Back up a damn minute: how did his first wife die? What happened to her?"

"Don't know the details yet. It was before the war and I've called for the file from the storage room in the basement. I'll have to let you know."

I couldn't lean on him any further or he'd get his ass in a knot again about sharing confidential police information. And there was no-one more stubborn than Detective Sergeant Frank Russo when he sat up tall in the saddle on his high-horse.

"Thanks, Frank. I really appreciate your help."

"Later," he said and hung up.

I set the morning mail aside, settled back in my chair and propped my feet up on an open desk drawer while I pictured that 'pillar of the community' looking down his nose at the hoi polloi so far beneath him. According to Vera's info, Peterson was not only a vice-president at Stelco, but the chairman of the Hamilton Progressive Conservative Party as well as Deputy Grand-Master of the Scottish Rite Masonic Lodge.

The toast of Hamilton's business world.

Then another image morphed into view: this was the carousing, 'call me Pete' version of the same man – dancing cheek to cheek with Ida Lucas or some other Betty Grable look-alike at the Circus Roof; buying another round of drinks for his table of after-hours pals and making plans to carry on at his penthouse apartment at the Pasadena after the lounge closed at midnight.

The toast of Hamilton's *demi-monde*.

My office door opened and Isabel said, "Oh-oh. He's communing with the spirits again."

I catapulted upright in my chair and had to hang on when it tipped forward and thumped to the floor.

"Welcome back to earth, Max."

I sent her a brave smile. "I get some of my best ideas from up there with the gods."

She was shaking her head as she sat on the chair beside my desk. "Emma Rose."

"What about her?"

"Remember that fraud case I'm working on with her?"

"Yep. Something to do with vending machines in some small businesses?"

"That's right – but not only small businesses. Those machines are becoming quite popular now – they're stocked with cigarettes, candy, soft drinks, and so on, and you see them now in a lot of busy locations, restaurants, hotels, bus and train stations, bars, nightclubs - those types of places. The vending company restocks the machines and retrieves the cash sales –"

"Hang on, Iz. How do the businesses that house those machines get paid?"

"The store owners are paid a commission. It's based on the volume of sales."

"All right, so what's fraudulent about that?

"That's what Emma's looking into. She was hired by the operator of a motel way out on Main Street East who's got some of these machines in his lobby. But he has no way of verifying the proper amount of commission he should get. Once a month the guy who services the machines will say, "Here's your share – it's $28 or whatever.""

"Sounds like it might be a racket. I bet the motel guy can't afford to hire someone just to keep track of those sales. So why doesn't he discontinue the service?"

"Emma says he tried but someone mysteriously trashed one of his rooms – set it on fire."

I shook my head. "Did he call the cops?"

"He did. They followed up with the vending machine company but nothing came of it."

"So why does Emma need your help on this case?"

"She wanted me to work with the motel owner to estimate the actual machine sales for a typical month. I've had one session with the man and I think we're making some progress. Already I can tell that he's being cheated out of half the commissions he should be receiving."

I thought about that for a moment. "Why don't I talk to Frank about this? If it's a problem for that motel owner then there must be other businesses in the same boat."

She bent over and pecked me on the cheek. "I knew I could count on you, Max. Now don't forget we're taking Bob and Aggie to Toronto today at one o'clock. It's all arranged."

I smiled at her, feeling the spot on my cheek where she'd kissed me. And I wondered what else she'd arranged.

Bob had told me a couple of weeks ago that the Department of Veterans' Affairs office had scheduled him for a medical review and that a consultation was booked at the Christie Street Veterans' Hospital in Toronto. At first he'd decided not to keep the appointment and we'd argued about it.

"I'm gettin' along just fine on my own," he said back then. "What're they gonna do? Fix me up with tin legs or a clunky pair of crutches? I can scoot around downtown and do my business just fine without their help. So to hell with that!"

I told him he was crazy.

"It's an assessment," I said. "You don't know what they might recommend. I read that there've been a lot of advances in the field of artificial limbs and you might be a good candidate. If you are, this could be your chance for a better life."

Then I waggled my index finger at him as though he were a naughty child. "And if you don't keep that appointment, by God, I'll rip your arm off and beat you over the head with it."

He gave me one of his guileless, altar-boy's grins, "Gosh, Max. You'd do that for me?"

We both laughed like hyenas.

"I still think you should go," I said. "You've got nothing to lose but your dignity."

CHAPTER NINETEEN

Isabel parked near the rear door of Bob and Aggie's apartment where they were outside waiting for us. Aggie joined Iz in the front seat while I held the rear door open for Bob. I was fumbling with his arm to assist him off his dolly when he told me to stand back. Then with one hand on the door's armrest and the other on the door jamb he vaulted himself up in a single smooth motion and plopped onto the rear seat.

"Quite a trick, Bob. I don't think I could do that."

"Nope. Your legs would get in the way."

He laughed out loud while I stared at him. "Let's go, Max. You can stash Aggie's suitcase and my duffel bag in the trunk. And they told me to bring my dolly, too. They want to see how mobile I am."

When I picked up his dolly I observed how well-made it was – some kind of figured hardwood, all corners neatly rounded and varnished to a high gloss. "I'm still wondering why you don't stick with your woodworking instead of selling your pencils."

"I told you before, Max, those small woodworking jobs aren't as steady as my pencil sales. And I enjoy being out-of-doors and meeting the people when they stop to chat."

"But I can't believe you'd make much money selling those things."

"You'd be surprised. I don't display a price list and when asked, I just say, 'Pay what you can'. But I rarely get less than two-bits, sometimes a half a buck or more. They're paying for my sparkling personality, you see."

I rolled my eyes. "Sure they are."

Isabel drove out York Street over the High Level Bridge to Burlington where she merged with the traffic on the Queen Elizabeth Way to Toronto.

Aggie turned in her seat and raised her voice. "We're really grateful for your kind offer to drive us. It's just too awkward to use the bus or streetcar so we usually take a taxi. That's okay for getting around town but way too expensive for a long trip like this."

Iz was shaking her head. "We're pleased to help. And we hope there'll be some good news for Bob."

"We've got our fingers crossed, "Aggie said, then she changed the subject. "I've been meaning to ask you, Max, about our young friend, Danny. We haven't heard from him lately."

"He's got the measles," I said, then described the sparse accommodations in Ida's apartment and the fact that he was practically living there on his own. I told them that we'd taken him to Grace's home where he was being nursed back to health.

Bob shook his head. "Boy, I'm relieved to hear that. We were worried about the kid. Is there anything we can do for him?"

"Not right now," Iz said. "Grace has a big home on Bold Street and a son who's a couple of years younger than Danny. In addition, Grace's sister has recently moved in there. We were over there just the other day and the boys are becoming good friends. We'll let you know when he's recovered – probably in a week or so, barring any complications."

When the women began to chat quietly, I turned to Bob. "Remember when I saw you reading the Daily Racing Form at Spiro's the other day."

"Yeah … what of it?"

"I'd forgotten that you're a horse player – maybe wager a few bucks every so often?"

He turned toward me, his eyebrows raised. "Sure – when I'm in the chips. Why do you ask?"

"Ever hear of a local businessman by the name of Peterson? Apparently owns some racehorses."

He paused a moment, looked out the window, then back to me with a question mark on his mug. "Yeah … what about him?"

"We're working on a case right now and his name came up. I'm getting the impression that there's more to this character than meets the eye."

It took him a moment to answer and that got my antenna waggling.

"You're right about that," he finally said. "There's a guy I know, hangs around Peace's Cigar Store – well, he's actually a bookie. He told me this Peterson guy's rollin' in dough, big job at the Steel Company with all the trimmings. And I've bet on his nags a couple of times."

"Did you win?"

"Yeah, I picked up a few quid. But I hear he's in a little hot water right now."

My ears perked up. "How hot?"

"It seems the Stewards' Committee at the Ontario Jockey Club is taking a dim view of some hanky-panky going on in his stables and –."

I stopped him there. "What do you mean by that?"

"The officials have a report that one of his winning horses was given a little booster."

"A what?"

He shot me a look that might've said: Where do *you* live – on the moon?

Then he explained: "Some trainers give their horses stimulants, such as cocaine, heroin or other drugs – to make them run faster. So the stewards have introduced saliva and blood tests to eliminate that practice and, in this case, Peterson's horse didn't pass the doping test."

"Ah-ha. Now what?"

"That could result in disqualification of his horse and a big fine. Or he might even be booted right out of the racing game."

"So that'll be the end of Peterson."

He shook his head. "Maybe not."

I was getting antsy while he decided to continue, but I managed to bite my tongue until he went on.

"I heard that one of the Jockey Club stewards is on the take from the Mob," he finally said. "And he might be able to make the case against Peterson go away. A little grease on the proper wheels – you know that game."

I considered this new info about 'call me Pete' then tucked it away, thinking it might come in handy later. Or maybe it would just gather dust in my memory bank.

"Don't tell anyone you got this from me, Max. I don't wanna get caught with my pants down over this."

I grinned at him then made a zipping motion across my lips. At that moment a huge Loblaw's transport truck rumbled alongside us and I couldn't be heard. After it passed, I said, "Thanks for this intel, pal. Anything else you know about him? Fancy women? Illegal drugs for humans?"

He shook his head. "Nah. I don't pay any attention to that kind of malarkey at Peace's."

As we approached the big city, I asked Bob, "What's the drill for your stay at Christie Street?"

"The paperwork they sent me said they'd take a bunch of x-rays, blood work, some other tests to measure my stamina and a psychological exam as well – 'all the basics' was how the letter described it. So when I'm recalled for the follow-up, the medics will have all that info about me. It'll take about two days for this first visit."

Aggie piped up, "I'll be staying next door in a hostel building where relatives from out of town can stay at no cost. We really appreciate all that you're doing for us and I'll call you when we're finished to confirm the time for our ride back home."

Isabel exited from the QEW in Toronto then turned onto Parkside Drive. "There's High Park on your left there," she said, "beautiful isn't it?"

We agreed that it was and Bob told her, "I don't know the way to the hospital from here. Maybe we could stop at a gas station and ask for directions."

Isabel was shaking her head. "No need for that. I called one of my former classmates at the University of Toronto who lives here and she gave me directions."

Past the park, she turned right onto Bloor Street then along to Christie Street where she made a left. "That's Christie Pits Park on the corner there. It was the site of a terrible race riot back in the early thirties – that's when Hitler was just coming to power and some of his Nazi sympathizers here in Toronto attacked the players on a Jewish baseball team, waving their swastika flags and swinging their billy clubs. Then the police had to be called when reinforcements for both sides joined in from the local neighbourhoods. It was a shameful thing and people still talk about it."

No-one spoke while Isabel continued along Christie St. to the veterans' hospital on our left.

"How do you know all that stuff?" Bob finally asked her.

"I was a student at the University of Toronto and it was the talk of the town for quite a long time."

We stopped at the front entrance where I got out with Bob and Aggie and we waited in the hospital's busy lobby for Isabel to park the car. I sighted a placard that gave a brief history of the place and pointed it out to Bob.

He was on his dolly, looking up. "Can't read it from down here. What's it say?"

I moved forward to read it aloud: "This building was a former factory, converted to a military hospital in 1919 to care for WWI vets and there were even some residents who survived the Boer War. But due to the large influx of wounded in WWII, residents here will be moved to a new and larger facility called Sunnybrook Hospital that will be officially opened in June of this year."

"Jeez, my timing couldn't be better, Max."

While Bob and Aggie checked in at the registration desk, Iz and I sat in the waiting area where we observed the passing parade – some veterans on crutches or in wheelchairs, others with arms and legs in casts or, in many cases, amputated. And to add to the hub-bub one man was wheeled in on a gurney from an ambulance, the attendant calling out, "Coming through, make way please. This is an emergency."

Unwelcome memories of my long rehab in that British hospital after I was wounded invaded my mind and for a vivid moment I become the body on that gurney.

"Are you okay, Max?" Iz was squeezing my hand. "You seemed to be somewhere else."

A shiver zapped through me and I stared at her. "I'll be okay, Iz. Sometime my mind plays tricks on me."

"This place must bring back memories that you want to forget."

I nodded my head. "You're right. But looking at these guys now makes me realize how lucky I am."

I read the empathy on Isabel's face as she watched these

wounded soldiers who'd come to Christie Street in hopes of a better life.

She turned to me, sadness darkening her eyes, "It's a shame that many of us who didn't go to war don't see the price that's still being paid by some of those who did."

Half an hour later, Aggie signalled us to join them across the room.

"A nurse is coming to take us up to Bob's room. The receptionist said she might be a few minutes."

A 'few' minutes turned out to be half an hour – what we used to call 'army time'. A nurse finally arrived pushing an empty wheelchair: she was short, slim and sharp-eyed. Her name tag read, Laura Anweiler, RN. Bob looked up at her and grumped, "I hope that chair's not for me. I get around just fine on my dolly – and it's a helluva lot more maneuverable than that thing."

She wheeled the chair closer and hunched down so they were eye to eye. "Oh, we're gonna have some fun with you, aren't we? What was your rank in the army, Mr. Muscles?"

Bob sat taller, his chest puffed out. "Corporal – Royal Hamilton Light Infantry."

"Well, you're in luck, bub – we just love the Rileys here. You boys are always so full of beans – and something else that I'm too polite to mention."

I smiled to myself, watching Bob staring at her for a moment, no doubt figuring how he was going to manage this spunky woman. "All right then," he said. "Let's get this show on the road."

Bob placed one hand on the floor to raise himself off his dolly and Aggie slid it out of his way. He signalled to Nurse Anweiler to hold the wheelchair steady while he clamped the arm-rest with his other hand then propelled himself onto the wheelchair. He turned to the nurse, a smirk on his puss that said, 'How d'ya like them apples?' She placed Bob's kit-bag on his lap then they swished down the hallway with Aggie in tow, carrying her brother's dolly.

Bob swivelled his head around the nurse to look back at us, wearing a wide grin as he sent us a big 'thumbs up' – the very picture of a guy who believed that his situation was firmly under his control. Some guys never learn.

Driving back to Hamilton, Iz and I talked about Bob's ability to accept the doctors' recommendations for improving his condition – especially if they advised him to consider the arduous and lengthy business of adapting himself to artificial limbs.

"I think he's got the strength of character to come through that process with flying colours, Max. I admire his determination to make a life for himself."

"You're right, he's certainly a courageous guy but that's similar to being stubborn. So I hope the hospital folks don't get his back up. He's used to his life right now and he won't find it easy to accept their advice."

She shook her head as she glanced over at me. "He's smarter than that, Max."

"He's smart all right, but he's still a man. And we tend to get pig-headed now and then – well, some of us do."

I watched her shake her head but she didn't respond. And once again I appreciated her ability to bite her tongue when she came face to face with the male ego.

As we approached Burlington, Isabel pointed out a large, empty plot of land beside the highway, where a billboard displayed a snazzy blue car with lots of chrome; the text shouted: ***Buy a 1948 Plymouth – made in Windsor by 2,265 skilled craftsmen of The Chrysler Corp.***

"Years ago, my father bought that property on a hunch that it might be valuable someday. Think he might be right, Max?"

Beyond the billboard, there was a huge weedy field, Lake Ontario off in the distance, and we were still a few miles from Burlington. "It's in the middle of nowhere so I don't think anyone will ever build this far out of town."

CHAPTER TWENTY

The following morning, I received a call from Wendy Crane who gave me the low-down on that Martin Investigation outfit in Toronto.

"One of my pals on the Toronto force remembered this guy's father as a good man, a legit investigator. But he says the son's a shyster. He took over the business when the old man died. And now he caters to people who can pay top dollar for a so-called investigative report that shows whatever the customer wants it to show. So, if you need photos to prove your Missus is running around on you, even though she isn't, then he's your man."

"Just a sec, Wendy. Those reports must get challenged in court. Why aren't they thrown out by the judges?"

"That's what I asked my friend. He told me this guy is slippery as well as being a fast talker – a real flim-flam artist. His photos are not quite in focus and they're cleverly shot from an oblique angle – or the subject is partly obscured. My friend thinks he's as crooked as a dog's hind leg, but he's still in business. At least, for now."

"Thanks for this info - you've confirmed my suspicion." I inhaled a deep breath before I continued. "Listen, I'm still feeling badly that I didn't stay in touch when I was overseas and I'm pleased to know that you're married now. But you didn't tell me your husband's name, and your name too, I guess."

"His name is David Hunter. A swell guy, Max - you'd enjoy his sly sense of humour. But I kept my maiden name because I've established my reputation with it and that's how people know me. After all, David doesn't own me like a piece of furniture – I'm my own woman with a different history and career than his. Now, that doesn't mean that I don't love the daylights out of him."

She surprised me and I wondered if Isabel might feel the

same way and wish to keep her maiden name. "Your hubby's okay with that?"

"Of course he is. If he weren't he wouldn't be my hubby."

Not five seconds after I hung up the phone, it rang again and I said, "Is that you, Wendy?"

Frank Russo said, "No, it ain't Wendy. It's your big brother calling. I have to pick up a parcel for Angie at the Post Office right now and afterward we could grab a cup of coffee. I'll meet you at that Russell Williams restaurant, across from the Cenotaph. Say yes or no."

"Yes."

"Okay. 15 minutes."

Then a dial tone.

I hung up the phone, wondering what the hell was going on. It wasn't in Frank's nature to be mysterious.

Fourteen minutes later, I cut across Gore Park and entered the restaurant, mid-block on the south side of King Street. Frank was leaning out from a rear booth, waving at me.

I hadn't been in here recently and the place had been renovated since my last visit. Now an eye-popping, candy-apple-red, arborite counter and stools ran along one wall and a row of booths upholstered in a similar shade of vinyl along the other.

And the big Wurlitzer jukebox in the corner could also be operated by those new table-top selectors at each booth. But the same goofy tunes were still on the playlist: some birdbrain had just selected Guy Lombardo's stodgy version of "I'm My Own Grandpa." No surprise that he was called Guy Lumbago by my army buddies overseas.

We ordered coffee from an end-of-shift waitress; her nametag read, *Olive.*

"And I'll have a donut with mine," Frank said. "One of those big honey-dipped thingees."

"Same," I said.

She looked us over, then rolled her eyes. "Cops," she said under her breath and clumped away.

Looking at the jukebox selector at our table, I realized that it, too, was a type of vending machine and I recalled that I had planned to talk to Frank about how those vending machine companies operated. When I put the question to him, he said, "Isabel's correct. There's a lot of hanky-panky going on in that business. I read a report from the U.S. saying these machines were becoming one of the biggest sources of revenue for the Mob. Only a fraction of the money collected gets reported for tax purposes. And if a nightclub, for example, refuses to place some machines in the lobby then the Mob arranges for certain 'accidents' to occur until they do. It's a big money-maker, Max, like many other cash businesses."

The waitress arrived and we made short work of the donuts then settled back to slurp some coffee.

"Now, what's all this cloak and dagger stuff, Frank?"

He yanked a couple of paper napkins from the chrome dispenser and whisked off the flakes of sugar decorating the front of his jacket, then sucked the sugary coating off his fingers. "That accident you asked me to look into? When Peterson's first wife ran off the road up on the Mountain?"

I leaned closer because he'd lowered his voice to a whisper, our heads almost touching now. "What did you find out?"

"I checked the files in the basement storage area. The old geezer who's in charge down there had a helluva time finding the proper file – the system we use is way out of date. Anyway, I looked through the contents, made a few notes for myself then returned to my desk. But within the hour I got a call to report to the Deputy Chief."

"Yikes. That old boy must've passed the word."

"Roger that. So I hot-footed it up to the Deputy's office. He's a conniving old fart so I didn't know what to expect. 'What are you looking for in the dead files,' he says, then he grills me for the next 10 minutes. At first, I thought he was gonna rip a strip off my hide."

"What did you tell him?"

"I said I was following up on a routine robbery case on James Street North some time ago – we'd nabbed a suspect named Peters but the file I was given referred to this accident with a Mrs. Peterson."

"Smart answer – you always were a good liar."

"Then I asked him, Why? Is there a problem? No, no, the Deputy says, but I happen to know this man, Peterson, and I wondered about your interest in him."

"Oh, shit."

"Yeah, it gave me a jolt, too." Frank made a quick scan of the restaurant again before he continued. "So I began to back out of his big office, explaining it was only a simple mix-up; then he gives me the cold-eye and says, 'Carry on, Russo. But don't poke your nose in where it doesn't belong.' "

"Close call, bud. He's gotta be covering for Peterson."

"Yeah, I got that message loud and clear. So promise me you'll keep me posted on any developments, eh? I don't wanna get caught by the short hairs."

"I promise."

He didn't speak for a moment and I had to goose him along. "C'mon, Frank. What was in that damn file?"

He tried to sip from his coffee cup but found it was empty so he signalled the waitress for a refill. We didn't speak until she'd tanked us up and left.

"Didn't find a helluva lot," he said. "That crash happened in December of '38. Road conditions were icy and she skidded at a curve near Albion Falls. The car smashed through a guard rail and rolled down the hill until it came to rest against a big boulder."

"No witnesses?"

"Nope. But a short time later a motorist called it in: officers were dispatched to the scene and the body was taken to the morgue - DOA."

"Follow up?"

"Coroner found no evidence of alcohol or other drugs. It was ruled an accident. But the investigating officer was killed during the raid on Dieppe in '42 so I can't talk to him. And I didn't see any evidence that the file had been tampered with at a later date."

I thought about that. "You think it was too clean?"

"That occurred to me. But maybe I was suspicious because you told me there might be something iffy about that crash."

I was disappointed that my hunch about Peterson's involvement in his first wife's death seemed to be going up in smoke. "What about her car? Anything in the file about it being monkeyed with?"

He was shaking his head before I'd finished speaking. "I'm a step ahead of you there. The file says it was taken to an auto wrecker's way the hell out on Beach Road so I spoke with the manager on the phone. He checked his records – the car was stripped then crushed for scrap. So that's the end of that story."

Dammit. We sat without speaking for a moment. "Not a good sign that the Deputy Chief was tipped off, Frank. I'm wondering why he's so interested in this old case."

"You ain't the only one, bud. Gotta be some kind of cover-up."

"What do you think we should do now?"

He fiddled with his coffee cup before he replied. "Maybe nothing. Is it worth risking my career for?"

I put myself in his boots – a wonderful wife, a pair of healthy, happy kids and another on the way. A promising career with the Hamilton coppers – promotion to Staff Sergeant on the horizon, and, if he kept his nose clean, even the possibility of becoming one of the 'white shirts' in a management position someday.

If it were me, would I risk looking into this cold case? Not bloody likely.

"Maybe we should just drop it now." I said.

"Hang on, there's still one more guy I can talk to but he's on leave until next week. I'll let you know what he says."

Damn – I felt crappy that he was willing to take that risk for me. But I didn't stop him. Instead, I said, "Thanks, pal."

We finished our java and were sliding our rumps out of the booth when he gestured with his chin and whispered, "Lordy, get a look at that babe sitting at the end of the counter - her skirt's hiked up so high you can see France."

I snapped my head around and got an eyeful. "I'm surprised at you, Frank. You're a married man."

"Hey, I'm just reporting."

CHAPTER TWENTY-ONE

Yesterday had turned out okay, all things considered.

But Saturday was another matter.

For most of this week I'd been staying over at Iz's home, but last night I'd stayed at my apartment to pack my stuff and clean up. I sorted my clothing, filling two large paper sacks for the Salvation Army with older items that I no longer wore and placed them on the porch for collection. Then I filled my duffel bag and a couple of cardboard boxes with the balance of my clothing from my dresser drawers.

Isabel arrived promptly at 0900 this morning to pick me up. I stashed the duffel bag in the trunk of her car, then we placed the boxes on the back seat and I laid my suits and new topcoat on top of them: pleased to see we could make the move in just one trip.

We'd just finished sweeping the floors and tidying up when the agent from the rental agency arrived for the final inspection.

"You should go with him," Iz said. "In case there's something you missed. What about the bedding – sheets, pillows, blankets?"

I shook my head. "They came with the apartment – and they've seen better days. If I left anything else, he's welcome to it."

When the guy had finished his walk-around, he joined us in the living room. "Looks good to me," he said. Then he gave me a cheque for the damage deposit that I'd paid when I moved in and I swapped him for the keys to the place.

"Last item," he said as he signed the inspection form on his clipboard and asked me to sign too. He gave me a copy then transferred a sheet of carbon paper under the next blank form.

We sat in Iz's car at the curb for a minute or two without speaking. Then she reached for my hand and squeezed hard.

"It's D-Day, Sergeant Dexter. Are you ready to jump?"

I slid closer and whispered in her ear. "Does Bogie love Bacall?"

She poked a finger in my ribs and as we drove away I waved goodbye to my old apartment.

And to my old life.

We parked in her driveway and I was staring up at her palatial home on Ravenscliffe Avenue at the foot of the Mountain. Only a 15-minute drive from my former apartment but a lifetime away from the tiny, cramped home in the North End where I grew up with Frank's family after my mother skipped town.

Isabel was becoming adept at reading my mind. She reached for my hand and held it in both of hers. "It's just a house, Max. It was part of my mother's estate and I did nothing to earn it. But now it's our job to make it a home – to be grateful and generous with our good fortune. And to raise our children in the same way."

I gulped. Was I dreaming in technicolour to think that I might become that devoted, loving father whom Isabel wished her husband to be?

Her bedroom – now our bedroom – was at the rear of the house on the ground floor. We carried in my worldly belongings from the car and set the cartons on the long bench at the foot of a bed the size of a trampoline. It took us only three trips from the car.

She opened the door to the walk-in closet and snapped on the lights in there. "This is your end, Max. Let's unpack your clothes."

This was the only closet in the room but it had two doors: one at either end of the 20-foot wall.

Iz removed my two suits and a sports jacket from their wire hangers and re-hung them on padded hangers embossed with the Holt Renfrew imprint.

"I've rearranged my dressers, Max. That one by the wall is

yours – the top two drawers are empty, and I can make more room if you need it."

As I unpacked the boxes and emptied the duffel bag, she put away my clothing, rhyming off the items like a quartermaster taking inventory. "Your suits and three pairs of slacks go in the closet; these white shirts and sport-shirts we'll put on hangers. Six neck-ties … hmm, we'll have to get you some new ones. Two pairs of dress shoes and one pair of loafers – they'll go on the low rack on the floor. We'll put your new topcoat in the closet by the front door along with your grey fedora, the toe rubbers and this pair of leather gloves.

"In the dresser there, you've got plenty of room for your underwear and socks. And here's your laundry bag – I usually drop the stuff off at Langley's every Saturday."

I couldn't keep the smile off my mug during this entire production; I made a wild guess that she was about 200% more organized than I was. If not more.

"One last thing, Iz. I also have my father's .32 police revolver and a couple boxes of ammo. I usually tuck them away in one of my shoes."

She paused for a moment, thinking. "Why not keep the ammunition apart from the gun? No point in making it too easy if someone wants us to shoot us."

"Smart," I said and handed her the ammo. "But don't forget to tell me where to find it."

When she'd finished, I stepped into the closet – my duds occupied less than 2 or 3 feet on the hanging rail – almost swallowed up by the array of women's dresses, suits, skirts, gowns, blouses and unmentionables that stretched to the far end where the image of a gawking male intruder was reflected in the floor-to-ceiling mirror.

We sat on the padded bench at the foot of the bed and looked at our reflections in the mirror over her dressing table. I saw a beautiful, uptown woman perched beside a country bumpkin who'd just moved to the city and was staying temporarily with a rich relative.

Iz slid her arm around my shoulder and pecked me on the

cheek. "There, that wasn't so hard, was it, Max? It took us all of 30 minutes – including the car ride."

We took a nap in the afternoon: this was something I'd never done until recently, when Isabel had introduced to me to its restorative powers.

When I awoke, she was propped up on a couple of pillows, reading a book. I turned onto my side to watch her until she lowered it, turning toward me.

"Good story?"

"It's sad, but heart-warming at the same time. About a poor family in the slums of Montreal at the beginning of the war. I think you'd be moved by this book, Max."

"What's it called?"

"*The Tin Flute* by Gabrielle Roy." Then she placed her bookmark between its pages, snapped it shut and placed it on her side-table. Snuggling up tight beside me, she said, "Now where were we before you nodded off?"

I was in the shower when Iz opened the bathroom door and called out, "Better shake a leg, Max. Our reservation is for 6 o'clock."

It was Phyllis's 21st birthday and we'd arranged a celebration dinner for her at the Innsville restaurant out on Highway 8 in Winona. When Isabel asked her if she had a special fella she'd like to bring as her date, Phyl said, "I have someone in mind – it'll be a surprise."

When I heard that story I'd laughed out loud, "Some surprise. Even her mother says that she's gaga over Trépanier."

We drove out Main Street East and I was gawking out the window as we passed the Stoney Creek Dairy Bar. "What was your favourite ice-cream flavour there, Iz?"

She didn't even hesitate. "Raspberry Swirl. I can still taste the tartness of those berries – they were picked nearby, you know. How about you?"

"Butterscotch Ripple – gooey and sweet. I met this guy from the Creek overseas, Terry O'Flanagan, and he told me that he had a boyhood ambition to eat a scoop of every flavour they offered in one sitting."

Iz shook her head. "Sounds like the kind of bone-headed scheme that only boys would try. Did he make it?"

"Nope. Half-way through the menu he ran outside and threw up in the parking lot."

We turned left off the highway at Lewis Road and parked near the small group of white-painted cabins beside the restaurant. "Cute little overnighters, Max. We could stay here if you get too tipsy tonight."

"That's not likely – I learned my lesson as a teenager in Jimmy Savatteri's basement when we got into his father's home-made vino."

A hostess met us at the entrance and led us past the lively bar area; we followed her downstairs where Phyllis and Trépanier were already seated in a quiet corner near the bandstand – quiet because the band hadn't set up yet. Rob jumped to his feet and went through his usual routine with Iz; then we examined the menus.

"It's cozy down here," Phyllis said as she looked around the room, "I love these red linen tablecloths and candles at every table. And that far wall is panelled with barn board – that's a nice touch too."

When our waitress arrived the men chose the prime rib speciality of the house and the women went with the more daring seafood platter. After careful study of the wine list, Rob finally chose a bottle – French, of course.

"I'll have a Peller's Ale," I told the waitress.

She glanced at Phyllis, eyebrows raised, "Everyone's over 21, right?"

Phyl gave her an ear-to-ear grin, "I wasn't yesterday but I am today."

The band arrived while we were eating and set up their equipment – which included a discreet sign on a tripod that read *The Gord Brown Quartet*. I recognized the leader as the same guy we'd seen at Robert's Restaurant last Christmas.

After dinner our waitress cleared the plates, then she carried out a small birthday cake and lit the candles at the table. The band swung into a snappy version of "Happy Birthday" and almost everyone in the room sang along.

Phyllis's face glowed as red as the tablecloths. But she stood and took a bow as she faced the happy singers and called out, "Thanks a lot, everyone," then she quickly sat down.

Later, with the cake eaten, another bottle of wine and glass of beer on the table, we joined the folks on the dance floor. After a couple of twirls, Iz said, "You probably don't notice it, Max, but you don't limp while we're dancing. So we should do it more often."

The band finished its set with a sensuous version of "Besame Mucho" and we approached the leader. He placed his big baritone saxophone on a stand beside his chair and I saw a clarinet beside an opened case on an empty chair. I shook his hand. "Pleased to meet you again, Gord Brown. We saw you at Robert's Restaurant with a trio and I'm guessing you've become so popular that you had to add another musician."

He looked me over with a grin then turned to Isabel. "You should bring your friend to the Brant Inn, Miss. We play with the Gav Morton Orchestra, the house band there. And Gav's looking for a guy with some snappy patter to keep the crowd happy when we take a break."

He and Isabel were getting quite a kick from the look on my mug and you would've thought that his little joke was a real knee-slapper. But some guys like to strut their stuff when they're in the presence of a beautiful woman, so I took his jibe in stride and I even begrudged him a little chuckle.

We returned to our table at the same time as Phyllis and Trépanier and I held Isabel's chair as she sat down. Rob glanced at me with a raised eyebrow as though he might've doubted my ability to behave like a gent.

Rather than take my seat, I said, "Excuse me, folks, but I have to see a man about a dog."

I skirted the dance floor and followed the arrow to *MEN* along a short hallway where I caught a glimpse into the rear of the kitchen. A couple of waiters and a guy in a chef's hat were leaning on their elbows beside a portable radio when Foster Hewitt raised his voice, "He shoots, he scores."

I stopped in my tracks and called over to them, "What's the score?"

The chef's hat said, "That makes it two-nuttin' Leafs. And if they hang on to win this baby, that'll make it three games to zippo. I gotta bet with Guido here for five bones that they're gonna sweep this series and so far, I'm lookin' good."

When I returned to the table, Iz grasped my arm and whispered, "Dance with me right now."

I was about to speak when she stood up with a look on her face that said, 'Make it snappy'.

I hummed along with the band's "Sentimental Journey" while Iz guided me toward the darker end of the room and signalled with her head toward a group of four patrons beside the far wall, a bottle of bubbly in an ice-bucket alongside their table.

I recognized 'Call me Pete' right away – he was sitting with a raven-haired beauty, her right arm curled around his shoulders.

"I watched them come in while you went to the washroom," Iz said. "I knew it was Mr. Peterson from the enlargement of that *Spectator* photo, but I don't know the woman with him. And – don't stare, Max – I don't know the other man either, but I'd swear that the woman with him is Ida Lucas."

A moment later, we danced near their table and I recognized the city's new mob boss; a smile on his kisser as Ida nuzzled close beside him, her lips against his left ear – the same routine I saw her use on J.B. O'Brien at the Connaught.

"You're right, Iz. She's with Vincenzo Belcastro; he's replaced Dominic Tedesco. And according to Longo, that dark-haired woman might be Ida's best friend, Trixie. He told me they often double-date."

"How would he know that?"

"Well ... he's a resourceful guy: he keeps a close eye on his customers at the Connaught – and makes himself useful for a generous tip."

Back at our table, I whispered to Trépanier that he should dance by the table in the darkened corner and tipped my head in that direction. "Let me know if you recognize anyone there."

He led Phyllis onto the dance-floor and I watched them foxtrot in that general direction, taking a roundabout route.

"They make a nice couple, don't they, Max?"

"Love in bloom," I said.

When they returned Phyl asked for another glass of wine. I wasn't counting but it must've been her third glass and I didn't think she was a practiced drinker.

"Sure you'd like another, Phyl?" I said.

"Of corth I am." Then she giggled like a school-girl.

I glanced at Iz and raised my eyebrows. The last thing I needed was Phyllis's mother phoning me in the morning to give me hell for allowing her daughter to become squiffy at the Innsville. I flicked my eyes toward the washrooms and Isabel caught my meaning.

She stood up, taking Phyllis by the arm, "Let's go powder our noses," she said. They skirted the dance floor as Gord Brown and his boys had the crowd on their feet and jitterbugging to a bouncy rendition of "In the Mood".

I moved over beside Trépanier.

"I should be watching Phyllis more closer," he said. "She looks *un peu pompette*."

"Yes – if that means 'too much to drink'. Maybe the French and the Italians have the right idea to allow their youngsters a bit of watered-down wine with their meals."

"You think I should I take her home now?"

I shook my head. "I wouldn't. Her mother might bite your head off. So let's wait a while longer."

He poured himself a half-glass of vino and took a tiny sip.

"Did you recognize anyone at that table in the corner, Rob?"

"*Oui.* Mr. Peterson with a woman I don't know. And Ida Lucas is with that Mafia man in the photograph at the horse race."

"Is your camera in the car?"

He nodded his head.

"Think you could get a photo of them when they're leaving?"

"Maybe. I can hide in those tall bushes beside the door."

"Is there enough light out there? You can't use a flash."

"I will try my best, Max, there's a big light over the door. But will a picture of Mr. Peterson and that dark-haired woman be enough to prove that Madame Gauthier is not the guilty person in his divorce case?"

"You bet it will. Pete hired the Nelligan law firm, claiming that his wife is guilty of adultery. And so far, we have your photos showing that she was with her brother and not some fictitious lover as he says. And now, if you're able to get a good shot of Peterson in the company of Hamilton's Mafia boss and two women of the evening – well, that should put this case on ice."

He raised his eyebrows. "On *hice*?"

When the women returned to the table, Phyllis's cheeks were pale and her manner subdued. Isabel flicked her eyebrows at me and I read that as a sign of mission accomplished.

Trépanier took Phyllis's hand and was whispering something in her ear as she gave him a wan smile.

I turned to Iz and lowered my voice, "She seems fine now. What did you do in there?"

"I splashed a little cold water on her face and told her how I handled my early experience with alcohol. She should be okay now – but don't give her any more wine."

Later, I was keeping an eye on Peterson's table in the corner and saw the men getting to their feet, readying to leave. I tapped Rob's leg with my toe to get his attention then tipped my head toward them.

He looked over then got to his feet. "Excuse me. My turn for the washroom."

I watched him skirt the dance floor and make a right turn through a shadowy area rather than left to the washrooms. Then he disappeared up the stairway to the front entrance like a phantom.

I turned to Phyllis, "I was watching you out there doing the jitterbug before. Where did you learn those jivey moves?"

She'd become quite talkative after she'd returned to the table and launched into a long story about the tea dances at Central High School, especially the annual Sadie Hawkins dance when the girls asked the boys for a date ... and on and on. I was impressed by her generous descriptions of her former classmates and their activities at Central High and at Wells Business College where she later attended.

Meanwhile, I glanced at Belcastro and Peterson as they

escorted their women to the door and left. I guessed that they'd only come here for dinner and were now on their way to some place more adventurous – maybe Pete's Pasadena Playhouse. And I hoped that Trépanier would be able to get a good shot of them while hiding in the shadows beside the stairs. But that was a long-shot.

A few minutes later, Phyllis was darting her eyes toward the washrooms, no doubt wondering why her date was taking so long. I was becoming fidgety too.

I got up from my chair and slid it toward the table. "I'm going to check on Rob. I don't know what's keeping him."

The band had returned from its break and some of the dancers were already on the floor waiting for the downbeat.

From the stairway, I looked back toward our table and was relieved that I couldn't see it from here. I mounted the stairs and stepped outside, my eyes searching the bushes on either side of the entrance.

Trépanier wasn't in sight.

Down the stairway, I parted the bushes and picked my way closer to the building. I found him slumped against the concrete wall, hair dishevelled, suit coat pulled down from his shoulders and his eyes were closed.

I shook him gently. "Are you okay, Rob?" I tilted his head toward me. "Can you hear me?"

One eyelid eased open – the other was puffy, swollen shut. His necktie was twisted from under his collar, maybe used to yank him over against the wall. He croaked like a bullfrog, "Is that you, Max?"

"Yeah. Are you okay? Maybe we should get you to the hospital."

Both eyes opened now. "Nothing's broken. I'll be alright."

"What the hell happened?"

He inhaled a couple of deep breaths and let them out in slow motion. "I came outside, got my camera from the trunk of my car, and I stand in the bushes where I'm able to get a good shot of the front entrance." He pointed with his head and winced, "Just over there. So when I see Mr. Peterson and the others coming out I get their pictures. But then I feel those bushes moving close behind me. I put my camera in the case right away and throw it under the stairs. Then two big guys grab me and start to punch – hard."

"I'm really sorry, Rob. It's all my fault – I should've realized that Belcastro wouldn't go anywhere without a couple of his goon bodyguards."

After a few moments, I was able to get him to his feet. "Here, lean against the railing and I'll get your camera." I couldn't see his right eye; it was swollen shut.

On my hands and knees, I found the camera under the stairs, relieved that he was able to get rid of it before those hoodlums noticed it. Then, with my arm around his waist, we limped slowly to his car. "I don't think you're well enough to drive, Rob."

He was about to argue and I cut him off. "How about this? We'll leave your car here overnight and pick it up tomorrow morning. Isabel and I will drive you both home now. How's that sound?"

He turned toward me and that caused him to wince. A pang of guilt shot through me as I helped him onto the rear seat of Isabel's car.

Hurrying back to the restaurant I was puzzling about what the hell I could say to Phyllis that would make any sense of the assault on Trépanier.

CHAPTER TWENTY-TWO

Monday morning got off to a late start.

I'd only been in my new digs for a couple of days and waking up in the morning with a warm body close beside me was still disruptive to my usual morning routine. But in a good way, of course.

After Isabel parked the car in the lot beside the Bus Terminal, we crossed King Street to the office. She continued on to Renner's drug store – "to pick up a few items," she said in that oblique way women adopt when they speak about their personal matters. There were some things a guy didn't need to know.

I was the only passenger when I boarded the elevator in my building. "Lookin' tired – but lookin' happy, Sarge," Tiny said. "You win the Irish Sweepstakes?"

I grinned at him. "In a manner of speaking."

He delivered a light punch to my arm. "Say no more, you lucky duck. Don't think I haven't caught the way that you and Isabel look at each other." Then he withdrew a small envelope from his jacket pocket. "Some character dropped this off for you. Said it was for that detective guy upstairs."

I looked at the envelope – my name in bold type, nothing else. "Old guy, young guy? Give his name?"

"No, yes and no."

I watched him smirking and I shuffled closer. "Would it help if I threatened you?"

"You just did. It's from Isabel's old man."

"He was here?"

He shook his head. "Nah. His chauffeur ran it in."

I pocketed the envelope. "This oughtta be good. Third floor please."

When I entered the office, Phyllis looked full of beans, typing a mile-a-minute, not a trace of that woozy imitation from Saturday night.

"Morning, Phyl. Get a good rest yesterday?"

She looked up with a grin. "Slept all day, Boss. And I'm really sorry if I embarrassed you and Isabel on Saturday night."

I shook my head. "We've all been there so forget about it."

"Rob phoned a few minutes ago. He slept late today and won't be in until this afternoon. But he'd like to speak with you, Max."

"Okay, how's he feeling?"

"He's still sore from his dust-up with those hoodlums."

"A night to remember, Phyl."

"I wish I could – but it's still kinda fuzzy."

Then she resumed her typing, a trace of pink on her cheeks.

I went into my office and called Trépanier. He answered on the fourth ring. "Welcome back to the land of the living, Rob. Phyllis says you're resting up and you'll be in later. But why don't you take the day off to recover?"

"*Non, merci.* I'm okay, Max. I'm a bit sore but it's better to move around. I will see you this afternoon."

I took a quick shuffle through the morning mail on my desk– a couple of bills, some advertising flyers, no cheques.

I looked up when the office door opened and Isabel entered with a smartly dressed woman about her age. I got to my feet when she introduced me.

"Max, this is my friend, Marilyn Edwards. We were classmates at Loretto Academy a few years ago."

"More than I care to remember," her friend said. She was a tall, slender woman wearing a green dress that was doing its best to cling to its owner's curves. She took a sinuous step forward, extended her right hand and I shook it. "Pleased to meet you, Handsome," she said in a breathy Rita Hayworth whisper.

I blinked, then glanced at Iz, who was trying to hide her smile as I shuffled my feet and tried to think of a suitable response. "Marilyn's a bit of a tease, Max. She's just having fun with you."

I smiled like a good sport who'd enjoyed their little skit.

"We ran into each other at the drug store," Iz said, "and we're going over to the Connaught now for a cup of tea and a little gab fest. You're welcome to join us, Max – I'm anxious to show you off to all my friends."

Was she pulling my leg?

Showing *me* off?

A gab fest?

I made a show of checking my watch. "Ah … maybe next time. I'm waiting for an important call-back."

After they left, I was seated at my desk when I remembered that envelope from J.B. O'Brien and wondered what the hell he wanted from me. I knew that Isabel had already informed him that his only daughter was now engaged to that two-bit private detective who occupied the bottom rung of Hamilton's social ladder. And the old goat certainly wasn't doing cartwheels about that – No-Siree-Bob.

Maybe he wanted to give me hell in person for moving in with Iz. But how would he know that? Unless she happened to mention it to him. And now, he wants me to pack my bags and bugger off.

I opened his damn envelope:

A small sheet of creamy vellum, his name imprinted on top.

A few cryptic words in black ink:

Hamilton Club
10:30
Ask for me

Shit, oh dear.

Should I or shouldn't I?

It was a few months ago when I'd last seen her father. We'd met in Isabel's room at St. Joe's Hospital after one of Tedesco's mobsters had forced her off the road and she'd crashed into a hydro pole. At that time, her old man had delivered a few choice words to Yours Truly, whom he'd blamed for Isabel's broken ankle. I didn't want to think about his reaction if he learned that she'd been shot in the arm while she was with me.

Later, I told Phyllis that I had a meeting with a prospective client and I'd be back in an hour or so. Iz had already left and was probably gab-festing right now with her chum.

It was another warm day for early April and the old guys on the benches in Gore Park were as numerous as the daffodils beginning to sprout around the statue of Queen Victoria. I hiked up James Street to Main where the Hamilton Club commanded the corner – windows heavily curtained, doors of solid oak and its nose in the air. According to Vera, it was *the* retreat for the city's male elite who preferred the privacy of their own company. Goes without saying that this was my first visit.

I tried the door but I should've known – locked as tight as a bank vault. A small engraved plaque read, *Deliveries at Rear Entrance* then I found the almost-invisible door bell. The bald guy who opened the door was dressed like a butler in a British movie – Jeeves or something.

"May I help you, sir?" And he sounded like Jeeves.

"I'm meeting Mr. O'Brien. Name's Dexter."

He bobbed his head and I followed him along a carpeted hallway; quiet as Dermody's Funeral Home in here.

He rapped twice on a solid oak door then opened it. "Your visitor, sir."

J.B. O'Brien appeared. "Come in, Dexter. Let's sit down."

The door snicked shut behind us and he bobbed his head toward a seating area across the room and I followed him. Without a doubt, his blue, pin-striped suit had been tailor-made and it fit him like a glove – a rubber glove. I deduced that he'd devoured too many of those fancy Royal Connaught dinners since I'd last seen him. And his thinning red hair was continuing to do so.

We sat in a couple of high-backed leather armchairs arranged in front of the largest fireplace I'd ever seen – but no fire today. A coffee service was laid on a small table between us and he poured two cups. "Cream? Sugar?" He pointed at them. "Help yourself."

He'd thrown me off-guard – his usual crusty manner wasn't on display this morning. And he'd actually smiled when I entered the room. Something ain't right, I thought, what the hell was going on here?

We sipped our coffee and he offered a plate of tiny

cupcakes. "Try a *Mont Blanc* –whipped cream with sweetened chestnuts."

I shook my head. "Thanks, but I'd prefer to hear why you summoned me."

He placed his cup and saucer on the table and dabbed his lips on a starched, white napkin. "As you wish, I'll get right to the point." He lowered his voice, "I'm going to take you into my confidence, Dexter – after all, you're engaged to my daughter and there's nothing I can do about *that*."

I wanted to smile but I forced a straight face and waited.

"I'm seeing a certain woman," his cheeks now beginning to bloom as he started to fidget in his chair. "Not a society woman, you understand. But a lovely person nevertheless, and she has a … complicated background."

He stalled for a moment and I let him sweat.

"You see, she happens to be acquainted with some men here in the city who operate … I guess you might say, on the outer fringes of the law." He paused and took a deep breath, letting it out slowly. "And I also know a few of those men."

"You do know they're criminals, right?"

He plopped back in his chair as though I'd pushed him, then slowly nodded his head. "Yes, I suppose they might be. Now … where to start?" His eyes roving about the room, unable to look at me directly.

I'd never seen him this befuddled and I recalled the lesson I'd learned from my old RCMP sergeant – "Just wait the buggers out," he'd said. "Give them all the rope they need to hang themselves." So I shut my gob and waited as he continued to stall for another tense moment.

"These … *criminals*, as you call them, they're pressuring me to sell them a parcel of land I own near Burlington, along the QEW. They happen to own the adjacent properties – one on either side of mine. Obviously, it makes sense to combine all three into one parcel for development purposes. But their offer to buy my land is a joke and I've refused to sell."

"How much did they offer?"

He hesitated, a grimace on his mug. "One dollar."

"And if you don't accept it?"

"Then …" his voice petered out and he took a deep breath.

"Then something will happen to my friend."

Damn … these boys were playing for keeps. "Did they give you a deadline?"

"Midnight," he said. "Three days from now."

I reached for my coffee and drank it all. "You're right to be worried, J.B. But what do you think that *I* can do about it?"

He sat a little taller in his chair. "I'd like to keep my friend from harm, of course. But not at the cost of losing my valuable property in the bargain. Now, I got the impression from my daughter that you have some acquaintance with these people so I'd like you to meet with Mr. Belcastro on my behalf and negotiate a fair deal for me."

I slumped back in my chair, thinking about the tight corner he'd backed himself into; glad that it wasn't me who was caught with my you-know-what in the proverbial wringer. But it would be a frosty Friday in hell when the Mob would allow an easy mark like J.B. O'Brien to slip through its sticky fingers. And I certainly wasn't anxious to let his problem become my problem.

"What do you consider a fair deal?"

"I want the fair market value for that land."

"Never mind what you want. What would you settle for?"

"I've already told you. So what do you think we should do?

Shit, now it was 'we'.

I didn't have to think twice. "If it were me, I'd sell the land for a dollar and get myself a new lady friend – one with no connection to the Mob."

He slumped back in his chair. "I can't do that."

"Can't or won't?"

Now he was on his feet and began pacing from one end of the room to the other. When he returned to his seat, he withdrew a small, narrow gift-box from the leather brief-case beside his chair. "I found this on my doorstep this morning," his voice a furtive hush. "In a plain brown wrapper."

He set the box on the table as though it were a live grenade and it seemed to pulsate between us.

"Open it," he said.

I stared at it – a blue gift box, *Birk's* imprinted on its top in silver letters.

When I opened it, I jerked backward and the lid tumbled to

the floor. Nestled on the cotton batting that lined the interior was a lady's finger – crimson polish on the nail – iron-red blood encrusted on the opposite end. And a silver ring on the finger, a sparkling diamond in its centre.

I let out the breath I was holding and it took me a moment to settle myself. "You believe that this is your lady friend's finger?"

He was staring into the fireplace and didn't speak for a moment. "I gave her that ring."

"Birk's must have sold many rings like this."

"I had it inscribed on the inside."

"Did you check?"

He turned to look at me, shaking his head. "No. I couldn't bring myself to touch it. But I know it's hers."

"Do you have a clean handkerchief?"

He removed his from the breast pocket of his suit jacket and passed it to me.

I lifted the finger from the box using the handkerchief and coaxed the ring off the finger. After I wiped the blood from the ring, I held it under the table lamp and read the inscription out loud – "Ida and Joe 1948." I hadn't known J.B. O'Brien's first name because I'd only heard him referred to by his initials, even by his only daughter. But this was a helluva way to learn it.

His face had drained of colour, his eyes beginning to flutter and … yes, there were tiny tears at their corners. "My God," he said. "What a mess. What'll we do now?"

That damn 'we' was back again.

I sat back in my chair, not pleased that he was trying to drag me into his dilemma with the Mob. Isabel's voice was whispering in my ear, *"He's a stupid man, Max, but he's the only father I have."* So, like it or not, there was no way I could turn my back on him.

I returned the finger to the box, set the ring alongside it and replaced the top. Then I slid it to his side of the table.

"What's your friend Ida's last name?"

He hesitated a moment, then said, "I'd rather not say."

"I can't help you unless I know her name."

His eyes were on fire when he whispered, "Lucas. It's Ida Lucas."

A gauzy image of Ida's son took shape in my mind. But his face wasn't Danny's face – it was a young Max Dexter's. And Ida's face had morphed into my mother's. In that moment Danny became my twin brother.

Someone was squeezing my arm and I blinked myself back to that plush meeting room in the Hamilton Club.

J.B. O'Brien was saying, "I repeat, what'll we do now?"

"Wrap this finger up and hide it in the freezer section of your refrigerator but don't tell a soul about it. I'll do some digging around and get back to you as soon as I can. And call me right away if you hear anything else from these guys.

"In the meantime, prepare yourself for the possibility of losing your land – that might be the least of your worries. If they contact you, try to stall them … tell them your lawyer's out of town or it might take a few days to get all the paperwork together for the sale of your property. You're a businessman – you'll think of some way to bend the truth to your advantage."

"But what are *you* going to do?"

"I'll try my best to save your ass – for your daughter's sake."

CHAPTER TWENTY-THREE

Back at the office, I made a lunch reservation for today at the sedate Green Room, up on the sixth floor at Eaton's – it was Iz's new favourite spot for lunch.

She was surprised when I invited her. "What's the big occasion?"

"No occasion – it's just because I love you."

"C'mon, Max. Spill the beans. You're a romantic, but not *that* romantic."

"After lunch."

This sixth floor addition at Eaton's was a recent development at Hamilton's largest department store. As well as this classy restaurant on the new top floor, there was also an auditorium for musical events, films and other presentations.

It wasn't busy today and we were seated at a window with a view of Hamilton Harbour at the foot of James Street North and we chatted our way through lunch. Isabel was becoming anxious with my delaying tactics until we'd finished eating.

I sat back in my chair after I polished off my dessert – a big slice of their famous butterscotch pie and I signalled for more coffee.

"Enough of this beating around the bush, Max. Now, tell me why we're really here."

I inhaled a deep breath, then another one, and passed her that tiny photo of Ida Lucas and her father in the photo booth at Niagara Falls.

She studied it for a moment, then raised her head, her x-ray eyes riveted on me. "Is that who I think it is? It looks like my father – and Ida Lucas."

"I'm afraid so."

"How long have you been holding this?" Her voice now an icy whisper.

"Not long. It's from our visit to Ida's bedroom."

She looked at the photo again and shook her head. Then she turned it face-down and slid it back across the tablecloth. "Why were you keeping it from me?"

I reached for her hand and squeezed it. "I was hoping there'd be no reason to show you – to spare you from being hurt. But now …"

I took a deep breath. She was right to be upset – she deserved the truth and I forced myself to continue.

"You already know that Ida has a reputation around town as a party girl. And Longo has been telling me about her adventures at the Connaught and elsewhere. He said that she prefers rich men who are eager to please her with expensive gifts. And this morning your father admitted to me that he's one of those men."

Iz was shaking her head, not wanting to believe me – but she knew me well enough to know that I wouldn't lie to her. Especially about a matter so close to her heart. "What do you mean, this morning?"

I inhaled a deep breath and continued. "He summoned me to his club while you were at the Connaught with your friend from Loretta. He told me it was urgent because someone had left a package at his front door this morning."

I lowered my voice. "It was a small box, containing one of Ida's finger."

Isabel gasped, covering her mouth with her right hand as she slumped back in her chair. It took her a moment to recover her voice. "My Lord, that's gruesome." She tasted my unwelcome words for another moment in silence. Then, "How could he know it was Ida's finger?"

"Because of the silver ring on it. He told me that he'd had it engraved – but he was too shocked and upset to touch it. I removed the ring and we read the inscription – it *was* the ring that he'd given her."

She didn't speak; staring out the window, trying to digest my news about her father.

After a moment, she said, "But that ring doesn't prove it

was actually Ida's finger. It could have belonged to some other woman."

"You're right. But it doesn't make any difference, does it? Your father believes it was Ida's and it's having the desired effect upon him."

"But who would do such a thing? And why?"

"It's a threat from the Mob. You remember pointing out that piece of land your father owns along the QEW when we drove by it the other day?"

"Of course, I do."

"Well, the Mob owns the properties on either side of it. Your father told me they've been pressuring him to sell his parcel to them so they could develop the entire site. So far, he's refused. And now they're turning up the heat with this finger – nudging him along so he'll change his mind. And with the unspoken threat that there could be other atrocities to follow."

"But why would these Mob people know anything about my father's personal life? I understand that they could easily find out he owns that property. But surely they wouldn't know about his *affair* – or whatever it is – with Ida Lucas?"

I was hoping that I wouldn't have to go into the unsettling details. I should have known better.

I reached across the table and held both her hands in mine. "We can't talk here. Let's go somewhere more private."

We walked a few blocks north on James Street and entered Christ Church Cathedral – as quiet as a tomb in here and we sat in a shadowy pew beside the south wall.

I slid my arm around her shoulders and spoke in a hushed tone. "Ida's connected to the Mob," I said. "The new boss, Belcastro's his name, has taken her as his 'special' friend. I learned from Longo that he sometimes uses women to entrap certain wealthy men so he can blackmail them to do something for him or face the consequences of being revealed to the public – or something even worse if they were slow to comply. Imagine the effect that such a revelation would have upon your father's standing in the business community or his position as a board member at St. Joe's Hospital. And it would certainly be the kiss of death for his hopes of becoming the Grand Poobah of the Knights of Columbus."

She didn't speak and I noticed that her eyes had misted up. I took both her hands in mine and brought her to her feet, my arms tight around her. "I'm sorry, Iz. He's not the first guy to be lured into a tight spot by a beautiful babe. And it won't be easy to release him from the clutches of the Mob."

She took several deep breaths to calm herself. Then her voice leaked out in a middle-of-the-night whisper. "It's hard to believe that people can be so cruel – blackmail, cutting off body parts. It's absolutely medieval."

As we walked back to the office we didn't speak until we got to King Street. "I'll bet you forgot that we're picking up Bob and Aggie," she said. "At the veterans' hospital in Toronto later this afternoon."

I gave her a self-conscious grin. "You know me too well. What time?"

"Aggie thought they'd be ready mid-afternoon so I agreed to get them about four o'clock. We can leave an hour before that, but I'd like to go home first to change into something more comfortable for the drive."

We were waiting for the elevator in the lobby of our building when young Rick hustled through the door waving a copy of today's early edition of the *Spectator*.

"Check the story on the Home page, Max. They jumped bail." Then he folded the paper, stuck it under my arm and ran from the building.

"Young man on a mission," Iz said.

I opened the paper to page three and we stared at the lead article that included two mug shots of those felons from the aborted payroll robbery at the Canadian Porcelain Company. They were identified as James LaBarde and Alain Pelletier of Windsor. They'd failed to appear in magistrate's court while they were out on bail and now a warrant had been issued for their arrest. The women had already been fined and released.

Isabel was studying the photos, absent-mindedly massaging her left arm where the bandage had been removed at her doctor's office yesterday. She'd come through her painful experience as bravely as some of the wounded soldiers I'd seen overseas.

"I wonder which one shot me," she said.

CHAPTER TWENTY-FOUR

I swung open the door to our office and stood aside for Iz to enter first. "Oh my," she said.

I looked past her into the startled eyes of Trépanier, his arms around Phyllis in a tight embrace. Phyl snapped her head around, her mouth open and her cheeks on fire as she squirmed free to straighten her blouse.

"Rob's back," she blurted out, her voice as loud as a fog-horn.

I grinned at her. "So I see. And I noticed you examining the swelling in that black eye he's wearing. Is he going to be alright?"

He stepped forward and shook my hand. "I am much better, Max. And I report for duty."

"Some duty," I said and waved my arm toward my office door, "C'mon in. I've got a job for you."

We sat at the table by the window. "You sure you're feeling okay, Rob? That's quite a shiner you've got there."

That stumped him for a moment. "Oh, you mean my eye. It is still sore but I'm okay."

"Good. Isabel and I will be in Toronto this afternoon and I'd like you to follow up on some information about Ida Lucas. Now that you know Longo over at the Connaught, I want you to question him about her. I'd like to know if she was working in the hotel over the weekend. If not, see if he knows where she might have gone. You could tell him we're concerned about her son, who's worried about his mother's absence. You know the drill, squeeze him for whatever you can get out of him. It might take a couple of bucks to loosen his tongue, so pay him if you have to."

I took out my wallet and handed him a five-dollar bill. "I

don't usually give him more than two bucks but you might have to go higher if the info is juicy enough."

He smiled at me. "I'm liking this work, Max. You get paid for being *fouineur*."

He read the puzzlement on my mug and said, "In French it means you are a noisy Parker."

I almost laughed out loud but I restrained myself. "Just so you know, we say a *nosy* Parker and I pointed at my nose. That's someone who sticks his nose into someone else's business. A *noisy* Parker would be someone who makes too much noise – too loud. But you were close."

Later, as we were driving past J.B. O'Brien's property along the QEW near Burlington, Isabel kept her eyes on the road ahead. I said, "There's your father's property–"

She flicked her eyes toward me for an instant, "I don't want to hear another word about him today. Maybe I'll feel differently to-morrow but I doubt it."

We arrived at the Christie Street Hospital at the appointed time and I spotted Bob and Aggie, waiting in the lobby – he was slouched in a wheel-chair, a sour look on his puss, and Aggie sat beside him on a bench with their bags.

"Boy, am I glad to see you two," he said when we approached. "Let's go."

An orderly wheeled him outside, then re-entered to return with Bob's wheeled dolly. "Sorry about that, buddy, but I just work here," he said. "Hospital rules: when you're inside, you walk or you're in a chair." Then he bent down to help him onto the dolly but he'd already swung himself aboard.

"Whew. That feels a helluva lot better," Bob said, "Now I'm in charge again." Then he scooted himself along the sidewalk toward the car while the orderly, his hands on his hips, stared after him.

Driving away, Isabel suggested that we might stop at a restaurant somewhere for an early supper.

Aggie shook her head, "Thanks, but I don't think so. It's difficult for Bob to manoeuver in those places. Besides, he still prefers his army grub."

Iz glanced over at her. "No, I don't believe it. What, for instance?"

Bob was listening to their conversation and raised his voice. "Wieners and beans are on my list of favourites and I often like a Spam sandwich for lunch."

I moved forward in my seat. "You hear that Isabel? I'm not the only one who's crazy."

"Besides," Aggie said, "I don't want to get back too late – it's my Euchre Night at St. Mary's Parish Hall and it starts at 7 p.m. sharp."

The women went off on another topic and I turned to Bob. "So what's the story? Did they give you another appointment?"

"Not yet. But I was really busy there – it seemed like they took a thousand x-rays, measurements and a bunch of tests. Can I do this? Can I do that? Does that hurt? You know – a lot of that poking and prodding. I thought it would never end. And after that, there were some psychological tests to see if I'd be able to handle the rehab."

"And what's the upshot, are they going to take you?"

"I think they might. They were talking about prosthetics, Max. They said it was a rapidly developing field. But the medics warned that the process wasn't easy. With a prosthesis, it could take a year or two – even more in some cases – for your body to learn how to navigate with it. And much longer, of course, with two limbs. Then they showed me a film. Oh, boy!"

"No walk in the park, eh?"

He gaped at me. Then we both laughed out loud.

Aggie turned to face us. "Would you boys keep it down, please? We're trying to have a conversation up here."

Bob gave her a quick salute and she turned back to Isabel. "By jingo!" she said. "They're like a couple of kids back there."

Bob lowered his voice and continued: "I think the highlight for me was meeting a guy who used to be in the same boat as I'm in now. He's undergoing a treatment that's similar to what they might recommend for me. This character was with the Hasty P's when he'd lost an unlucky encounter with a German landmine during the battle for Ortona late in '43. The blast sheared off both his legs above his knees. He lives here in Toronto and was at the hospital for a check-up."

"You were lucky to meet him, bud."

"I'll say. He doesn't know it but he might've given me the courage to allow these guys to go to town on me when they call me back for a second visit."

"But you didn't seem too happy about being in that wheelchair, eh?"

"Hell, no. It's a cumbersome thing to wheel around and outside, of course, it's almost impossible to get the damn thing over the curb and onto the sidewalk when you're crossing the road. One of the guys I met there said, 'The world ain't ready for wheelchairs yet.' But I did hear about an engineer at the National Research Council in Ottawa who's developing an electric wheelchair. Now, that might be just the ticket."

"Knowing you, the cops would probably take it away from you for speeding."

He turned toward me with a grin and I noticed that he was wearing a small blue service ribbon with red and white stripes in its centre pinned to his jacket. I was surprised because he never spoke in detail about his service overseas. "Isn't that the ribbon for the Military Medal, Bob?

He frowned, then finally admitted it. "Yeah. Aggie made me wear it at the hospital. She thought I'd be treated better by the staff. And maybe she was right because, all in all, they were pretty good to me there – aside from that damn wheel-chair."

I knew that the medal was awarded to non-commissioned soldiers for individual acts of bravery in battle and it sure as hell wasn't doled out two-for-a-penny. "Can you tell me a bit about it?"

He made a face, then turned toward the window for a moment. "I don't make it a habit, Max. I lost a lot of my pals during that raid on Dieppe."

Aggie must have overheard us speaking and now she reached over the seat for her brother's hand and squeezed it. "I think you should talk to Max. After all, he was wounded over there too."

He didn't say anything for a full minute as he stared out the window; then he turned back to me. When he spoke I could feel the pain of his remembrance in his voice. "Everything went wrong with the plan. As we were approaching the shore, the Germans were waiting for us, dug into caves along the cliffs; their aircraft were swooping down to strafe us and their snipers could pick us off as easy as targets in a shooting gallery. Our landing craft were under heavy fire; many of our tanks didn't make it to shore and some that did were hit and foundered on that stony beach. We finally had to retreat. I blame those high mucky-mucks, sitting back in London, who dreamed up the attack plan without knowing the difficulty of the landing area there. It was doomed to fail.

"A lot of guys in my platoon were wounded and couldn't get back to the boats; many of them drowned that morning or were shot dead in the water by the snipers. I was a strong swimmer back then and managed to get a number of the wounded back to the landing craft waiting for us off-shore. On my last trip back to the boat, there was a huge underwater explosion; the guy I was carrying flew into the air and my whole body went numb before I blacked-out. Somebody managed to drag me into the boat and when I woke up in a British hospital I discovered that my legs were still in the English Channel."

Nobody spoke much for the rest of the journey.

I tried to help Bob out of the car at their apartment and onto his dolly, but he did most of the work.

Aggie gave us both a hug. "Thank you Isabel and Max. We couldn't have done this without you."

"Make sure you call us for the next appointment," I said. "We're hoping that Bob will regain some of his old mobility."

As Bob scooted away from us toward their apartment, Aggie lowered her voice, "He's wavering because it won't be easy for him – so I'm saying my prayers that he'll go back for the return visit. It could make a big difference in his life – well, in both of our lives."

CHAPTER TWENTY-FIVE

The following morning I phoned Grace Clark to inquire about Danny's measles.

"I'm glad to report that he's well on the road to recovery, Max. His rash is almost gone and he's feeling peppier. He'll be able to return to school soon – probably Monday."

"That's good news. I got a look at his mother recently but I didn't have a chance to speak with her. As I suspected, she's leading a very active social life. She's running with a fast crowd and I'm beginning to think that she's simply deserted her son."

"Yes, you could be right. Yesterday I dropped in to see Mrs. Macaluso at the Langley Cleaners shop. She told me that she'd seen his mother leaving the building with a couple of tough-looking men – they were carrying out armloads of her clothes and her suitcases – then they drove away. Not a good sign for Danny."

"I'm sorry, Grace. It seems that I've left you with the problem of what to do about the boy if Ida doesn't return."

She didn't take a second to respond. "I've already given that some thought. He'd be more than welcome to stay with us while we search for any other family members that he might have. Failing that, well, we'll cross that bridge when we come to it."

"Thanks, Grace, did–"

"And before you ask, yes, I spoke with my friend in the lab about Ida's pills."

"Thank you. What are they?"

"They're bad news for Ida, that's what they are. They're a fairly new class of drugs called 'amphetamines'. My friend told me this drug was developed about 15 years ago and was first marketed in the U.S. as Benzedrine – an inhalant for use as a decongestant. Later on, in the more concentrated pill form, it was prescribed for obesity, low blood pressure, depression, chronic pain, – a whole slew of ailments. However, it also has a euphoric, stimulant effect and it increases stamina. But they're addictive if taken too long, so doctors won't renew prescriptions if they suspect their patients are abusing these pills. As a result, he said there's a big black market demand for them."

"Yes, I've heard about that," I said. "If fact, I believe it might've been the same drug that was given to some servicemen during the war. I remember hearing that aviators were given pills to keep them alert on long flights and to submarine crews when they were submerged for lengthy stretches. Now you've got me wondering if Ida might be addicted to these pills."

"I think that's a strong possibility, Max. It might explain why she's lost interest in Danny and has apparently left him."

We didn't speak while we contemplated that possibility.

"I appreciate your help, Grace. I'll let you know as soon as we learn anything more about Ida."

I replaced the receiver in slow motion, imagining myself in Danny's shoes, knowing exactly how it felt to be abandoned by your mother; then reliant upon the goodwill of others to give you shelter. And after a while, if you were very lucky, they might even show you some love, as the Russo family did for me.

The phone jangled me from that reverie.

"Max, it's Frank. Meet me at the Majestic – 10 minutes. *Capiche?*"

"See you there."

I hiked up King Street and turned right onto James North for a short block to Market Square where the busy Majestic Grill faced the south side of City Hall. I heard a commotion across the street and watched a frantic farmer chasing a chicken that had escaped from his stall at the busy, outdoor Hamilton Farmers' Market behind City Hall. A small group of boistrous onlookers appeared to be cheering for the chicken.

When I entered the restaurant, I saw Frank in a booth near the front window and I slid in across from him.

"Don't look now," he said, "but that's Mayor Lawrence in the booth across from us."

I turned to look and he thwacked my arm with his hat. "Hey, I just said don't look. You never listen, do you?"

154

"Good morning to you, too, Frank. What's up?"

Before he could answer, a waitress appeared and doled out menus. "Two coffees and two of your cinnamon rolls," he said.

She slid the menus back under her arm and stooped down close to him. "Your mommy never taught you to say 'please'?"

As he stared at her, I watched his dark eyebrows knitting together in a puzzled frown. In a situation like this, I knew from experience that he always had trouble deciding between apologetic and smart-ass.

"Please," he said, sounding contrite. Then, "If it ain't no bother."

She rolled her eyes and retreated.

"You're a smooth operator, Frank. Now tell me why we're here."

He gave me a withering look as I smiled back at him.

"Remember that collision when the first Mrs. Peterson slid off Mount Albion Road and was killed?" he said.

That wiped the smile off my puss. "Of course I do."

"I spoke to that guy I told you about … his name's Todd Lantz, a staff-sergeant now and he just returned from vacation this morning; he was a good friend of the original investigator and he told me what he remembered about that crash. Don't forget that it happened way back in December, 1938 – damn near 10 years ago. So his memory is kinda fuzzy. But he recalls that his partner suspected that the dead woman's husband might've had something to do with it."

"Now we're getting somewhere. What else did he say?"

"At first, it looked like a straight-forward investigation – wintry weather, slippery roads, and maybe she was taking a corner too fast when the car crashed, killing her. Then he interviewed Mr. Peterson and got the impression that he knew a helluva lot more about it than he let on. And when he spoke to the manager at the auto wreckers where they took her car, he got the run-around. A couple of days later, he returned for another crack at that guy and was told that the car had already been crushed flat and hauled away. That's when the investigator's boss took him off the case and assigned him to another unit."

"Dammit. Who was his boss?"

"Staff Sergeant Nichols."

155

That name rang a bell. "Nichols. Isn't he –?"

"Yep. He's now the Deputy Chief."

We didn't speak for a moment – allowing that info to percolate.

"Sounds like the fix was in, Frank."

"That's what my friend said. Then the case was closed and there's no way to re-open it after 10 years when there's no remaining evidence."

"Shit," I said.

"I second that."

Our cinnamon rolls arrived and Frank made a production of thanking the waitress.

When we left the Majestic, he walked back to my office with me.

"I appreciate the risk you took by looking into that old case for me, Frank. But I think you should back away from it now – I don't want you to get your ass in a sling with the Deputy Chief, especially when that evidence from the car crash has conveniently disappeared."

"You're probably right but I hate to let it go. It's such a piss-off when the rich and powerful get away with murder – literally."

We'd arrived at the entrance to my building and I shook his hand. "Some days you're the pigeon, Frank – and other days you're the statue of Queen Victoria in Gore Park."

When I approached my office door I heard laughter inside. It sounded like Trépanier was entertaining Phyllis while he awaited my arrival.

"I just got the prints from our night at the Innsville," he told me. "Let's go into your office and I'll show you."

He laid out five photos on the table by the window and set three of them aside. "These two here are the best. Take a look."

"It's a wonder that any turned out at all," I said. "You had to take them in a hurry and ditch your camera before those mugs beat the crap out of you."

He sloughed off my remark and pointed to the photos.

The first one showed Belcastro snuggling close to Ida in the doorway; Peterson was beside her but shown here in profile. In the second photo, both men were smiling at her and her left hand was touching Peterson's cheek. It didn't escape my notice that Ida's ring finger was intact – and ringless.

"Enlargements –" I said but he cut me off.

"Already ordered, Max. It's easier this time because I have the negatives. They should be ready later this afternoon."

I took a quick look at the other photos. None was as good as those he'd selected. "Very good work, Rob. These photos should be evidence enough to sink Peterson's phony divorce case and the cops might like to know about his close connection with the Mob boss. Now, were you able to get anything from Longo while I was in Toronto yesterday?"

"He's a different sort of man, Max. I like him but he always looks for a special deal or anything that will profit him. I don't know how to say that exactly."

"But you do know his character type. He's 'on the make' as we say in *anglais*. Meaning that he's always alert for private information that he might be able to sell for a few bucks or trade for other info. And if you need hard-to-get tickets for a special event, then he's your man. I'll bet he sold you some intel when you talked to him, right?"

He gave me a sheepish grin. "When he saw I had a $5-dollar bill, he said it was exactly the cost of his new information about Mr. Peterson."

I delivered a light punch to his arm. "And whatever he told you was worth it because you also learned never to show him the colour of your money before you get the goods."

Now he was blushing, "A good lesson, Max, but expensive for you. I don't think he would charge that much if you were there."

"Forget about it – now you know for the next time. So, what did he say?"

"He told me Mr. Peterson went to Buffalo for the weekend with the Big Man. I guess he was meaning that Mob *chef*, I forget his name."

"Vincenzo Belcastro. He's the head of the Hamilton Mob and he reports to Stefano Magaddino who's the big boss in Buffalo – maybe they had a meeting arranged. So I guess it was just a lucky chance that we happened to be at the same place for dinner."

"Less lucky for me than for you, Max," and he pointed to his black eye.

I clapped him on the back. "Good thing you're one of those brave Van Doos guys. Did he say what they were planning to do in Buffalo?"

He withdrew a small notebook from his jacket pocket and flipped it open. "Longo didn't drive them because he was booked for a special event at the Connaught. But he got a friend of his to drive. Longo said they usually take the girls to have a good time at one of the clubs there. Their favourite is … a place called the Moon-Glo on Michigan Avenue. And they always stay at …" he glanced at his book again, "The Hotel Lafayette downtown. The following day, they planned to look at some race horses with somebody he called 'Don'. But I didn't get his last name."

I tried to keep the grin off my mug. "The big boss of a Mafia family is sometime called 'The Don' – it's a title of respect. Did he say anything else about their plans down there?"

"Not much. He said they were going to stop for dinner on the way there, then go on to Buffalo for a 'floor show' but I don't know that term."

"It's a type of musical show at a nightclub – apparently some of the Buffalo clubs have nude dancers."

"They don't wear any clothes? Is that allowed there?"

"Everything's allowed there. It's the U.S. of A. and they're not as civilized as we are."

CHAPTER TWENTY-SIX

We were invited for dinner at Grace's home and I was cooling my heels in the living room at home while Iz was getting ready. I picked up one of her art magazines, something called *Art in America*, and I leafed through it.

I stopped in my tracks when I came across a large painting titled *Full Fathom Five* by a guy named Jackson Pollock. It looked like an atomic explosion in a paint factory and I read on. This painting was described as *'great arcs of paint cover the canvas apparently at random to produce an intense and energetic abstract plane.*

What the hell did that mean?

Jackson is one of the most famous American abstract-expressionist painters, earning the name "Jack the Dripper" because of his method of dripping and splashing the paint onto a canvas laid on the floor. Shocking to some – a breakthrough to others."

And here was a photo of the guy, sloshing paint straight from the bucket all over a carpet-size piece of canvas on his studio floor.

Isabel entered the living room and watched me puzzling over the so-called painting.

"What do you think of that, Max?"

"I hate the result, but the guy's smart."

"What d'you mean?"

"I admire his craftiness because he's become famous for being lazy: just look at all the time and bother he saves by avoiding all the tedious brush work that other painters spend so much time on."

She rolled her eyes and I guessed that was the end of that subject.

According to the weather forecast on the radio, there was a risk of heavy rain so we drove the short distance to Grace's home on Bold Street. I caught a glimpse of the Pasadena Apartments in the next block but I didn't notice 'Call me Pete' coming or going.

Danny answered the door wearing a good-sized shiner on his left eye. "You bump into a door or something worse?" I asked him.

"Something worse," he said and led us into the living room where Grace bustled toward us with open arms.

"Welcome, you two. It's grand to see you both."

Samantha came in from the kitchen wearing a yellow souvenir apron emblazoned with a map of Jamaica and we went through the same routine with her. "Have a seat and relax," she said. "Dinner will be ready soon – it's my speciality but we'll have a drink first."

Isabel gave her a quizzical look and Grace said. "You're in for treat - Sam's made the Jamaican national dish in your honour. We hope you like it."

Sam returned to the kitchen and we sat in the living room where Grace and Isabel chatted on the settee.

I plunked down on the couch between the two boys and turned to Danny. "How'd you really get that black eye? And I don't want to hear any malarkey."

He gave me a weak smile. "Well, um … Vince and me were shootin' baskets in the schoolyard across the street yesterday. And these tough guys who hang around that confectionery store near the corner of James Street tried to take our ball."

"Of course you couldn't just let them have it."

He gave me a tiny grin. "'Course not."

"Then you had a little dust-up and the big guys pushed you around, took your ball, shot a few baskets then moved on to terrorize some other kids."

They both stared at me.

"Happened to me too," I said. "One time I got two shiners when the big guys took my football and when they finished, they sliced it open with a jackknife."

Vincent hunched closer to me and spoke in a half-whisper.

160

"This was different. They were teasing me – calling me names, spitting at me and shoving me around. They yelled at me to go back to the jungle where I belonged. And when Danny tried to help me, they held him down on the ground and kept calling him a 'nigger-lover' and other rotten names."

"That's terrible," I said. "How'd you get away?"

"A man and lady were walking by and saw the fight. The man was a big guy and those boys ran off when he yelled at them and came over to help us."

"I'm sorry that happened. Do you get teased a lot, Vincent?"

He shook his head. "Not too much at my school anymore. Most of the teachers watch out for that and stop it. My mom used to tell me to ignore it and not make big a fuss. But sometimes you gotta fight back."

"I guess so," I said. "But it can't be easy." I jerked a thumb toward Danny. "Good thing you've got a body-guard looking out for you now."

They were both grinning as Vincent gave Danny a light punch on his arm.

"Game four," I said. "It might be the final game for the Stanley Cup tonight – Leafs could sweep this series."

"Vince and me got a bet," Danny said. "He's got Toronto by two or more goals in regulation time. But I'm betting they'll win it in overtime."

I nodded my head. "I think you're gonna win, bud. But it'll be a close game – it might even go into double overtime. You can bet those Wings don't want to lose the series without a single win."

Sam returned from the kitchen. "Soup's on, folks. C'mon through to the dining room."
When we were seated, she filled the plates and we passed them around the table.

"Do tell us what's in your national dish," Iz said. "It has such a spicy aroma."

"It's called ackee and salt fish," Sam said. "The fish is salted cod. We usually let it soak for an hour or two before cooking – but some folks soak it overnight. And ackee is a pear-shaped fruit. There's a little store just off Market Square where you can buy it by the can. Then you debone and flake the fish and sauté it with the ackee, adding onions and tomatoes; then the spices – garlic, scallions and Scotch Bonnet peppers, if you can get them."

"What a cute name," Iz said. "What is a Scotch Bonnet?"

"It's a variety of chili pepper that looks like a tam-o'shanter hat." Sam lifted a piece with her fork to show us. It looked like an ordinary pepper to me.

"Do you serve it with anything else?" Iz asked her.

"We usually eat it with peas and rice."

When my plate was passed to me, its spicy aroma washed over me. "It looks benign but I guess you can't tell a pepper by its looks," I said. When I took a big forkful and chomped on it, my mouth exploded and my eyes began to spout tears. I reached for my glass of water and gulped it all down. When I could speak, I said, "That sure lifted *my* bonnet. I might need a fire extinguisher."

Vincent and Danny hooted at me while the women grinned. Sam said, "Would you like another helping, Max?"

Somehow I was able to eat most of what I was served and I celebrated my survival from the Jamaican traditional dinner by washing it down with another full glass of water. I noticed that Vincent had cleaned his plate while Danny ate most of his serving with the exception of the Scotch Bonnets.

When I'd finished, Grace said, "You're brave to try it, Max. For non-Jamaicans, it's an acquired taste."

I glanced at Iz who was trying to keep her grin to herself. "It's zesty," she said, "and it certainly gets your attention."

I reached for the pitcher that Grace had set before me and poured myself another glass of water.

After dinner, the boys went upstairs to get their hockey cards and I went with them. They both had complete sets of the Leafs but not the Red Wings; so they'd made cardboard cutouts for the Wings players' cards they were missing. On a large piece of cardboard they'd drawn a hockey rink and they showed me how they could follow the game with their cards as Foster Hewitt gave his play-by-play commentary.

"It must be pretty tricky," I said. "I don't know how you can keep up with the pace of the game."

Danny grinned at me. "Yeah, you've gotta be quick

because the coaches are changin' the lines all the time."

"We're takin' turns being the Leafs," Vincent said, "and tonight's my turn because Danny won the coin-toss for the first game. So if Leafs can win tonight that'll make it four straight – and they'll win the Stanley Cup while I'm their coach."

I grinned back at him. "Don't get over-confident. It's not easy to win four games in a row in a seven-game series. Did you bet anything on the game?"

Danny pointed at Vincent. "Loser has to dry the dishes for two weeks."

We gathered around the big Crosley radio console in the living room and all talk ceased when we heard Foster Hewitt say, "Hello Canada and hockey fans in the United States and Newfoundland."

Vincent tugged my sleeve and whispered, "Why does he always say that? Isn't Newfoundland part of Canada?"

"Not officially," I said. "It's still under British rule but they're holding a vote this summer about joining Canada."

"You mean they have their own money and everything?"

"Yep. They have the Newfoundland dollar – it's worth the same as ours. I've got a few bills and coins at home. If I remember, I'll bring you some."

Between the second and the third periods, Sam got busy with the boys making popcorn in the kitchen.

"Looks like Danny's become part of the family," Iz said to Grace.

"He's a good boy and he's appointed himself as Vincent's protector when he gets picked on by the bullies." Then she glanced toward the kitchen to make sure we weren't overheard. "And we're not looking forward to the day when he goes back to his mother. That is – if she plans to return."

You could probably hear the cheers at the North Pole when the game was over. The Leafs had thrashed the Red Wings 7-2 and the boys were jumping up and down as though they had springs on their shoes. It was impossible to tell which kid had won the bet. Of course, we had to stay tuned for Foster Hewitt to describe the presentation of the Stanley Cup by NHL President, Clarence Campbell, to Leafs' captain, Syl Apps.

When the cheering died down, Grace pointed at the boys. "Upstairs, you two. I'll be there in five minutes and I want to see you both in bed."

They waved good-bye to Iz and me and hustled up the stairs, pushing and shoving at each other. I heard Vincent teasing his new roommate. "Two weeks drying dishes – that'll teach you to bet with me."

Later, we were saying our good-byes in the front hallway and I pointed to side-by-side pencil drawings of the art deco T.H. & B. train station over on Hunter Street. I turned to Grace, "You told us that Sam liked to draw and these are very good. You should have them framed."

Iz stooped down for a closer look. "They *are* nicely done, but I don't think they're by the same hand."

"You've got a discerning eye," Sam said as she joined us. "I did the one on the left and Danny drew the other."

"Did he copy from yours?" I asked her.

"No. If you look closer, you'll notice they're drawn from different perspectives. I've been helping him with that and he's a quick learner. Later on, we're going to work on portraits."

It was raining now as we dashed to the car at the curb. "Let's drive past Peterson's apartment on the way home," I said, then paused. That was the first time I'd referred out loud to Iz's place as 'home'. But she didn't appear to notice.

Instead, she frowned. "Nobody will be out in this rain, Max."

"Just humour me. Please. I've got a hunch."

She drove down Bold Street toward James Street South, where the Pasadena was in the next block on our right. But there was nobody on the street and no lights were burning in the top floor apartment.

My fiancée turned toward me, her eyebrows raised, but she didn't say a word.

"Well, I did say it was just a hunch," I said.

I watched her shake her head, then she changed the subject.

"I'm pleased that Grace and Sam have welcomed Danny so warmly. Those boys are like real brothers, aren't they? It may sound cruel, Max, but I think Danny would be far better off if his mother didn't return."

Isabel was right. And I was struck again by the similarity between Danny's situation and my own when I was living with Frank's family. For the first few months I'd fall asleep at night by fantasizing about my mother's imminent return. I had convinced myself that it wasn't her choice to abandon me. That she'd been taken away against her will and was trying her best to escape so she could be reunited with her only child.

I gradually accepted her absence from my life and was grateful to Frank's family for treating me as one of their own. I wished the same good fortune for Danny.

CHAPTER TWENTY-SEVEN

"This Peterson character has turned out to be a real lulu," I said to Jackie Nelligan when we met in her office in the Pigott Building early the following morning.

She leaned toward me, a determined look on her handsome face. "Don't leave anything out, Max. I need to hear it all."

From her briefcase, Isabel removed the photos that Trépanier had taken of Peterson, Belcastro and their dates at the Innsville restaurant and passed them across the table.

Jackie took her time examining them. "I recognize Mr. Peterson, of course, but not the others here."

I pointed out Vincenzo Belcastro. "He's replaced Dominic Tedesco as Hamilton's new mob boss. The woman beside him is Ida Lucas; the other woman is Trixie, a friend of Ida's. They're hostesses at the Connaught and a lot more."

"They're certainly glamorous creatures, but in a blousy kind of way," she said. "Almost like ladies of the evening."

"Not almost – that's exactly what they are. They're attracted by the high life as well as the dangerous thrill of associating with criminals."

"So you're saying that Peterson and one of these women are having an affair?"

"From what I hear, maybe with both women. This photo was taken at The Innsville last Saturday evening. The four of them were on their way to Buffalo for the weekend."

Jackie seemed to simmer in silence for a moment, scrutinizing the photos in minute detail. Then she slapped the flat of her hand on the table – a thunderclap that startled Iz and me back in our chairs. "I just don't get it!" she said, her voice raspy with anger. "What is the matter with a man who has all the advantages in life? A beautiful, intelligent wife, a gracious home in Westdale, a top executive at the Steel Company. And yet – he risks it all by fooling around with known criminals and their floozies. I swear, *this* takes the cake."

I'd never seen her so agitated and I wondered if there might've been some parallel in her own experience, maybe with a relative or close friend. I reached for the water carafe, poured a full glass and set it in front of her.

"Thank you," she said in a subdued whisper. "Pardon my outburst. But some men – they just infuriate me."

I gave Iz a quick glance and she signalled me with a tiny shake of her head to keep mum and allow Jackie to simmer down.

She drank most of the water I'd given her and inhaled a couple of deep breaths before turning back to me. "You were saying, Max?"

I remembered a bit advice from a Dorothy Dix column I'd read in *The Spectator*. 'When in doubt during an awkward social situation, simply ignore it.'

So I topped up her water glass and pressed on. "I was saying that this photo proves your client is consorting with Hamilton's Mafia boss. In addition, he's violating his marriage vows by living it up with a pair of women of easy virtue."

I tapped the photo in front of her. "And this should put the kibosh on Peterson's divorce case."

She placed her hand on mine. "Thank you, Max. This is excellent work. Is there anything else?"

"There is. I spoke again with my RCMP contact in Toronto. She learned that Peterson's so-called investigator has a shady reputation as a swindler for hire. Those photos he sent you are likely to be staged, apparently this guy's specialty."

She was nodding her head before I'd finished. "That's all I need to hear. I'm going to file a complaint with the Toronto police department about that guy."

Then she withdrew a letter from a file on the table and held it up. "In this morning's mail, I received this registered letter from Mr. Peterson notifying me that my services in his divorce case are no longer required. And he's also requesting that I return his entire real estate file because he's hired another lawyer."

She read the concern on our faces and Isabel was about to respond. "Don't worry," Jackie said, "I'm glad to wash my hands of the man. He was a good client in the past but somehow he's become a different person – and certainly not for the better. No doubt the Mob has a lawyer he can use – one who's willing to hold his nose and look the other way if the price is right."

She closed her file and stood up from the table. "Send me your bill," she said. "I have a contingency fund to cover cases such as this."

Isabel zipped up her brief case and I stood with her. "I'm still wondering about Mr. Peterson's divorce case," Iz said. "Do you think he might try the same tactics with his new lawyer?"

Jackie nodded. "Probably. But even if he were successful, his wife would still be much better off without that snake. And she certainly doesn't need his money."

She walked us to the doorway and shook our hands. "By the way, Isabel, how's your arm?"

"Thanks for asking." Iz pulled back the left sleeve of her blouse, revealing a slim red scab on the inside of her left forearm. "It's on the mend and I don't notice it much anymore. My doctor says I'll probably be wearing a battle scar."

Returning to the office, we crossed to the east side of James Street and were passing Birk's Jewellers on the corner of King Street where a large shiny object in the window caught my eye. I held Iz's arm and guided her to a stop. "Looks like a streamlined kettle," I said, "but it's got an electrical cord." I shuffled closer to read the card aloud – "*Amazing new way to boil water* – **GE Electric Kettle** – *unbelievable speed, it boils water in just 3 minutes.* **$17.50**."

I turned to my partner, "What d'you say, Iz? This kettle could save us a lot of time."

She turned from the window, shaking her head. "How long does it take to boil water on the stove, Max?"

"I'm not sure; I've never timed it. Five minutes, more or less?"

"There you go, then. It's never been a problem in the past so why should get this contraption to boil our water quicker? What's the big rush?"

I nodded my head. "Good point."

As we were walking away, I glanced back. "But it sure looks nifty."

Trépanier didn't arrive until mid-afternoon because his boss needed him to complete some work on a rush job. "Don't sit down," I told him when he entered my office. "We're going across the street."

He raised his eyebrows. "Okay. But why are we doing that?"

"I've got an idea."

We crossed King Street and boarded the elevator in the Connaught's lobby. In the main dining room, I spotted Longo talking with the head waiter. When he saw me, I angled my head toward the hallway and we waited for him there.

When he arrived, he said, "You guys are here more often than I am. What's up now?"

"We want to talk to Trixie – see if she'll open up about Ida."

He was shaking his head before I'd finished speaking. "She'll just clam up – unless I'm with you. Of course, there'll be a small fee for my time."

I stepped closer to him. "What's this? You're her manager or something?"

"Do you want to see her or not, Max? It makes no never mind to me."

When I scowled at him, he gave me his Mona Lisa smile and waited with an open palm.

I forked over a couple of bucks and we took the elevator to the Circus Roof where a team of women was preparing the tables for another evening of dining and dancing and whatever else they did up here. On the bandstand, a piano player was rehearsing a young singer who was stumbling her way through a fast-paced version of "Lady Be Good" and we stopped to listen for a moment.

"No way she'll have that tune ready for tonight," Longo said. "She sure ain't no Ella Fitzgerald."

We followed him along a dark hallway into a large dressing room: lacquered wooden lockers along one wall, and at the far end, shower stalls, sinks and toilets. Against the opposite wall was a long make-up table with individual bench seats. Above it a mirror that ran the length of the room – enough seating area here to accommodate eight or nine women at one time. And on the end wall, near the doorway, we could admire our reflections in the floor-to-ceiling mirror.

Trixie sat alone at the first dressing table, repairing the hem of a red silk gown with needle and thread; I noted that she had all her fingers. She looked up as we approached, focusing on Longo. Then she gave Trépanier and me the once-over as we followed in behind him.

"What's this? You guys can't read the sign, *Women's Dressing Room*?" She turned back to Longo. "They can't be your pals. They're too well dressed."

Longo ignored her barb and introduced us.

"We're private detectives," I told her. "We'd like to talk to you about Ida Lucas and we understand that you and she are good friends."

She jabbed her needle into a pin-cushion with a determined look that said she wished it were my rear end. "Oh yeah? Who told you that?"

"We've been asking around. That's what detectives do."

"What d'you wanna know?"

"We're concerned about her son, Danny," I said. "Ida hasn't been home for almost a week and her boy's very concerned about her. Did you know she had a child?"

"Of course I did. We're good friends, Ida and me. But she never talks much about him."

I shook my head. "He's only 12 and she's left him on his own. He's worried that she might not return, so we'd like to speak with her about that. Or maybe the boy's father – do you know who he is or where he lives?"

She took a deep breath and let it out slowly, her eyes squinting. "No and no," she said. "Ida never talks much about the boy's father or her son, so I'm in the dark about both of them. I met Ida a few years ago when she began working at the Connaught and we hit it off right away. She told me the boy can look after himself now, so she doesn't have to worry about him. And I got the strong impression that the father was a one-night stand; I'm not sure that she even remembers his name."

Trixie swivelled her eyes between Trépanier and me.

"C'mon, what's this really about? Have you guys talked to Ida?"

Trépanier shook his head. "No, we haven't. When did you last see her, *Madame*?"

She took her time looking him over and nodded her approval. "Say, I like your accent, big fella. What are you, Italian or something?"

He kept his smile in place. "We heard that you and Ida are friends with the Mob men," he said, his voice calm and unaccusing.

She straightened in her chair and rounded on me. "What's goin' on here, Mister? I don't have to answer any of these dumb questions. So why don't you both hit the road?"

I removed one of the photos from my jacket pocket; the one showing Trixie with Ida and the two men at the Innsville restaurant, and placed it in front of her.

At first, she ignored it. Then she moved closer and studied it, being careful not to touch it. Her gaze was steady when she lifted her head and glared at me. "So what does that prove? A couple of guys bought us a drink."

"You know very well they're not just a couple of guys," I said. "We know who they are and what they do. But we're only interested in Ida. We want to talk to her about her plans for her son's future – that is, if she intends to return at all. When my partner and I met young Danny we discovered that his mother had been gone for days and she'd left the boy with a good dose of measles. Did you know that they can be a life-threatening disease? And it can make you vulnerable to other serious illnesses. You want to help your friend and her son, don't you?"

She began to squirm in her chair, her eyes flicking between the photo and me. She remained quiet for a long beat and when I noticed that Trépanier was about to speak, I tapped his shoe with my foot and gave my head a tiny shake when he glanced at me.

Then Trixie drew in a deep breath and let it out slowly. Finally, her voice leaked out in a quiet whisper. "After dinner at the Innsville, the men took us to Buffalo for the weekend. Ida stayed on with Mr. Belcastro and I came back to Hamilton with Mr. Peterson on Sunday evening. I haven't seen her since and, yeah, I don't mind saying that I'm worried about her."

"Why did she stay there?" I said.

"I don't know the details. Mr. Belcastro had some business in New York City and he wanted to take Ida with him."

"Does she do this type of thing often? Just go off and leave you?"

"No, not usually. But she always loves visiting New York. We don't know this Belcastro man well yet but he's a real twitchy guy – you've gotta be careful not to upset him."

"Did she say when she planned to return?"

A shake of her head. "And that's not like her either – she usually tells me everything. She just said they might stay there a few days but it might take longer."

"What might take longer?"

"She said she couldn't tell me that. But I suspect it might have something to do with the drug business the men are involved in."

An image of that unmarked bottle of amphetamine pills that Iz had found in Ida's bathroom flickered in my mind. "Was Ida using drugs?"

"She told me her doctor had prescribed something for her low blood pressure."

I reached for Trixie's hand but she placed it on her lap. "I can see why you're worried about her," I said.

"You bet I am," her voice with some muscle now. "These guys can do nasty things if you happen to displease them."

"Did that ever happen to you?"

"Just once."

"What happened?"

"It was a misunderstanding."

"Were you injured?"

"That's none of your business."

"But you continue to be involved with them."

She stared at me for a long moment then gulped a deep breath before she spoke. "I've got no choice, Mister. I've got two kids and my mother who depend upon me. I know it can be dangerous but this is the only kind of work I know. And I'm going to lose my looks before too long so I've got to put some money away while I can."

She became silent again but we waited for her. "Just the other day," she said, "I heard that a hostess at the Golden Rail had one of her fingers chopped off as some kind of punishment from a Mob guy."

"Good Lord. Why?"

"I don't really know. She was a girlfriend of one of those gangsters and I was told that she stepped out on him with somebody else. But maybe she was lucky."

"That's your idea of lucky?"

"Well, it could've been her entire hand and she'd never work again. According to the grapevine, that's what happened to Ginger."

"Who's she?"

"Ginger was one of the hostesses here – when she got out of the Hamilton General last year she moved to Vancouver and nobody's heard from her since."

We didn't speak for a moment then she picked up the dress she'd been sewing and I got the message that this interview was over.

"We appreciate your help," I said. Then I placed my hand on her shoulder. "Please be careful, Trixie – you're in a dangerous business for a mother."

As we walked back to the office, Trépanier said, "I want to get two tickets to that Barbara Ann Scott ice-show in Toronto for Phyllis and me but they are all sold." He hesitated for a moment. "I'm hoping you could ask Longo if he can get some."

"You know him well enough to ask him yourself, Rob."

"Yes, but I can't make a bargain with him like you do. If that is all right."

A Belt Line streetcar clanged past us, its wheels squealing and we couldn't be heard for a moment. "I'm happy to help," I said. "How much do you want to pay?"

"It doesn't matter. "I'd like the best seats for the lowest money."

"Okay. I'll see what I can do."

CHAPTER TWENTY-EIGHT

Isabel entered my office at closing time. "Don't forget it's movie night, Max, and I have a little plan."

"I'm not surprised."

I watched her lips press tightly together and I grasped both her hands in mine. "Just kidding, Iz. I always love to be planned."

She shook her head, her red curls dancing. "You're a tease, Buster, and sometimes I like it."

"Other times?"

Her eyes held steady on mine and I felt a tingle up my spine. I kept my smile in place as she pinched my arm – hard.

"The movie starts at 7 o'clock," she said, "and it's about three hours long. So we could have an early dinner at the Wentworth Arms over on Main Street, then stroll back down James North to the Tivoli theatre. It's supposed to be a warm evening. What d'you think?"

"I think I like your little plan."

Meandering down James Street after dinner, I asked her, "What's the name of this movie again?"

"'The Best Years of Our Lives' – it's the story of three American soldiers who return from the war and how they're able to cope with their re-adjustment to civilian life. This film won the Academy Award for Best Picture of 1947. You might find some similarities to your own situation, Max."

During the intermission the house lights came up and many patrons stood to stretch their legs. Others made a dash for the snack bar or the washrooms – maybe both, but not in that order.

"How do you like the movie so far, Max?"

"I think it's true to life. And that guy who lost his hands is a fine actor; I didn't realize that you could become so skilled at manipulating those hooks."

"I read a story about him and he's an actual veteran of the U.S. Army. During the war he was training paratroopers at an army base stateside and he lost both his hands when some TNT that he was handling exploded. Then he was fitted with hooks on his wrists and he became so adept with them that he was chosen to make a training film on their use. One of the producers of tonight's movie happened to see that film and that's how Hollywood discovered him."

As the credits were rolling at the end of the film, we did the slow shuffle with the crowd toward the double doors into the lobby. Several extra ushers seemed to be on hand and I noted a growing sense of urgency in their manner as they herded the moviegoers along like cattle as we got closer to the main doors.

Acrid smoke swirled in the air when we exited onto James Street, accompanied by the wartime-wail of sirens close by. We were caught up in the crowd milling around us in confusion, trying to see the source of the commotion out here. A moment later, a wave of anxious people was pushing us along with them in the smoky darkness; as though the crowd had made a collective decision to witness the fearful blaze now invading the sky like a giant volcano behind the James Street Armoury a couple of blocks northward.

I clung tightly to Iz's arm as we were jostled forward to Cannon Street where wooden barriers were erected by the police. The sprawling Armoury complex was in the next block and the crowd of onlookers released a collective gasp as flames burst through the roof of the massive, old building on Hughson Street just behind it.

An eerie silence gripped the crowd; then even the sidewalk seemed to quake beneath us as a thunderous explosion from the interior of that building catapulted a giant fireball into the sky above us, cascading sparks like Satan's Roman candle.

I'm not ashamed to admit that it scared the hell out of me and some folks began to scream as they attempted to fight their way back up James Street to escape this holocaust. For an anxious few seconds, my mind transported me to that London bomb shelter where I'd shivered in the crowded Underground as German bombs exploded above us and our senses were invaded by the eye-watering sting of the hot smoke from the street above.

Now a police van, its siren still whining, disgorged a platoon of cops onto James Street who began pushing the crowd back from the site of the flames, ashes now sifting down upon us as the wind shifted and the rain began to fall in earnest. An old duffer who'd squeezed in beside us said, "I just prayed for more rain and the good Lord heard me."

Downtown traffic was as snarled as I'd ever seen it and it took Iz twice the usual time to drive home. Once there, we showered off the odour, but not the memory, of that stupendous fire. Isabel had hung our smoke-soaked clothes in the sun-room at the rear of the house and opened a window in there.

Now in the living room with our cups of Mother Parker's tea, I tuned the radio to CHML to catch some news of the big fire and we listened to a live report from Paul Hanover at the scene.

"… the blaze is almost under control now but Fire Chief William Murdoch fears there won't be much left of the three-story Burrow, Stewart and Milne building, a former foundry, that occupies the entire block bounded by Cannon, Hughson, John and Robert Streets. The Chief said that all but two pieces of the city's fire equipment are at the scene right now.

"It's a sight to behold, folks, and it might've spread to other nearby buildings if it weren't for the speedy response from the Central Fire Station crew only three blocks away. Captain Murdoch believes the building was unoccupied when the fire broke out but that's unconfirmed at this time. He also credited the rain with preventing numerous other fires as sparks were driven over the business area on James Street by stiff winds. The origin of the fire is still a mystery. It was reported by a member of the RHLI Sergeants' Mess at the James Street Armoury who noticed the red glow in the second story windows of the doomed building.

"The Chief also said that the building contained 10 separate businesses but none of them could be saved. A fire here in February had destroyed part of a wing of the furniture company that owns this building and it had just wound up a fire sale of furniture damaged in that blaze. But it's unlikely there will be anything that can be salvaged this time.

"There are scores of broken windows here and you can see the wreckage of furniture and machinery inside – everything's been twisted and burned to a crisp.

"Now, I just noticed Mayor Sam Lawrence arriving at the scene and I'm making my way over to speak with him. Mr. Mayor …"

In the morning, Iz stopped at the dry cleaners on the way to the office and I dropped off our smoke-sodden clothes.

"You're not the first one this morning," the clerk said, and she pointed to a full rack of suits and dresses reeking of smoke and fumes. "I can't wait for the driver to pick this stuff up and take it to the plant – it smells like a bomb shelter in here."

I gave her an inquisitive look and she smiled.

"I was in England with the Canadian Women's Army Corps."

When I returned to the car, Iz said, "Let's get this show on the road, Max. What took you so long in there?"

I grinned at her. "Just keepin' up the morale of the troops."

She shook her head and drove on.

I called Frank Russo mid-morning to ask him about last night's fire because he lived nearby. "Guess you heard about that big fire last night, eh?"

He humphed. "Don't be a wise-ass, Max. You know as well as I do how close it was to our place on Mulberry Street. We were lucky it didn't spread – that rainstorm prevented a lot of damage to the homes and businesses nearby."

"Also a good thing that it broke out after business hours when nobody was in the building," I said. "Otherwise, there'd be no escaping that inferno."

Silence on the line for a strained moment.

"Frank? You still there?"

"Um … there was somebody there."

"What? C'mon, bud, out with it."

"We haven't released this info to the public yet. So if there's a leak, I'll know it came from you."

"Sure, sure. Now, who was it?"

"We don't know yet. After the fire was out, the charred remains of a body were discovered among the debris in a small kitchen area on the second floor at the rear of the building. It was a cabinet-making business so it was probably one of the workers there."

"Or maybe a night-watchman who got trapped by the flames and smoke."

"Could be, Max. When I called Doc Crandall at the morgue this morning he told me he wouldn't be able to examine the remains until this afternoon. In the meantime, keep your lip buttoned. We're not releasing any info until we can identify this body."

Just before lunch young Rick dropped off an early edition of *The Hamilton Spectator*. Iz and Phyllis crowded around the long table in my office where we examined the shocking photos from the fire scene.

A six-column photo of that block-long building, swallowed in flames, dominated the front page. And the Home Page was entirely devoted to scenes showing the firemen in action, hosing down the building, and a panoramic view of the crowds of onlookers drenched by the rain. And here was a handsome photo of three-striper Paolo LaRosa who was the first to report the fire when he discovered it from a window in the RHLI Sergeants' Mess across the street.

There was also a list of the 10 businesses housed there, whose employees would be out of work indefinitely.

Phyllis spoke in a whisper. "Oh, gosh. I hope there was no-one caught inside there."

I kept my trap shut about that corpse in the morgue.

CHAPTER TWENTY-NINE

At noon, Isabel and Phyllis had gone to Fischer's Hotel on York Street for what they called their 'Monthly Catch-up Meeting and Lunch' so I asked them to bring me back a sandwich from Spiro's on their way back.

While I was sorting through the Peterson file I heard a tap on my office door and Longo waltzed right in, sat on the chair beside my desk, and started in with his business.

"A couple of nights ago, I was about to drive Mr. Peterson home from the Connaught and Mr. Belcastro also needed a lift. Turns out they live at opposite ends of the city but anyway … they were in the back seat talking so they weren't paying any attention to me. I'm just the help, of course, and they presume I'm too stupid to understand what the big, important men are talking about. They were arguing about Pete's upcoming appearance before the Steward's Committee at the Ontario Jockey Club. You heard about that, Max? It's happening next week."

"Yeah, I heard."

"Well, Pete was half in the bag, as usual, but Belcastro, see, he was dead-sober. And he was trying to rehearse Pete for his defense at that hearing – coaching him on what to say, so I figured that it must involve him too. Pete kept objecting to the plan; he was reluctant to feed a phony story to the committee. Finally, Belcastro became angry and ordered him to stick to the script – or else. When he spelled out the 'or else', I was really afraid for my guy because the very last place you want to be is on top of the Mob's shit-list.

"I got them both home all right but I'm still worried about Pete – I can't afford to lose my best customer, Max. I think he's making a big mistake by defying Belcastro so I'm hoping you can help me out here. I know that you and Trépanier have been investigating him so I'm wondering if you've learned anything that could help Pete with the boss-man."

"Like what?"

"I don't know what … that's why I'm asking you. I'm at my wit's end and I need your help to save my guy."

I stood up and walked over to the window, staring at the weathered brick wall next door, waiting for some inspiration – I'd never seen Longo looking so anxious. Sure, he was a two-bit chiseler, but he operated at a much lower level than those Mob mutts. And I sure-as-hell wouldn't give him any info, even if I'd had some, to help a scheming rich guy like Peterson who was cheating with his race horses, not to mention cheating on his wife. After a moment, I returned to my seat with half a plan.

"How about this? I'll tell you all that you need to know about Peterson if you'll get me a pair of rinkside tickets for a performance of the Barbara Ann Scott ice show at Maple Leaf Gardens next month. I'm willing to pay cost plus 50%. That's $4.50 for a three-buck ticket. What some folks might call 'highway robbery'."

"Are you nuts? What makes you think I've got a guy at The Gardens who'll whistle me up some tickets whenever I want them? And on the street, those babies will fetch at least double the box office price."

"No, no, no," I said, shaking my head. "That's B.S. You've always got a guy who knows a guy – so don't give me any of that guff." Then I fixed him with my hard stare and said, "Take it or leave it, Mister."

He dithered … tapping his fingers on the desk, then he closed his eyes for a moment. When he opened them, he said, "When's this ice show?"

"Not til next month – May 6, 7 and 8. Doesn't matter which date – evening performance only."

He stood up to leave. "What if your info about Pete doesn't help me a damn bit?

I let him squirm for a moment then gave him a Longo smirk. "You'd still be making a nice profit on the tickets and you'd have the satisfaction of helping out your second-best customer."

He rolled his eyes and headed for the door.

Longo called me 20 minutes later. "The best I can do is six bucks a ticket and that's rock-bottom. They're in short supply, Max, so you have to tell me right now."

I thought about it for two seconds. "Deal."

"Now, what about that inside dope about Pete?"

"When I've got the merchandise in my hot little hand, bud."

I replaced the receiver on its cradle, thinking of a story that I might give Longo when the phone rang before I'd removed my hand. I figured he was calling me back because he'd already thought of a way to jack the price of those tickets.

I picked up and said, "The ticket price has doubled, right?"

"Pardon me?" J.B. O'Brien said.

I felt my face flush. "Oh, sorry about that. I was expecting someone else. What's happening?"

"Nothing's happening! That's why I'm calling you. Have you made any progress on my … little problem?"

I wouldn't have called a human finger left on my doorstep a 'little problem' but I didn't occupy a suite on the top floor of Hamilton's business world. I said, "Progress is slow because –"

"Don't give me any lame excuses. I hope you realize that my arse is on the line here. I –"

"Hang on now. I've made some headway but it's a delicate situation. I learned that the finger you received probably does *not* belong to Ida Lucas – so if you were worried about her well-being, which I doubt, that might set your mind at ease. That finger may belong to a hostess at another club in town. But it doesn't mean the Mob's threat is off the table. So I strongly recommend that you accept Belcastro's offer to buy your land for a dollar. If you don't, the Mob is sure to ramp up its scare tactics. And that might include some larger body parts, maybe your own this time."

"What the hell, Dexter? That's no solution. I told you that I don't want to sell that property but if I'm forced into it, then I want fair market value."

"You still don't get it, do you? You're dead wrong if you think you can negotiate with the Mob. They dictate the terms. And if you don't play ball then your house blows up or someone close to you 'accidently' drives off the top of the Mountain. And that treatment continues until you give them what they want. Or you're dead."

He didn't respond for a moment and I could hear his raspy breathing in my ear. "That can't be true. People don't negotiate like that."

"We're not talking about *people*. We're talking about the damn Mob – they live in a different world than *people*. It's how these guys operate. Ask the Chief of Police or Mayor Lawrence if you don't believe me. You have to cut your ties with the Mob or they're going to squeeze your private parts for everything you own. If you try to reason with them, you'll lose. Or if you decide to simply ignore them – you'll still lose. So please take me seriously: sell them your damn land for a dollar, then have nothing more to do with them. Otherwise your daughter and I will be attending your funeral and that's not something she'd wish to do."

He didn't respond but I heard him muttering under his breath, as though he were having an argument with himself. After a long pause, he said, "We O'Briens never turn tail and run from a fight."

I huffed out the breath I was holding. "Even when the odds are a million to one against you?"

"Especially then."

"Then you leave me no choice. I'll have to tell Isabel about your problem and you know as well as I do that she'll be on your doorstep two minutes later. And she'll be madder than a hornet that you're determined to fight a losing battle. In fact, you'd be committing suicide by Mob."

A deafening silence dragged on so long that I thought he might've walked away from the phone.

But he finally said, "So be it."

After she returned from lunch, Iz and I sat in my office, not speaking for a tense moment after I'd told her about my phone conversation with her father. She reacted just as I'd predicted: she reached across my desk to dial the phone. After a red-hot exchange with J.B., she said, "Don't go anywhere. I'm on my way over to see you."

After she'd cooled down to a slow sizzle, I said, "I'll go with you; we're in this together now."

We marched north a block to King William Street and walked west, past the police station, and two blocks further on, we had to cross to the other side of the road at John Street because much of the fire station's equipment was hanging outside to dry after last night's big blaze. At James Street North, we entered the Lister Block on the corner, where we took the elevator to the top floor. On the entrance door to the suite of offices at the end of the hallway, a gold-lettered sign announced, *O'Brien Chartered Accountants*.

Isabel hadn't spoken on our way here and I worried that she might've built up such a head of steam that she wouldn't be able to control her temper with her father – not that he didn't deserve a swift kick in the keester for getting himself into this dilemma.

She powered through the entrance door, steaming straight for his office with me close behind her, limping on the double. A receptionist was on her feet now, extending her arm, hoping to restrain her.

Iz kept marching and pointed toward his office. "No calls for 10 minutes. Then we're leaving."

The startled young woman bobbed her head and said, "Yes, Ma'am."

J.B. stood up from his desk when his daughter bee-lined right up to him. "Sit back down," she said. "We're going to make a decision right here and right now."

Iz and I sat on the hard chairs in front of his desk and he sank slowly onto his leather executive's throne.

"Max has told me all about that gangster's offer to buy your land," she said, "and your refusal to sell."

He stared at her and I couldn't read the look on his mug – startled and angry at the same time and I wondered if he might become downright hostile and throw us both out. Or maybe he'd try to reason with his only child and heir.

Isabel laid out the situation in her clear and logical manner but the look on her father's face told me that he wasn't buying any of her wares.

"If you persist in dealing with these gangsters," she said, "you could be signing your own death warrant. This entire affair just doesn't make sense. You told me that you paid about a thousand dollars for that acreage before the war. That's small change for you. And it's worth every penny to get free from these people."

He shook his head. "You don't understand. It's not the money but the principle. I refuse to be pushed around like this."

Iz stretched across his desk and clamped both his hands in hers. "You're the one who doesn't understand. This is the price you have to pay for getting into bed with these Mob characters – not to mention that Ida woman at the Connaught. You are not their friend, Dad – *you're ... their ... target.*"

A silent battle, fought with their eyes, raged for a few tense moments and even the room temperature seemed to be rising.

Finally, he pulled back his hands, holding them up in surrender and I felt the tension in my neck and shoulders relax. "All right," he said. "I promise to think about it. But I'm very busy right now, so you'll have to excuse me." Then he strode from his office into the boardroom at the end of the hallway, his head held high. Through the doorway I could see the men in suits who were seated around a long table, scrambling to their feet as he marched into the room. I had to limp on the double to catch up with my fiancée as she bustled toward the elevator. I heard her mumbling to herself, "He says he'll think about it – my God."

CHAPTER THIRTY

The following morning, Iz and I were waiting for the elevator in the lobby of our building and when it arrived we stood aside to allow an old woman to shuffle in before us. Her spring coat smelled of mothballs and she was carrying a shopping bag imprinted with *The Right House.*

Tiny closed the doors and turned in my direction. "Heard the news, Max?"

"What news is that?"

"They say Princess Elizabeth is preggers."

"No, not already. Who told you that?"

"I overheard a guy saying he read it in the *Toronto Telegram.*"

"Oh, crumbs!" the old woman chipped in with her two-cents-worth, "I wouldn't believe anything in that rag."

When we entered the office, Frank Russo was parked on the corner of Phyllis's desk where he was chatting with her. He didn't like to discuss confidential police info over the phone and his office was less than a block away on King William Street, so we often saw him here.

"He could do a lot worse than the Hamilton Police Force," Frank was telling her. "I'd be glad to speak with him if he's interested."

He got to his feet when he saw us approaching.

"You're recruiting for the cops now, Frank?"

"Just part-time," he said with a smile. "Phyllis says that your pal, Trépanier, is thinking about becoming a police officer."

"Huh. I didn't know that. But he'd be good at it. Come on into the office."

We sat at the long table by the window where Frank

dragged a chair over to join Isabel and me. "Got some news about that body in the fire," he said.

"Yeah …?"

"I've just come from the morgue. Doc Crandall has finished his examination of what was left of the corpse. He said he's never seen anything like it – the body was so badly burned that most of the flesh was simply gone, evaporated by the intense heat. He showed it to me and I wished he hadn't. It reminded me of the photos I'd seen of those blackened skeletons in the rubble of the fire-bombed buildings in Dresden during the war.

"Doc determined that the victim was a male because of the size and structure of the few remaining bone fragments. The poor devil had been trapped face-down on the floor with his arms beneath him. Some tiny scraps of burnt flesh were all that remained on the underside of the body. And a solitary piece of evidence – so blackened by the flames that Doc almost missed it."

He paused, waiting for the desired reaction. "C'mon, Frank," I said. "What the hell was it?"

"A wrist-watch. The band had been burned off – disintegrated. And the watch face was a black crisp. But you could still make out a bit of engraving on the back of the watch."

He sagged back in his chair, staring out the window: he'd clammed up again, maybe seeing that corpse again in his mind's eye.

Isabel had to prod him. "What did it say, Frank?"

"After Doc cleaned it up, we were able to see a tiny symbol – looked like a triangle. And a name … 'Peterson'."

I glanced at Iz when I heard her gasp and she blinked her eyes. "Our Mr. Peterson?"

"I think so," he said. "I wasn't able to contact him at his business or his home. And no-one seems to know his whereabouts. His secretary said he'd missed several important meetings that he'd scheduled for this morning. Then I had quite a time getting in touch with his wife – turns out she works in Toronto and she still uses her maiden name in her business. She's on her way back to Hamilton now and I'm meeting her in an hour or so."

I shook my head. "I don't envy you, pal. It's one of those situations when they can't pay you enough to do a cop's job."

"Yeah, I'm not looking forward to it. We'll meet in Doc

Crandall's office and he'll explain the condition of what's left of the corpse. That way, we hope she won't ask to view the remains. But if she's unable to identify that watch, then we might have to chalk this guy up as just another John Doe."

Isabel said, "Just a suggestion, Frank – but maybe you could bring one of the women police officers with you to that meeting. Mr. Peterson's wife might talk more freely to another woman – under the circumstances."

He didn't speak for a moment, flashing me a 'what-the-hell' look, then he turned back to Iz, his face flushed. "Ah … we don't have any women who are sworn police officers. There are some women working in the office – typing and record-keeping and so on, but not on sensitive or criminal, investigative work."

She stared at him, her eyes squinting, "Are you saying that women couldn't handle those situations? Such as consoling another woman who's just lost her husband in a horrible fire? That a male cop is more … 'sensitive' in a situation like that?"

I could see that she was still steaming after our heated encounter with her father: now there was a fiery light in her eyes as she fixed them firmly on Frank and leaned forward in her chair.

Frank glanced at me but I kept my face blank while I waited for him to fend for himself. He cleared his throat and turned back to Isabel. "Of course, we have some women in uniform but they look after parking offences and some domestic concerns, especially where children are involved. But they're unarmed and they don't have the authority to make arrests."

Isabel shook her head but her lips were clamped tightly together. She glanced toward me, passing me the ball.

"Iz makes a good point, Frank. And I'll bet that Angela would agree with her."

He got to his feet and nodded his head toward us. "Gotta run," he said as he strode quickly to the door and closed it behind him.

Isabel pulled me to my feet and squeezed me in a hug. "I don't want to come between you and your best friend. I know he's like a brother to you."

"He'll get over it – he always does."

"I hope so. But he's like a lot of folks who seem to have

forgotten that many women served bravely overseas as well as on the home-front where they took over much of what was considered 'men's work' in the factories and offices. So it's disappointing that they're now expected to return to their so-called rightful places. I think it's unfair that women who resist going back to full-time housework are regarded as uppity and, in some cases, even as 'unfit mothers'. Likewise for police work – I can't think of any reason that women couldn't perform as well as men. Remember meeting my friend, Marilyn Edwards, the other day?"

"How could I forget her?"

"Well, she told me about her sister, Michelle, who worked at that big Westinghouse plant on Longwood Road before the war."

"What happened to her?"

"She worked in the Finance Department and several of the senior people there – men, of course, volunteered to work at the War Planning Office in Ottawa during the war. She's a smart woman and because she has an accounting degree, Michelle was promoted to Acting Manager of the department and did a great job. Of course, when the men returned at war's end –"

"Don't tell me. She was shunted back to her old job."

"That's right. And I understand that the same thing happened in many other businesses as well. But times are changing, Max, and many women don't want to go back to how things were before the war."

"I can't argue with that. But lots of guys, including Frank and me, might need a little more time to get in step with that."

"Your heart's in the right place, my dear." Then she pecked me on the cheek. "But you're still a man."

Jeez. Did that mean what I thought it meant?

Later that afternoon, Frank called me again. "Holy cow," I said. "I'll bet that I'm hearing from you more often than Angie does."

He chuckled. "God, I hope not. But I just got back from the morgue. Thought you'd like to hear about my meeting with Doc Crandall and Peterson's wife."

"We sure would. But this time we'll meet you in the dining room at the Connaught for a change – our treat."

I heard him chuckle before he spoke. "You're gettin' to be one of the swells, Max. Hangin' out at that ritzy joint."

"I'll never be welcomed by the upper crust – but it's fun to watch them parading about in their finery, their noses in the air. See you there – 10 minutes."

We chose a quiet table in the corner of the dining room and I waved at Frank as he entered. After he settled, I signalled to the waiter hovering nearby – a well-muscled guy with a too-tight shirt whom I hadn't seen before, his nametag read, *André*.

He poured our coffee and returned a moment later with an assortment of Danish pastries on a serving platter, offering it to Isabel first. She chose something chocolaty and he placed it on her plate with a pair of silver tongs. Then he offered it to Frank who glanced at me, raising his eyebrows. He selected two fat delicacies and smiled as the waiter served him. I chose an éclair, then the waiter bowed and left.

 Frank tapped me on the arm. "Didn't take you long to fit right in here. And now I can see why."

After we'd re-fueled, Frank set his linen napkin aside. "Okay, down to business."

Isabel touched his arm, "Before you begin, did Carole Gauthier expect to see her husband at home for the weekend?"

"She did until she found a note that he'd left on the kitchen table. It said he'd be in New York on business for a few days and he planned to return on Tuesday or Wednesday."

I puzzled over that, recalling what Trixie had said about Ida Lucas going there. "I don't suppose that note said anything about what he was doing down there or who was with him?"

"Nope, not a word. Then Doc told her about the body found in the cabinet-maker's shop in that burned-out building – that it was incinerated beyond recognition and the only means of identification was the wrist watch inscribed with her husband's name."

Iz nodded, "A terrible shock, I imagine."

"Yeah. But she didn't fall to pieces as we feared she might. She was subdued and kept a tight rein on her emotions. When she didn't insist on viewing what little remained of the body, Doc looked as relieved as I was. She told us that Peterson was a long-time member of the Scottish Rite Freemasons who hold their activities in that big stone mansion on the corner of King and Queen Streets. He received that watch last year as a memento of his election to Deputy Grand Master of the Lodge.

"When I asked her about that triangular shape just beneath his name, she remembered it as some kind of Masonic symbol but she didn't know what it meant."

I stopped him there. "But did she have any idea why he might've been in that burned-out building in the first place?"

"Nope, she didn't have a clue. I told her that we'd return the watch to her when we'd finished our investigation but she didn't want it. She said that it would only stir up bad memories."

"She's right about that," Iz said. "If I were in her shoes, I wouldn't want it either."

"When we'd finished, she told Doc that he could send her husband's remains to the Dodsworth and Brown Funeral Home and she'd make arrangements with them."

"But what about their families?" I asked him. "They'd wish to attend the funeral, wouldn't they? Did she say anything about them?"

"Not much to tell. Her family's in Montreal and she said they never got along with Peterson – they'll be coming to be with her but they wouldn't wish to attend a funeral service. As for his family, he was a young man when he emigrated from England with his parents after WWI. He was an only child, and she told us that his folks had passed away. And she's not aware of any other relatives because he'd never spoken of them."

Iz gave him a puzzled look. "Then why did she mention a funeral service?"

"She said the Masonic Lodge would insist on having one – he was a big-wig there and they liked to dress up and conduct their rituals on special occasions – and this funeral would certainly be one of them."

We didn't speak for a moment when the waiter returned to top up our coffee cups. After he left, I said, "Doesn't sound like his wife would care to attend the funeral anyway, Frank."

"You're right. She said she'd tell them that she's too distressed to attend."

"A wise woman," Iz said. "I like her even though we've never met."

Frank didn't speak for a moment, tapping his finger on the rim of his cup. "I still feel like I'm missing something about this Carole Gauthier – did you get the impression that she's almost too good to be true?"

"What do you mean?" Iz said.

"I presume that she was aware of Peterson's intention to divorce her – no doubt they talked about it, maybe for years. But I was wondering if she might be involved in his death somehow."

I shook my head, "Jeez, Frank, I don't think so. She's hardly the criminal type – a clean record, a good career and she comes from a respectable family. Trépanier checked that out with the Montreal cops where she lived before relocating to Hamilton about 10 years ago. What's making you wonder about her?"

He sat forward in his chair and turned to Isabel. "Are you as certain as Max that she's not involved. What's your gut feeling about her?"

"I agree with Max but I was unsure at first. On the surface, she and her husband appeared to lead completely separate lives but no-one knows how a couple gets along behind closed doors. For all we know, they may have been quite content to live as apart as they did. And such an arrangement may have gone on for years.

"What we don't know is *when* his wife learned the truth about him," she said. "Was it only recently when he filed for divorce? Personally, I don't think so. It's not likely that Mr. Peterson's behavior changed overnight – I believe his wife began to see the changes in him over a period of years. She might even have considered divorcing *him* before she learned of his intention to do so.

"She's a smart, successful woman so in order to prevent any scandal on her husband's part from tainting her own business, perhaps she decided to let the divorce takes its course, then just carry on without him. I think the last thing she'd do is involve herself in her husband's death. Especially in the grizzly manner that he died."

I watched Frank nodding his head while he was listening to Isabel. "Interesting," he said. Then he folded his napkin into a perfect square, opened his mouth to speak, but nothing came out.

He cleared his throat and tried again. "Ah …" another pause.

It wasn't like Frank to stammer like this; usually, when he had something to say, he spit it out without fanfare. Then he took a deep breath and turned toward Isabel, "You were right about having a woman constable at the interview – sworn police officer or not. The lady was very guarded with Doc and me: I had to coax out bit by bit what little info we got from her. And I still don't think I got everything."

She gave him a sweet smile. "Thank you, Frank. I appreciate that."

CHAPTER THIRTY-ONE

The following morning, I heard a single tap on my office door then Longo breezed in and sat on the chair beside my desk. He withdrew a small envelope from his jacket pocket and I reached for it. "No, no, no," he said, leaning away from the desk. "You don't get these duckets until you give me the promised info on my guy." He slapped the envelope on my desk, his right hand glued to it.

I dug out my wallet and laid a sawbuck and a deuce on the table, securing them under my hand as he had done. "Tickets first," I said.

He shook his head. "Age before beauty."

I glanced quickly at my office door and when Longo followed suit, I snagged the tickets from under his hand.

I pushed the bills toward him. "As we agreed."

"Hold on, Buster," he was half out of his chair, leaning toward me. "What's the dope on Peterson?"

I let him sizzle for another moment, then I moved forward, our heads almost touching, and I whispered, "*He's dead.*"

"**WHAT**?" On his feet now, both hands on my desk, craning his angry red face at me.

"You heard me," I said. "He's dead, *morto*. He was burned to a crisp in that big fire behind the Armoury the other night."

He slumped down onto his chair. "No, I don't believe it. Why the hell would he be anywhere near that place?"

I shrugged my shoulders. "Dunno. But I'm willing to bet that Belcastro had something to do with it."

He was still simmering as he continued to glare at me. "So, I don't get nuttin' out of this deal? I went to a helluva lot of trouble to deliver the goods here."

"Like I said before, you made a nice profit on these tickets.

And you've got my undying gratitude."

Now he pushed back his chair, almost toppling it, then stomped toward the door as he pocketed the cash. At the doorway, he snapped over his shoulder, "You can't spend gratitude."

Isabel stood at my office door, hands on her hips, watching Longo storm past her and out the main door.

"What did you say to the poor man, Max? You certainly got his dander up."

I signalled for her to close the door and waved her in to sit at the desk beside me. "I don't want Phyllis to overhear us," I said. "And I wouldn't worry about Longo – he's all show. I just bought a pair of tickets from him for that Barbara Ann ice show that Phyl's been going on about. I planned to give them to Trépanier so he could take her to see her idol."

Iz reached for my hand and squeezed it. "Aren't you the generous boss, Max. She'll be tickled pink. But why did Longo go off in a huff like that?"

"I just told him that his main benefactor, Peterson, is dead. And you know Longo – he's big on theatrics."

After Iz left the office, I'd just opened the new account file for the Wentworth Insurance Company case and Frank phoned me – again.

"Holy cow, I hear from you more often than anyone else I know, Frank."

He ignored my remark and started right in with his business. "Remember that I told you there was a guy in the radio room who's a member of the Masons?"

"Yeah."

"Well, he's back on duty this morning and he told me that the square and compass emblem on the back of Peterson's watch represent architectural tools that are used by masons and they're displayed together to form a triangle – it's a religious symbol for Freemasonry. The letter 'G' in the centre represents God as the Great Architect of the universe."

"Well … that doesn't help a helluva lot. Is that all he gave you, Frank?"

"Yeah, I was disappointed too."

Then he paused for a moment. "Speaking of Masons

reminds me of that old witch, Sister Gabriel. Did you have her for religion class at St. Mary's?"

"Huh? What's she got to do with anything?"

"Is that a yes or a no?"

I thought for a moment, wondering where he was going with this. "No, I don't remember her."

"Maybe she retired before you got there. Anyway, she taught us that Masons were in league with the devil and it was a sin for Catholics to have any truck with them. You believe any of that guff, Max?"

"Of course not. But don't tell me that *you* still do."

"I did when I was a kid. Some folks say that beneath all their regalia and mumbo-jumbo, the Masons are just a Big Boys' club."

"In that respect they're like the Knights of Columbus," I said. "I've seen those boys on parade in their ceremonial capes, feathered hats and swords."

"I've gotta run, Max. Believe it or not, I've got my own work to do."

I'd just hung up and opened the Wentworth Insurance folder when the damn phone rang again. It felt like some mysterious power was keeping me from reviewing this file – maybe a Masonic curse.

When I picked up the receiver, an anxious-sounding woman said, "Max, is that you?"

I didn't recognize her voice. "Yes, Ma'am. How can I help you?"

"It's Sophia, Max. I hope you remember me from Central High."

Sophia … Lord love a duck!

I knew her a million years ago and now here she was on the phone. Sophia DeStefano and I were classmates when we attended Central High School; not sweethearts but just good friends who shared a similar quirky outlook on life. I hadn't seen her since graduation and that was five years before the war. In the meantime I'd moved to Regina for RCMP training and later I was posted to Prince George in British Columbia. Later still, I moved to Toronto.

Then came the war. Little wonder, therefore, that I hadn't recognized her voice.

"Of course I remember you, Sophia. I'm just surprised to hear from you now. How long has it been? It's gotta be … 14 or 15 years ago since we last saw each other. "

"That's about right. I'm calling you now because one of my friends from school told me you were back in town – a private detective now." She paused and I heard her take a deep breath. "My family is in trouble so I'd really appreciate getting some advice from you – if you wouldn't mind. I was hoping that I could meet with you."

Sophia's voice was hesitant, almost pleading, and it made me wary. But for old time's sake, I said, "Okay, I suppose I could do that. When would you like to get together?"

"As soon as possible, Max. It's urgent."

"Well … could you tell me a little more about your problem?"

"Not on the phone. Maybe we could meet at that diner where the gang used to go after school. It's still on the corner, across from St. Pat's Church at King and Victoria."

"I remember it." A lively image bounced into my mind – a bunch of noisy teenagers, laughing, talking, sipping Cokes, some even jiving in the aisle to the jukebox tunes of the day. The big favourite back then was "Stompin' at the Savoy" by Chick Webb.

"Cosentino's," I said.

"That's right. Can you make it this afternoon – about 3 o'clock or so? We're in a real bind, Max, and we'd be very grateful for your help."

"Well … I'm working on a big case right now –"

"Please, Max. It's urgent and I promise I won't take too much of your time."

I'd always been a marshmallow when I heard a woman's pleading voice. "Okay, I'll be there."

I hung up the phone then finally had a chance to review some notes I'd made on that Wentworth file.

Later that afternoon, I was leaving the office to meet Sophia and I asked Phyl when she expected Isabel to return.

"She said it would be close to 5 o'clock."

"I'll be back before then. I'm off to meet a prospective client."

I didn't see any cabs in line at the Connaught so I boarded a Belt Line streetcar heading east on King Street and got off at the Victoria Street stop. On the way here, some of my happy high-school memories were colliding with the distress I heard in Sophia's voice.

When I entered Cosentino's, she was waving at me from a booth at the rear of the restaurant. She hadn't changed much since I'd last seen her: her dark hair was cut in the same short style and she wore a stylish, green dress that emphasized her still-trim figure. But her ebony eyes were overflowing with worry as I reached forward to shake her hand.

"Great to see you again," I said. "You still have your high-school good looks."

She squeezed my hand. "And you're still a smooth-talker."

I slid along the bench seat across from her and looked at the menu.

"A cherry Coke and a side of fries, Max?"

I set the menu aside, shaking my head. "Nope. I've given up my teenage grub."

When the waitress appeared I ordered coffee; Sophia preferred a cup of tea. "And I think I'll have one of those jelly donuts in that display case on the counter," I said.

Sophia shook her head. "Same old Max."

While we waited for our order, I gave her a quick summary of my time in the RCMP and my injury during the war. "When I couldn't get hired by the police because of my limp, I decided to go into business for myself as a private investigator. How about you?"

She told me about her job as a teller at the downtown branch of the Bank of Commerce. "After high-school I married Carlo DeLuca. He's a cabinet maker and he worked in his father's shop along with his two younger brothers; I look after the books for them. My Carlo walks like you do, Max – he had polio when he was a kid and suffered nerve damage in his right foot and leg."

"What about family," I said. "Do you have any children?"

"Twins – a boy and a girl. They're in Grade five now. How

about you, Max? Has some lucky lady been able to drag you to the altar yet?" She smiled at her little joke.

"Coming soon. My partner at the detective agency and I are taking the plunge in September."

"I'm happy for you," she said while she nodded her head.

The waitress returned with our order. Sophia held up her hand when I offered to share the donut so I was forced to eat it myself.

After I set my empty plate aside, I said. "Now tell me about your family's problem."

She fussed with her teacup, moving it round and round on the saucer. "Um … I don't where to start."

"Take a deep breath and try to relax. I'll help you if I can."

"Well …" she'd removed a small handkerchief from her purse, dabbing at her eyes. "It's about my husband, really, but it involves the whole family. His father is Guido DeLuca. Have you heard about him?"

I shook my head.

Her eyes made a quick sweep of the few people nearby then she bent closer, lowering her voice. "He used to be part of the Rocco Perri gang – bootlegging and all that stuff before the war. Then Guido quit the Mob to join the family cabinet making business. That was before Rocco's crew was rounded up in 1940 and imprisoned in Camp Petawawa. But the truth is – you can't really retire from the Mob; so once in a while Guido's forced to do certain favours for them."

"What kind of favours?"

She paused to sip her tea, then she lowered her voice to a whisper now, our heads almost touching. "The business has a couple of vans to deliver the finished cabinets to our customers. But once in a while, the Mob boss calls my father-in-law to arrange for the pick-up and drop off of certain large items."

"Stolen property, that kind of thing?"

"Yes. But once or twice I suspected that the property was recently deceased."

I jerked back in my seat. "Oh … that kind of property."

Her eyes said 'yes', then she drank the rest of her tea in one long gulp.

I signalled to the waitress to bring her a refill; we didn't speak until it arrived and the waitress departed.

"I'm guessing that it might be your husband who's now under pressure to deliver that 'property' and that's why you're upset."

The jittering in her eyes told me I was on the right track. It seemed like a full minute passed before she could respond.

"That's right, Max. I'm worried sick that my Carlo might already know too much … and now I'm afraid that he may be forced to cooperate with the Mob on other jobs as well."

She added a bit of sugar to her tea and the small jug of milk almost slipped from her fingers while she poured.

I lowered my voice as she had done. "Tell me what's frightening you now, Sophia. You know you can trust me."

It pained me to see the tears in the corners of her eyes when she raised her head. When she attempted to speak, no words came out. I waited while she gathered her courage.

"Last week, Carlo's dad got a call from the Mob boss ordering him to pick up a certain 'delivery' then dispose of it in the Bay. But when Carlo's father told him to look after it, Carlo refused. He tried to convince the old man that it was too dangerous to continue doing these 'favours' because it put the entire family at risk."

She pushed back from the table to blot the tiny tears now trickling down her cheeks. I waited in silence until she was able to continue.

"It took a lot of talking but Carlo finally convinced his father to tell the Mob boss that he wouldn't do these jobs anymore. But when Guido spoke to the big boss, he was given 24 hours to reconsider his decision – or else. That was the day before that big fire in the north end."

She paused to gulp a deep breath. "That fire was devastating for us, Max, because our family business was housed in that building: we suspect that the Mob's plan was to dump that dead body in our shop, then set it on fire to teach us a lesson. But the blaze got out of control and the entire building went up in flames along with all the other businesses there. We believe that's what the boss meant by 'or else'. Now I'm scared to death because we don't know what'll happen next. We don't know if our family is still in the Mob's sights even though our business is gone."

She slumped back in the booth, exhausted by relating her family's dilemma – especially   the lingering threat of the Mob's next move.

"And you haven't heard anything further from the Mob?" She shook her head.

"I don't suppose that Carlo has gone to the police for help?"

"No, he was afraid of implicating his father because of his past history with the Mob. He feared the big boss would find out, then retaliate in some way."

My heart went out to her. I could only imagine the anguish suffered by a family besieged by the Mob's vicious tactics.

Before we parted outside the restaurant, I shook her hand, "I'm sorry for your family's distress, Sophia. I have some contacts with the police and I may be able to get some advice about your problem."

She pulled back from me, her eyes brimming. "No, I don't think that's a good idea. If those criminals find out, they're sure to retaliate then we'd be in worse trouble."

"You remember Frank Russo, don't you? He's a sergeant with the Hamilton Police now; I can speak with him off the record. We can trust Frank to help and to keep quiet about it."

"I don't know …"

"Talk it over with your husband and assure him that I won't do anything unless you both agree. And I'd like to have your phone number in case I think of anything else."

I jotted her number in my notebook then passed her my card after I'd added my home number. "Let me know after you discuss it with Carlo."

As I was waiting for the streetcar on the other side of King Street, I observed a slick young guy in a dark suit standing outside the smoke shop next door to Cosentino's – he folded his newspaper and walked casually in the same direction as Sophia had taken.

CHAPTER THIRTY-TWO

When I returned to the office, it was near closing time and I called Frank. "See you at Duffy's in 10 minutes?"

He muffled his phone, speaking with someone in his office. Then he said, "No can do. Better make it half an hour."

We sat near the doorway, the farthest table from the hoo-ha of the regulars crowded along the bar. Frank waved to Liam to catch his eye, holding up 2 fingers. I watched a music lover at the Wurlitzer as he dropped in a nickel, then the room was regaled by Spike Jones playing "Yes, we have no bananas." When Liam dropped off a couple of Peller's Ale at our table, I asked him, "That tune on the squawk box – does that mean we have some or we don't?"

He bellowed a laugh. "You're the second guy who's asked me that today."

"What did you tell the other guy?"

"We have no bananas today." Then I heard him laughing like a loon as he hustled away.

Frank and I clinked bottles then glugged some beer. He lowered his voice, "Listen, Max, we've gotta stop meeting so often. People might start talking about us. Now, tell me what this about and make it quick – I'm a busy man."

I gave him a summary of my meeting with Sophia and sat back in my chair.

He'd nodded his head when I referred to her husband, "I remember that guy," he said. "Yeah, there was a DeLuca on Cathedral High's football team: he played the centre position on the offensive line. Not a real big guy, but as strong as Charles Atlas. And I think, yeah, he was a gimpy guy, too – just like you. I guess that's why he only played on the line – not much running required."

"Did you know that his old man was a member of the Mob?"

"Yeah, we try to keep track of these guys but I thought that old Guido had retired."

"According to Sophia that's a helluva lot easier said than done. He still gets roped into performing certain favours for the Mob from time to time. Disposing of Peterson's corpse was one of those times. But at Sophia's urging, Carlo had finally convinced his father to take a stand against the Mob. When the big boss ordered Guido to dump that body in Hamilton Harbour, the old man refused. That's when all hell broke loose for the DeLuca family."

Frank stopped me there. "What kind of hell? Gimme the details."

"Carlo believes that Belcastro had a couple of his thugs deliver that body to the DeLuca cabinet shop in that building behind the Armoury – then set it on fire. The Mob's way of showing Guido and his family what happens when you don't follow orders. They probably didn't intend to burn down the whole damn building but I don't think the Boss and his goons have lost any sleep over that."

Frank took a steelworker's glug of Peller's that emptied his bottle. He covered his mouth when he burped, then waved at Liam to bring us another round. "So the fire was meant as a lesson to Carlo's family?"

"They believe that it was. Of course, it had the added advantage of disposing of Peterson's body at the same time."

Frank turned up his nose. "Well … I suppose it might've happened that way. But it sounds a little too pat to me."

"Do you have a better explanation?"

"No. But I've learned to avoid the easy answers."

I finished off my beer and set my bottle aside. "I gave Sophia your phone number. And I suggested that she have Carlo give you a call. You don't mind, do you?"

"No, it's a good idea. I'd be glad to talk to him – but I'd be surprised as hell if he came forward as a co-operating witness."

I recalled Frank telling me about a survey of the workers in that building at the time of the fire. "Anyone missing in that roll-call you were conducting?"

"Almost everyone's accounted for."

"Almost?"

He pulled a long face. "Yeah, the building owner hired a night watchman after the previous fire a couple of months ago. But the bugger took a powder on the night of this fire. Don't think we won't sit him down for a nice, long chat if we can find him. He's moved from the address that he gave the building owner – no forwarding address."

Liam arrived with more beer, noting our sombre demeanour. "Cheer up, fellas," he said. "This one's on the house." Then he hustled away with our empties.

Frank leaned toward me. "You're certain that Sophia's telling the truth?"

"I believe she's on the level. Why would she make up something like this?"

"Okay. But I don't know how the hell Peterson would've posed a threat to the Mob in the first place."

"That's another story."

"Well, damnit, Max – let's hear it."

I wet my whistle with a gulp of Peller's, then leaned toward him. "I learned that Peterson's in trouble with the Ontario Jockey Club officials who suspect him of doping some of the horses that he races on the Ontario circuit. As a result he was scheduled to appear before the Stewards' Committee next week. As it happens, Belcastro was his partner in that doping scheme so it wasn't in his interest to have Peterson spill the beans to the Committee. They could've been fined and banned for life from racing in Ontario. And publicity like that ain't in the Mob's interest. That's one reason why they turned up the heat on Peterson – literally."

Frank was nodding his head while he digested my intel. "How'd you get all this stuff?"

"I have an inside source. But I've been sworn to secrecy."

"How reliable is this guy?"

"He's gold-plated. This info comes straight from the horse's mouth."

"I don't suppose that he's going to come forward to testify?"

I leaned toward him, "It's not in his best interest."

"Of course it isn't. It's risky as hell for him. But how are we gonna stop these Mob buggers if nobody's willing to stand up in court – or at least co-operate with us?"

I shook my head. "Life is hard, Frank. Then you die."

On my way to the office, the following morning, I spotted my friend, Bob, at the entrance to the Capitol Theatre where he'd set up his array of pencils for sale and I stopped for a chat. "Did you hear anything from the veterans' hospital yet?"

"Sure did, Max, and I was hoping to spot you today. I got a letter yesterday: they've completed their assessment and my next appointment'll be on 26 May."

"Good news," I said. "I'll make a note of that so we can drive you."

"We really appreciate your help, Max. You two are the best –"

I cut him off there. "We're not doing anything you wouldn't do if our positions were reversed. But maybe you can help a friend of mine. Her hubby and his two brothers are cabinet makers whose shop was destroyed in that big fire last week: as a result, they're out of work. You told me about your former job at the Evel Casket Company so I wondered if you still had a contact there you might call on their behalf."

"Sure do, Max. I know the foreman pretty well – we stay in touch. I'll call him today then let you know. Do they happen to be veterans? That would help their chances."

"Don't know about that, so don't contact him until I find out. I'll get back to you as soon as I can."

"Roger that. Speaking of vets, Max, did you happen to see that item in the *Spec* about the Veterans' Disability Allowances program? It's gonna affect you."

"No, I haven't read the paper yet."

He was searching his jacket pockets. "Here it is – I clipped it out." He read it aloud for me: "The Government of Canada has raised disability allowances for military personnel from a maximum $750 to $1,400 yearly, depending upon the degree of disability. The minimum allowance has been raised to $480 yearly – up from $250."

"It's good that it's gone up," I said. "But it doesn't sound like it's enough to live on."

"Well, if you're gettin' the maximum allowance it's because you need a lot of help. But if you don't have a family member to provide it, then you have to hire someone and, POOF, there goes your damn allowance. You ain't gonna get rich on this pension, Max."

"So it's still not enough."

"It is, if you only eat a light meal once a day and sleep in Victoria Park."

I could still hear him laughing as I limped away, thinking – everyone's a comedian these days. I blamed it on the radio.

Back in my office, I called Wendy Crane at the RCMP headquarters in Toronto.

"It's Max Dexter calling," I said when she picked up. "Got another question for you, if you don't mind."

"Still no 'Hello, Wendy – how are you?'"

I felt my face flush - again. "That's what I was about to say."

"Sure you were. Now go ahead, ask your question."

"Witness protection. I recall hearing about a program in the U.S. which made me wonder if the RCMP has adopted something similar here."

"Not much info on that, Max, however there isn't a program in the States yet. The FBI is still exploring that possibility along with the U.S. Marshal Service, but it'll be years before it gets off the ground. It's complicated – state and local governments would be involved. In addition, it's very expensive. So if your next question is about a similar RCMP program, ask me something else."

"Okay. How are you today?"

I listened to her laugh. "I'm fine, thanks. You have some witnesses to protect?"

"Yeah. I'm trying to help a family threatened by the Mob and wondered what advice I might give them. A witness protection program might've been a possibility."

"Yes, it would. But if the Mob were after me, I'd change my name, move to Edmonton and leave no forwarding address.

But it means starting over from scratch in a new place and that wouldn't be easy – especially if you have kids."

We chatted a bit longer then after I hung up the phone I imagined myself in the DeLucas' shoes – Mom, Dad and the twins standing on the sidewalk in front of a small house for rent in a different city. A new school for the kids; new jobs for the parents if they could find them. Perhaps worst of all, they'd have to sever their connections with their close-knit family and friends back home to ensure that no word of their whereabouts would leak out.

On the other hand, if they decided to stay in Hamilton and tough it out, they'd risk retaliation from the Mob for talking to the police.

It was like the executioner's offer: 'You have a choice – would you prefer the gallows or the electric chair?'

Later, I checked my notebook for the phone number then called Sophia, hoping to speak with her husband and I was in luck.

"It's Max Dexter calling. Is that Carlo?"

"That's right. Sophia told me that you were old friends from high school and you've offered to help us. I appreciate that, Max."

"You're welcome – I'm glad I caught you. I wanted to tell you that a friend of mine was a woodworker at the Evel Casket Company before the war and he's still friendly with the foreman there. I told him that your family had lost their business in that big fire and now you're looking for work. It might be your lucky day, Carlo – he's offered to speak to the foreman on your behalf."

"That's good news, Max. Lord knows, we're in short supply of that right now. But caskets? Jeez, I don't know about that. And that company name – Evel? It looks like evil. That's two strikes against the place right off the bat."

"I had the same reaction but they pronounce the name so that it rhymes with 'level'. My friend says there's nothing creepy or ghoulish about the work. He told me that it's just woodworking, whatever the hell the product might be."

I listened to him laugh. "Yeah, I guess he's right. Wood's just wood; it doesn't care what it's used for."

"Also, my friend wanted to know if you and your brothers

were veterans. If so, you'd go to the head of the line for an interview."

"Well, both my brothers were Armoured Corps – tanks. They were in the thick of the battle in Sicily, then later in Normandy and Germany. But I was rejected because I had polio when I was a kid and that left me with nerve damage in my left ankle and lower leg so the Army wouldn't take me. Sophia says that my limp is similar to yours – but on the other leg."

"We'll have to compare them when we meet sometime," I said. "Did you work in your shop during the war?"

"No. It was my father's shop but without my brothers there, he decided to mothball the business until the war was over. Then he worked in a friend's shop until '45. After the war, he moved our shop into the Burrow, Stewart and Milne building for a fresh start – you must've heard that the damned place burned down."

"Yeah, that was bad luck. But what did *you* do during the war?"

"I worked at that big factory on Victoria Avenue that was formerly the Otis Fensom Elevator plant. The government had taken it over to produce Bofors anti-aircraft guns. Now the new Studebaker plant is at the same location."

"Why didn't you stay there, work on the line?"

"I could've but I'm a good cabinet-maker so I wanted to stay in that trade. Right now my brothers and I are working part-time at a friend's lumber yard in Dundas until we find something better."

"Well, thanks for this info. I'll let my pal know and he'll pass it along to the foreman at the Evel shop."

"Okay, Max, we're grateful for your help. You have my phone number but if we're not here, I'll give you my parents' number. My brothers still live at home so someone's usually there to take a message."

He recited the number and I noted it in my book. "Now with your shop destroyed, do you think the Mob will back off from your family?"

"We sure hope so. For our part, we're trying to keep the old man from contacting any of those mob guys. Both he and my mother are eligible for the Old Age Pension but that's peanuts; you can't live on that. I know he's got some savings but we'll have to look after the old folks. Not that we mind, of course."

"What about insurance on your business?"

"Luckily, we have some. In addition to the shop equipment, we had a couple of vans housed there and they went up in smoke along with everything else. But with 10 businesses involved, plus the building owner's insurance company, it's gonna be a nightmare to sort out who gets what. My guess is that all the claims will end up in court for settlement. That'll probably take forever and a day so we're not holding our breath on that score."

"One last thing," I said, "you might consider speaking with my friend, Frank Russo. He's a Hamilton cop who's familiar with the Mob's operations. He's a good guy, Carlo, even though he played football for Central Collegiate. He might be able to help your family."

The line went silent for a moment until he finally said, "Well … the cops … I dunno … I'll have to think about that."

I gave him Frank's phone number in case he decided to call him. "Good luck, Bud, from one limper to another."

Over dinner that evening, I told Isabel about my meeting with Sophia and my later phone conversation with her husband, Carlo.

"Before the war, Bob worked for the Evel Casket Company and he's agreed to put in a good word with the foreman there on behalf of the DeLuca brothers."

"I'm sure they appreciate that, Max. But now you've got me wondering if you're planning to get in touch with all your former girlfriends."

We stared at each other in silence for a moment until she began to laugh, pointing a finger at me. "I'm pulling your leg, Max, don't look so worried. I think it was generous of you to offer them help – it's one of the reasons that I love you."

CHAPTER THIRTY-THREE

Isabel was working with Emma Rose at her office the following morning and I was down on my good knee searching for a file in the bottom drawer of her desk. I heard someone entering the office, then Frank's voice asking Phyllis, "Is his nibs around?"

"He's on the floor behind you."

He wheeled around and bent down to help me up. "You okay? Did your leg give out?"

I extended my right arm and he yanked me upright. "Nope, I was just looking for something. C'mon in."

After we settled in my office, I said, "Is this just a courtesy call or did you have something on your mind?"

"Nothing special. I have to pick up Angie's wrist watch at Gaul's Jewellers next door." He checked his own watch – "and I'm meeting somebody in 15 minutes so I can't hang around."

"I'll give you two minutes," I said. "I spoke with Carlo DeLuca yesterday and he might call you about his family's situation. Naturally, he's not anxious to talk to the cops."

"Nobody's anxious. But I'd be glad to talk to him."

"You think there's anything the police can actually do for the DeLucas?"

He shrugged. "There's not a helluva lot we can do. As a rule, people threatened by the Mob are afraid to come forward, fearing retaliation. And I can't blame them – from time to time these mob guys will make a public display by leaving the body of a tortured victim strung up on a telephone pole or in another public place as a warning to people who try to resist their demands or go to the cops. Blowing up your car in your driveway is also effective, especially if you're in it at the time.

"My guess is that only one in a hundred people will come to us if their problem involves the Mob. But in the case of the

DeLuca family, since old Guido was a low level member and they no longer have a business, maybe they'll have a better chance than most of staying under the Mob's radar."

I left the office with Frank and he went next door to the jewellery store. I walked in the opposite direction to the Capitol theatre where Bob was set up in the entranceway.

"I told you about the DeLuca brothers looking for carpentry work." I said.

"Yep. And you were going to find out about their military service."

"Turns out, the older brother, Carlo, had polio as a kid and he's a limper like me. He was ineligible for military service but during the war he worked at the former Otis Fensom plant that was re-tooled to manufacture those big anti-aircraft guns. His two younger brothers were both Armoured Corps – all over Hell's half-acre in Europe during the war."

"Good stuff, Max. The foreman at Evel's will be impressed by all that. I'll call him today and get back to you pronto."

As I was returning to the office, I noted a chauffeur standing beside a gleaming, black Cadillac at the curb and when he saw me he waved me over. "Mr. O'Brien would like a word," he said and he opened the rear door for me. From the glistening chrome grill to the stylish tail fins on the rear fenders, this car thumbed its nose at all the others on the road and shouted, 'I'm a shiny new 1948 Cadillac Fleetwood and you ain't.' I slid onto the back seat beside J.B. and the driver closed the door behind me. He remained outside on the sidewalk. As I settled onto the plush velvety seat, I caught a whiff of that distinctive new-car aroma that only lasted a short time.

"Smells like a brand new car," I said when I was seated.

J.B. bobbed his head. "Just took delivery this morning – a special order through Hamilton Motor Products over on Main West. But that's not what I wanted to discuss with you."

'Discuss' had the connotation of reasonable people sitting down to talk something over in the hope of reaching a mutual agreement. But that wasn't this old fart's style.

"All right." I said. "Let's discuss."

"I thought I should tell you about my plot of land near Burlington."

"What did you decide?"

"Well, it's against my better judgement but I'm ready to sell it."

I raised my eyebrows, wondering what happened to change his mind. "Will they pay you the market value you were holding out for?"

He scowled at me. "No – but close enough."

That probably meant he'd caved in and sold the entire acreage for a dollar but I didn't press him on it, allowing him to save face. "What did your daughter say when you told her."

"I haven't spoken with her since she made that big fuss at my office. But you could do me a favour and let her know..."

"She's *your* daughter."

"She's *your* fiancée. Besides, I'm tired of talking to her. She wants to stick her nose into every damn thing that I do – even the women I see from time to time."

I shifted in my seat and leaned toward him. "It's because she's concerned about you, J.B. She's afraid that your association with those mobsters and their women will cause you no end of grief – blackmail, extortion and maybe even a slab in the morgue. And I agree with her; there's no 'happily ever after' with these guys."

The blank expression on his face hadn't changed while I spoke. I couldn't tell if my little speech had registered or not. After an awkward silence he changed the subject. "Now, what should we do about that finger in my freezer?"

That damn 'we' was back again. I let him simmer for a moment longer, then I told him, "**You** could tape it to a brick and drop it in the canal – the fish will look after it."

"I was hoping you'd take care of it for me."

"Look here, Mister, it wasn't sent to me. You're the new owner of that finger. And you don't even have to get out of your car – just open the damn window and toss it over the bridge railing into the canal." I bobbed my head toward his driver out on the sidewalk, "Or you could have your man there do it for you."

"Hell, no. Then he'd have something to hold over me."

"Well, that's your problem. I've told you what I'd do." I

reached for the door handle and he grabbed my sleeve, yanking me back.

"I need your help here, Dexter. And I'm willing to show my gratitude – within reason …"

I was shaking my head before he'd finished speaking. "No can do, bub. It's time for you to be a man here – and clean up after yourself."

I hoisted myself out of the back seat and slammed the car door with a satisfying thunk. When I steamed past the chauffeur, he was swivelling his head between me and his boss who was glaring out his shiny new window at me.

Later that afternoon, I got a phone call from Longo. "Trixie wants to see you about Ida," he said. "I'm busy with a private reception this afternoon but she's upstairs in the dressing room right now – same place as last time."

"Thanks. I'll get over there in a few minutes."

"Right. And don't forget that you owe me for this."

"Put it on my tab. I'm sure you'll remind me."

I intended to call Isabel on the intercom but Phyllis answered. "You dial 2 for her and I'm number 3," she said. "I didn't think you needed a list to remember that, Boss."

"Don't get snippy, young lady. A little respect for your elders, eh?"

I heard her chuckling as she hung up her phone. Then I dialed 2.

"What's this? A roll call?" Iz said. "We're all here, Max – both of us."

Now I could hear Phyl laughing in the background and I sighed. It wasn't easy working with comediennes. "I got a message from Trixie at the Connaught and she'd like to talk," I said. "Do you have time to go with me now?"

"Sure thing. Just give me five minutes."

We crossed King Street to the Connaught and when we entered the women's dressing room upstairs, Trixie was ironing a blouse. "The laundry here does a crappy job with our outfits," she said. "So I have to get the creases out myself." She set the iron on

A DEVIOUS DAME

a metal stand and I introduced her to Isabel. Then we sat at a small table in the corner of the dressing room.

"Max and I are partners at the detective agency," Iz said, "and he's told me about his last visit with you."

Trixie was looking closely at her. "I think I've seen you here in the Circus Roof, Miss. It's nice to meet you."

"Don't be so formal. Call me Isabel. We understand that you have some news about Ida."

She withdrew a pack of Black Cat cigarettes from her purse and offered them to us. After we shook our heads, she hesitated, then put them away. We didn't speak, allowing her to set the pace. She inhaled a deep breath and let it out slowly, "How's the boy?"

Iz smiled. "Danny's doing pretty well, under the circumstances: he's just recovered from a dose of the measles. And he's staying with a good friend of ours who has a boy a bit younger than he. Of course, Danny's quite concerned about his mother. She didn't tell him that she was going away."

"That's Ida – she's a single-minded woman. Full speed ahead and damn the torpedoes."

"Longo told me you got a letter from her," I said.

A grimace on her face as she shook her head. "I'm really worried about her this time." She removed a letter from her purse and passed it across the table toward us. I slid it from its envelope and we stared at the cream-coloured page: an embossed letterhead from the Waldorf-Astoria Hotel at 301 Park Avenue in New York City.

Dearest Trixie,
I'm in love with the most darling man and I can't wait until you meet him. I hope you're sitting down when you're reading this because we're planning to be married in Havana next month when he'll be down there on business.

I knew it was true love by the size of the sparkler he gave me at our engagement party at this real swanky place called the Stork Club here in New York.

Mr. Gambino is married but he's certain that his divorce will be finalized any day now.

He's put me up at this wonderful hotel for the time

213

being and I'll let you know when I get something more permanent. Then you must come down for a nice long visit.

I'll write again soon when everything is settled.

Love and kisses,
Ida

We didn't speak for a pregnant moment as we digested the contents of Ida's letter.

Then Iz passed it back to Trixie. "Thank you for showing us this. Do you think it means what I think it does?"

"Well, if you're thinkin' that Ida is crazy to believe this Gambino guy is going to marry her, then, yes – that's how I read it, too."

"Were you aware that Ida may be hooked on drugs?" I said.

A grimace on her face. "I warned her about those damn pills but she wouldn't listen.
I tried to convince her they were habit-forming and could take over her life. One of my girlfriends who worked at the Brant Inn died from a drug overdose last Christmas. Such a waste of a life."

"Let's hope that Ida comes to her senses" I said.

Iz leaned closer to her, "For Danny's sake, at least."

Trixie sat back in her chair and I noticed that tiny teardrops had formed in the corners of her eyes. "I hate to say it, but the boy is probably better off without her."

It saddened me to hear her opinion. "You don't think she'll come back to Hamilton? Even for Danny?"

"No, I don't. Ida's main concern in life is her own well-being. In fact, it's her only concern."

As we were about to leave, I folded a $5 dollar bill around one of my business cards, then slipped them to Trixie when we shook hands. "Thanks again for showing us the letter. Here's my card - we'd appreciate hearing from you if you get any more information about Ida."

Walking back to the office, Isabel said, "It wouldn't surprise me if Ida disappeared somewhere between New York and Havana."

"That's a pretty good guess. Now we need to speak with Danny about her, but I'm not looking forward to that."

Later, I called Grace and briefed her on Ida's situation. "We'd like to see Danny after dinner, if you don't mind. Then we could tell him the bad news."

"Of course," she said. "I was afraid that his mother might be involved in something like this, especially when we learned about those pills. But most of all, I feel badly for the boy. Of course, he's welcome to stay with us until we know for sure about his mother. And I think that you should be the one to tell him about her. He talks a lot about you, Max. You're his hero: a real, live, private detective. I allow the boys to listen to a few of those private eye serials on the radio – Boston Blackie and that bunch. Danny often says, 'I wonder if that's how Max Dexter would solve the crime?' But before you tell him about his mother, you could let them show you their hockey stuff – they're still excited about that Stanley Cup business."

"Thank you, Grace. You've been very generous to take Danny in and treat him as your own child. But I think we should talk to the Children's Aid Society soon about where he might go if Ida doesn't return at all."

"Let's not rush into that yet," she said. "We've got lots of time to consider a longer term arrangement. I think you know very well that the boy has captured our hearts – all three of us here. And if there's a way of keeping him here with us then we'd like to explore that. So let's not make any hasty decisions that we might regret later."

After supper, we were standing on the porch at Grace's home, inhaling what remained of a warm spring day. According to *The Spectator*, the high today had reached 68 degrees, not bad for mid-April.

Grace fussed over us at the entranceway before leading us into the living room where the coffee table was covered with a pile of Toronto Maple Leaf clippings from the newspaper and a huge scrap book. Danny knelt on the floor beside Vincent and they waved me over to join them.

I heard Samantha calling 'hello' from the kitchen then

Grace and Isabel were quick to join her there. It made me wonder why so many women didn't enjoy yakking about hockey – maybe they didn't realize the fascination of player trades, team standings, goals and assists, shots on goal, face-off percentages and all that interesting stuff. So far, Isabel appeared to have a bit of interest but only in tiny doses.

Vincent was using a bottle of LePage's glue to stick the clippings into their album and Danny was cutting them to size. I got down beside them and looked over the photos they'd clipped from *The Spectator*.

"That big one shows the crowd in front of Toronto City Hall where the victory parade ended," Vincent said. "See – that's Syl Apps holding the Stanley Cup over his head."

"You could stick that on the cover of your album," I said. "It tells the whole story in one photo."

Danny glanced across the table at me, "That's what we're saving it for."

After another page was completed, I said to Vincent, "I hope you don't mind but I'd like to talk to Danny upstairs – I've got some news about his mother."

Vincent nodded but didn't speak, an anxious look on his face.

"Have you seen her?" Danny said.

I shook my head and took his arm. "No, but I'll tell you what I know upstairs."

I closed the door to the boys' room and we sat together on the edge of Danny's bed.

"Did your mother seem different to you before she went away? Really happy or sometime very sad?"

He thought about that for a moment, a frown on his face. "I guess so, yeah. And she was taking a lot of pills; she said they were for her allergies but she never said what she's allergic to. And when she got real sad, she took another kind of special pill and then she felt better – but only for a little while. She was never just ordinary like she used to be. But why are you asking me about this?"

"I'm trying to understand why she might have gone away. This afternoon, I spoke with one of your mother's friends who works with her at the hotel. This friend got a letter from your mother who's now in New York City."

His eyes lit up and he gripped my arm. "A letter for me?"

I shook my head, "'Fraid not, bud. It was for her friend."

"But why is she there? Is she coming back soon?"

I took a deep breath to steady myself before I replied. "Maybe not. She says in that letter that she plans to keep travelling – maybe to another country. And she might be gone for quite a while, but we just don't know yet."

He sat as still as Queen Victoria in Gore Park for a long moment and didn't speak. Then his shoulders began to shake as tears trickled down his cheeks. In that instant I envisioned a sorrowful image of a young Max Dexter when I received a similar message from Frank's mother all those years ago.

I slid my arm around his shoulders, then I held him as he sobbed against my chest.

After he'd calmed himself, I said, "Same thing happened to me. My father died when I was seven years old and soon afterward my mother moved away without telling me and now she lives in Florida."

"What did you do then?"

"A family who lived in our apartment building took me in to live with them. They had a boy who was a few years older than me and he became my big brother. But I won't lie and tell you that it was easy. I used to cry myself to sleep at first. As time passed, I began to worry less about my mother. And it took me a long time to learn to live without her. Once in a while, I still think about her,"

"You really think that I'll feel better after a while?"

"I know you will – you're a strong boy. In my case, I was very angry at first but later I got busy with school and sports and I gradually felt part of my new family. If your mother doesn't return, I'll bet the same thing might happen for you. But it takes time – and it's not easy."

He didn't speak, lips pressed tightly together, maybe feeling the same mixture of hurt and anger that I had felt. Blaming himself, maybe thinking that it was his fault.

I got to my feet. "I'm going downstairs now, but think about what I told you. You're doing a lot better than I did when my mother left me. C'mon down when you're feeling a bit better."

In the living room, the women were chatting quietly while Vincent continued cutting and pasting in the album. Grace stood and gripped my arm when I entered. "How did Danny take the news? Was he heartbroken?"

We sat on the sofa. Four pairs of anxious eyes trained on me, waiting for my report. "He's upset, of course, trying to understand why his mother has gone away. I think it'll take him a while before he accepts the fact that he's not responsible for her leaving."

I looked directly at Vincent, now sitting close beside his mother. "Danny's a lucky boy to be here with a family that welcomes him. He might be moody and upset for a time but he'll get over that with your family's help."

Grace stood and took Vincent's hand. "Let's go up and see him."

We could hear Grace's muffled voice taking charge of the situation upstairs.

"Big sister to the rescue," Samantha said.

Iz smiled at her. "Those boys are lucky to have her."

"She's always had that special knack of smoothing over a difficult situation. It makes you feel safe when she's beside you," Sam said. "That's what makes her such a great nurse – and sister."

When Grace came downstairs with her son, Sam went up with a plate of cookies and a glass of milk. Isabel glanced at me with a look that said, 'We don't have to worry about Danny. He's in good hands here.'

I waved Vincent over to sit beside me on the sofa. "I brought you some Newfoundland money. Here's a one-dollar bill; there in large letters, it says, 'Government of Newfoundland' and here, in the centre, that's a picture of King George." I dug into my pants pocket, "Here's a small collection of coins – some pennies, nickels and dimes and a couple of quarters; it's similar to Canadian money."

He got busy examining his loot – then he totalled it up. "Almost three bucks. Thanks a lot, Max. I'm gonna save these."

"Good idea because this might be the last of the Newfoundland money. Remember that I told you they're planning to hold a vote down there this summer on whether to join Canada? If the voters decide to become our tenth province, then they'll switch over to Bank of Canada money – same as we use here. And that's your civics lesson for today."

After we'd said our good-byes and were walking to the car Isabel pointed to a large black sedan parked on Bold Street, near Central Public School.

"I think I noticed that car when we arrived, Max. But it was parked in the next block."

"If you're worried that we're being followed, drive by and we'll have a look at it."

"I'm not worried. It was just an observation."

Nevertheless, Iz drove past the car, a sleek, black LaSalle, but we couldn't see anyone in it. It was parked in front of a large home with two cars in the driveway and a couple more on the street nearby.

"Looks like they're having a party, Iz. And the owner of that car might've gone out to pick up more booze or something."

"Liquor stores are closed by now."

"In this town, you can get booze anytime. You just have to pay more for it."

CHAPTER THIRTY-FOUR

At breakfast the following morning, Isabel poured us a second cup of coffee. "I was proud of how you handled that delicate situation with Danny last night," she said. "I'm sure that you'll treat our own children in the same sensitive way."

My antenna sprang to parade-square alert. "Trying to tell me something, Iz?"

Her brow wrinkled for a moment, then she shook her head. "I'm not pregnant, dear boy. If that's what you're worried about."

"I'm not worried. It's just that … well, maybe I am a bit concerned – husband, father and all that. I just hope that I'm up to the job."

She got up from her chair, placed her right arm around my neck and squirmed herself onto my lap. "I'm certain you'll be up to the job, sweetheart."

We were late arriving at the office.

"Heavy traffic this morning," I said to Phyllis as we entered. "Any messages?"

"Just one from Rob. He won't be in this morning."

"He's not sick, is he?"

"No, no." She began to rub her hands together, eyes downcast.

Isabel said, "I hope he hasn't been in an accident."

Phyl shook her head and took a deep breath. "He has a job interview at the police station this morning and I'm worried sick. Just the thought of him being involved in that dangerous work scares me silly. I don't want to risk losing him."

Iz placed her arm around Phyl's shoulders when they began to shake then she guided her over to the couch where they sat. "Let's talk this through, Phyllis …"

I made a bee-line for my office.

Isabel joined me later. "Phyllis has the jitters – she's afraid that Rob will get beaten up or shot in the line of duty. And that could happen, of course. But I reminded her that I was shot even though I was only a bystander during that attempted robbery. We talked it over and I hope she's thinking a bit more clearly now. Were you ever injured while you were an RCMP officer, Max?"

"No, I was lucky. A couple of close calls but I only received some scrapes and bruises. I'm not worried about Trépanier. He came through the war all right so he knows how to look after himself."

I'd been dithering about informing Isabel about my meeting with her father. I hated to stir up the disappointment she was feeling about his behaviour with Ida and his stupid involvement with those Mob guys. She was about to leave, but I held her arm. "Hang on a moment," I said. "I saw your father yesterday and I've been putting off telling you about it."

She sat back down, straight-backed and alert. "I'm almost afraid to ask," she said. "What's he done now?"

"He finally sold his land along the Queen Elizabeth highway to those mobsters. Remember they offered him $1 for that big parcel?"

"I remember."

"He told me that he was holding out for the 'fair-market value' and they've finally reached a compromise."

She was nodding her head before I'd finished speaking. "That means he accepted the dollar."

I smiled as I pointed at her. "Exactly what I thought. Then he wanted me to dispose of that finger with Ida's ring on it. It's still in his freezer."

"But why would he ask *you* to do that?"

"Because he thinks I'm a chump – he expects that others will be glad to do his dirty work, just to curry favour with him. But I refused."

"Good for you, Max. I'm glad you're standing up to him. And I'm sorry he's trying to take advantage of you."

"That's his nature." I held her hand and planted my lips on it. "I'm happy that you're nothing like him."

"So what's he going to do about that finger?"

I shrugged. "I don't know and frankly, my dear, I don't give a damn."

Later, Frank burst into my office and leaned against the door, out of breath. "Whew, I just escaped from Phyllis and Barbara Ann Scott."

I laughed, knowing exactly how he felt.

"I spotted that doll on her desk," he said. "Then I made the mistake of asking her about it and, oh-boy, did that set her off. She began to list a long string of the skater's activities, including an offer from a Hollywood studio for a film deal at $3,000 a week, then a possible appearance at the Canadian National Exhibition this summer, if they can figure out how to keep the ice frozen. I'm tellin' you, she was making my head spin and I couldn't get away fast enough."

He took a seat and I grinned at him. "I'm glad she's found someone else who shares her enthusiasm, Frank. Now you know what I go through every time Barbara Ann scores another earth-shattering achievement."

"Do you think it's true though – that she'd get three grand a week to make a damn movie? Those labourers at the Steel Company bust their asses for only two grand – and that's per year! Something ain't right in the state of Denmark, Max."

"Well, it's Hollywood, eh? And everything's out of whack down there. Anything else on your mind today?"

He seemed to relax at the change of subject. "Yeah. I just had a cuppa coffee with Carlo DeLuca over at the White Spot. It's just across the street so – I stopped in to tell you about it."

"I'm glad he had the nerve to meet you. He sounded reluctant when I spoke with him on the phone."

"Everyone's reluctant to talk to the cops but I don't take it personally anymore. And this Carlo guy showed me some backbone by meeting me and speaking up. His old man has put the family in a bind with the Mob but Carlo and his brothers are determined to steer clear of those guys. I explained to him how little the cops could do for them unless his father is willing to testify against the Mob and that ain't gonna happen. But he did offer to talk to me on the q.t. if I'd treat him as a confidential informer and not reveal him as my source. Of course, I agreed. Finally, he told me about the possibility of working at the Evel Casket shop. He said that he called the foreman there and all three of them will be interviewed next week. They've got their hopes up."

"Good news, Frank. Thanks for seeing him – and for letting me know."

Later, Isabel and I were at the Connaught for lunch when I caught sight of J.B. O'Brien. His right arm encircled the waist of a foxy, dark-haired woman who was smiling up at him as they swished from the dining room, heading toward the elevators.

I caught Isabel's eye and nodded toward them.

She did a double-take, then turned back to me. "Was that who I think it was?"

At that moment Longo appeared with our drinks. "Here we go, folks. Are you ready to order now?"

I grabbed his arm and drew him closer. "I just noticed J.B. O'Brien leaving with a good-looking woman."

"So did I."

"Do you know her?"

He leaned toward us and lowered his voice. "That's Linda. She's the new Ida."

"Hell's bells!" Iz said. "Here we go again."

When we returned to the office, I noted an early edition of *The Spectator* on the corner of Phyllis's desk and I brought it into my office because a teaser above the fold caught my eye – "INQUIRY INTO MILLION DOLLAR FIRE – see page 3."

I opened the newspaper at the long table in my office and I read the brief update.

"Provincial Fire Marshall W.J. Scott has ordered an investigation into the two recent fires at the historic Burrow, Stewart and Milne building in downtown Hamilton. Deputy Fire Marshall, J.E. Ritchie, will preside at the hearing next month at the Central Police Station on King William Street. More than 20 witnesses will be called by Hugh Brown, assistant crown attorney."

I sat back in my chair, staring out the window, wondering

what that inquiry might uncover. And I finally concluded – bugger all. Even if a few witnesses had seen some suspicious characters anywhere near that building before the fire broke out, they'd be smart enough to keep their lips buttoned. From an early age, Hamilton's north-enders learned the fine art of looking the other way, especially if the Mob might be involved. "Fire? What fire?"

CHAPTER THIRTY-FIVE

The telephone was ringing as we were entering Isabel's home at the end of the day.

She answered it while I hung up our spring coats.

"No, no," I heard her saying, "it's no trouble at all. Max and I will be there in 5 minutes."

She didn't speak until I prompted her. "What's happened?"

"That was Grace. Danny hasn't returned from school and she's worried about him." She glanced at her watch. "It's almost 5:30, Max."

"Let's go," I grabbed our coats as we were hustling out the door.

Grace was in a tizzy; as anxious as I'd ever seen her. She fumbled with the front door as she was letting us in and she was still fretting when we sat at the kitchen table.

"Vincent and Samantha have walked down to James Street for a few groceries," she said. "They should be back soon."

Iz scooted her chair closer to Grace and held her hand. "Has Danny been late like this before?"

"Yes, a few days ago," she said. "I meant to tell you about it last evening but we got on to something else and I forgot all about it. On that day, I drove over to his school and I didn't see him around. I asked some boys there if they'd seen him and they told me he was walking back home right after school let out.

"I drove around the neighbourhood and couldn't spot him: then I went over to his mother's apartment on York Street on the off chance that he might be there. Mrs. Macaluso thought she noticed him going upstairs but she got busy and forgot all about him. She knows the woman in Apt. 1 who buzzed the door open for me and I went up to check the apartment. Of course, I didn't really expect to find Danny up there and I didn't have a key. But the door was wide open and I was horrified to see that the apartment was in a shambles: clothing strewn about, shelves emptied onto the floor, drawers with their contents spilled out – it was a terrible mess."

Grace withdrew a handkerchief from her apron pocket and dabbed at her tears. "I found Danny in the bathroom with a broom and dustpan, trying to clean up the litter on the floor – perfume bottles, make-up containers, everything from the shelves was spilled out all over the room. It was a terrible, smelly mess. At first, I thought that he might've done the damage himself. But when he caught sight of me in the doorway, he burst into tears and clung to me, crying. After I calmed him down, he told me that he came to see if his mother had returned and discovered the apartment had been broken into and ripped apart. It almost broke my heart when he told me that he had to clean it up before she returned and that's why he was late.

"I helped him tidy up a bit; there wasn't much we could do and I told him we'd get a cleaning company to fix everything up. I've booked them for tomorrow."

We didn't speak for a moment, imagining that scene of destruction – and Danny's fear for his missing mother. I figured it must've been those mobsters who were responsible but I had no idea what they might've been searching for.

"What time does Danny usually return from school?" I asked her.

"Well, it's only been a few days since he got over the measles. I've been dropping him off on my way to McMaster in the mornings. This semester, I'm finished my classes at noon so Danny walks back here after school – about 4:30 or so, depending on how long he stays with his friends on the playground. But he's not been this late before."

"Name of the school, Grace?"

"It's Hess Street Public – about a 20-minute walk and he should've been here by now."

She paused. "Do you think I should call the police, Max?"

"Not yet. He's probably just lost track of the time. You stay here, in case he calls. Does he know the phone number?"

She nodded. "Yes, I gave him a card."

"Okay. Iz and I will drive to the school, see if we can spot him along the way then we'll come back here."

She jumped up from her chair and opened the front door for us. "I'll see you soon – with Danny, I hope."

Isabel turned north onto Hess Street and I scanned the foot traffic, searching for the boy as she drove. We moved slowly through the downtown area until I caught sight of the school at the foot of Cannon Street. A couple of cars were parked on either side of the school's main entrance, and a classic 1940 LaSalle sedan was nearby, on the street – it looked like that car Iz had noted near Grace's home last night and maybe she was right to be concerned about it. I read somewhere that General Motors had ceased production of the LaSalle brand back in 1940, so you didn't see many of these cars on the road. I looked again and didn't see anyone in it. Then I made a mental note to check it after we'd looked around the school.

Iz parked close to the school's main entrance. Through the windows in the double doors we watched a couple of janitors with push-brooms cleaning the floor at the far end of the hallway. I checked the doors – both locked.

The shouts of kids playing got our attention and we walked behind the school where a half-dozen boys kicked around a soccer ball on the playground. Danny wasn't one of them. When we got closer, I waved at the biggest kid to come over. He booted the ball toward the far end of the field before he walked toward us.

"What's up, Mister? You lookin' for somebody?"

"Yeah," I nodded. "We're looking for Danny Lucas. Was he playing with you guys?"

"Nah. He's been away 'cause of the measles. So he leaves right after school."

"But did you see him today?"

"Sure I did. I 'member 'cause I seen a couple of guys pick him up and drive away with him."

"Did it look like they were taking him away against his will?"

"Huh?"

"Were they kidnapping him?"

"Don't think so, Mister. He didn't try to run away or nuttin' so I guess he knew 'em."

Most boys of this kid's age knew the make, model and year of every car on the road so I asked him, "What kind of car were they driving?"

"Was a big, black '47 Buick Roadmaster."

Isabel moved closer to the kid, "In which direction did they go?"

He bobbed his head eastward. "Drove down Cannon Street, Ma'am."

I reached into my pants pocket for some change and flipped him two-bits that he nabbed on the fly. "Thanks for your help, bud."

We were rounding the corner of the school building, heading back to Iz's car, when we were grabbed from behind: Iz cried out when a muscled, hairy arm reached around her and clamped a beefy hand over her mouth. Her jittery eyes bugged out at me, pleading for my help as she struggled to get free, trying to kick at her attacker as she was hoisted off her feet. But I couldn't help her; my right arm was pinned behind me and when I tried to swing my left, my attacker grabbed it in mid-air and twisted it back so hard that I almost passed out as the pain jolted through me. I tried to call for help but only a gargle escaped from my mouth.

Arms firmly clenched behind our backs now, we were frog-marched out to that LaSalle at the curb. Its motor was running and a slim young guy in a black suit was perched behind the wheel.

We were still panting, trying to catch our breaths, when we were shoved into the rear seat; the biggest thug sat between us so he could control us by squeezing my left arm and Isabel's right. His grip felt like an iron clamp. I glanced over at her: she was gritting her teeth and her eyes were flame-throwers.

The other guy slid onto the front passenger seat. "Let's roll," he told the wheel-man who squealed the tires of the big car away from the school and headed east on Cannon Street.

I figured these guys had to be here on the Mob Boss's orders but why would Belcastro arrange such an elaborate scheme? And what could he want from us?

The driver swung over to Burlington Street where we drove through the heart of Hamilton's smoke-filled steel industry, then out to Beach Boulevard.

A few doors past the busy Dyne's Hotel, he turned onto the double driveway of a substantial, two-storey beach house on the Lake Ontario side of the road.

Isabel said, "Why are we stopping here? What –" She startled me when she cried out, "THAT HURTS!" as the big guy squeezed her arm again.

"Then shut up, Lady."

The driver parked behind a black '47 Buick Roadmaster, just as the kid at the school had said. Then the thugs hustled us out of the car and onto the side porch. A cool breeze off the lake sent a chill through me; maybe an omen of what was to follow inside.

The guy who'd been gripping my arm rapped on the side door and a grey-haired woman in a black dress opened it and stood aside as we entered. "Straight ahead," the guy said as he pushed us forward and we stumbled along a dark hallway.

We were passing a storage room and I slowed to peek in through the partially opened door: a boy's bicycle and some sports equipment: hockey sticks and a goal net as well as a number of cardboard boxes stacked along the back wall. Our guide stopped and reached past me to close that door then prodded us forward into a spacious living room with floor to ceiling windows that afforded a stunning view of the wide beach-front and Lake Ontario beyond. I could see an old duffer walking a French poodle along the water's edge and a long freighter steaming in to pass through the canal into Hamilton Harbour.

This large room was furnished with bamboo armchairs and a couple of matching sofas; on the walls were colourful scenes of Mediterranean beaches – someone was singing in Italian from a floor-model radio/record console in the corner of the room.

Vincenzo Belcastro rose from his chair, turned off the music and waved us closer. I'd only seen him in photos and from a distance at the Innsville, so I had the impression that he was of medium height; but standing before us now, I saw that he was as stubby as a fire hydrant – but with a muscular body and steely grey eyes that could pierce your skin with a sharp glance.

When Danny caught sight of us he wriggled out of his chair and ran over to stand between us, gripping my arm like a drowning swimmer. The big guy who brought us in, now stationed by the doorway, moved to grab the boy but the Mob boss held up his hand. "Leave him be." Then he motioned with his head toward the doorway, "I'll call you when I need you."

He pointed to a two-seater sofa near his chair and we sat with Danny wedged in between Isabel and me.

"We finally meet," he said, then he zeroed in on Isabel. "I'm acquainted with your father. We've done a little business together."

She sizzled him a sharp look, "Yes, I'm aware of how you blackmailed him into selling you his property near Burlington at a bargain-basement price."

He raised his eyebrows then waved his hand in dismissal, "It was just business."

No-one spoke for a moment and he was content to let us stew. I broke the aching silence, "Why are we here?"

"I wanted to clear the air between us," he said. "And also to establish a few ground rules for our future relationship."

Isabel leaned forward, fire sparking from her eyes and I recognized that same feisty woman who was giving hell to J.B. O'Brien in his office. "We don't want any kind of relationship with you. And you can stick your ground rules into your hat."

Her outburst didn't seem to faze Belcastro one bit. In fact, a tiny smile flickered across his lips before he continued in a soft voice, "I enjoy a feisty woman; one who's not afraid to speak her mind. But I can't allow you folks to pry into my business affairs. So I've invited you here to discuss our mutual concerns."

I glanced at my partner, her face now aflame and I knew she was about to explode again. I cleared my throat to get Iz's attention then I forced myself to speak without emotion when I turned to Belcastro. "You have a different definition of 'invited' than we do. And it's time for some straight talk now. We didn't choose to be here and I can assure you that we have no 'mutual concerns' other than the release of this boy. We were kidnapped, man-handled, and we're here against our wills - all three of us. And we know how you threatened Isabel's father into selling you his property by sending him that 'package' to nudge him along."

I took a deep breath and leaned closer to him. "But scaring the wits out of a young boy and using him as a bargaining chip is despicable." I slowed my speech, delivering my words like fiery arrows, "It's not the behaviour of an honourable man."

He blinked as my remark struck home but he waited for me to finish my little speech. "We're asking you to back off now– to leave this boy alone and the family he's staying with during his mother's absence. They've done nothing to harm you, nor do they intend to interfere in your business. As for Isabel's father – well, if he wishes to continue his association with you then that's his decision."

I leaned back on the sofa, reaching behind Danny to place my left hand on Iz's shoulder as we waited for Belcastro to respond.

His eyes moved back and forth between us, taking our measure. Beyond that, I couldn't read his body language. Then he looked at Danny, trembling beside me, and that gave me the heebie-jeebies.

When he finally spoke, his voice was quiet, his words coated with ice. "I can assure you that I *am* an honourable man."

I realized that I'd struck a nerve with my remark and I forced myself to bite my tongue until he'd finished.

"We do have a code of honour that my men and I live by," he said. "And I grant you that it's different than yours." He shifted in his chair and leaned forward, his dark eyes levelled at me. "Nevertheless, I'll agree to release this boy on the condition that you keep your noses out of my business."

I'd suspected that he might make some kind of offer but it stunned me that he wouldn't have demanded more from us. It made me wonder if his offer might serve some other purpose that we didn't know about, maybe part of some larger plan.

Our eyes locked for a tense moment and I felt a shivering sensation streak down my body all the way to my toes.

Then Belcastro got to his feet and we followed suit, still stunned by his offer to allow us to leave. He took a couple of steps toward me and grasped my arm, lowering his voice to an ominous whisper, "I spoke on the telephone with a certain Mrs. Black in Miami earlier today and she agrees that my proposal to you is a fair one. But if you don't keep your end of the bargain, remember that I know where this boy's now living."

I felt a volcano roiling inside me. That 'certain Mrs. Black' to whom he referred was my mother who'd abandoned me all those years ago – just as Ida Lucas had left young Danny to fend for himself. But I wondered, did Belcastro actually contact my mother? Or was he just using her name to secure my agreement. She was now an important figure in the North American mob hierarchy. And no doubt he knew that I wouldn't be anxious to contact her to verify his claim and put myself in her debt.

I could feel Danny shivering beside me and I squeezed his hand. Isabel leaned forward, close to Belcastro, "How can we trust your word – after what you've done today – snatching this boy, scaring the wits out of him?"

He darted a sharp glance at her. Then his eyes locked onto mine in an iron grip and I gulped as we awaited his response. He took a step closer to me and my knees began to wobble. When he spoke, his voice was firm, sounding like Moses delivering the Ten Commandments. "You have my word."

He made a move to leave then stopped himself. "I almost forgot," he said and withdrew a small envelope from his jacket pocket. "Before I left New York, Ida asked me to see that her son received this note. Of course, I had to open it to protect my interests."

Danny gripped my arm with both his hands as Belcastro leaned forward extending the envelope toward him.

I whispered a few words of encouragement to the boy and he extended his shaking left hand for the envelope as though it were a stick of dynamite with its fuse sparking. Then he whispered a hesitant, "Thank you, Sir."

Belcastro nodded to Danny then walked smartly from the room without another word.

A moment later, the driver looked in and motioned for us to follow him out to the car.

We sat on the back seat with Danny between us.

"Back to the school?" the guy said.

I leaned forward, "If it ain't too much trouble,"

When I sat back, Danny linked arms with Iz and me;

staring straight ahead, his lips sealed, still shivering from his ordeal.

I nudged his arm and when he looked up at me, I pointed to the letter, now clamped in his right hand. "You can read your mother's letter,"

"I'm afraid to. It might be more bad news."

I silently agreed with him. "Would you like me to read it?"

He bobbed his head and passed me the envelope. Inside was a single sheet of note-paper, the same Waldorf Astoria Hotel stationery that Trixie had received. And a crisp, American hundred-dollar bill was paper-clipped to it. Danny squeezed my arm with both his hands and I held the letter so that Iz and he could also read it.

> *Danny,*
> *I finally caught that big break I've been waiting for all my life. I'll be living in New York and maybe Cuba for some time. I don't know when I'm returning to Hamilton.*
> *But you're a smart kid and I'm sure you can figure things out, just as I did at your age.*
> *Here is some money to get you started.*
> *Good luck,*
> *Ida*

His hand began to shake as tears dribbled down his cheeks. When he removed his hand from my arm, I returned the letter to its envelope and passed it back to him along with my clean handkerchief. "Let's talk about this later."

We continued to Hess Street Public School in guarded silence. As we got out of the car, the driver held me back and lowered his voice, "Mr. Belcastro had a son about the same age as this kid here but his boy died from measles a coupla months ago. The Boss liked the way you been helpin' this kid, havin' him looked after by that Negro family. That's probly why he let you walk away with just a warning. But if it was up to us guys, we woulda dumped you and the red-head in the Bay for stickin' your noses into our business."

Back at Grace's home, Danny was as welcome as the prodigal son; hugged and kissed by Grace and Samantha. And the two boys jostled and bumped one another in the way that young guys released their tension and showed their affection for one another.

Samantha whipped together a light supper of cold beef sandwiches, salad and potato chips. While we ate, I kept my eye on Danny. He only nibbled at his food so I had to eat half of his sandwich. After supper, Vincent couldn't stop peppering him with questions: "Did you see the Mob boss? What did he look like? Did he have a gun? Did they tie you up? Were you tortured?"

Grace was able to steer the boys' interest toward their hockey scrap book and the adults drifted back into the kitchen.

I described our meeting with Belcastro at his beach house and the contents of Ida's letter. "Isabel and I agreed to butt out of the Mob's business in exchange for Danny's release. He's got his mother's letter now and I'm sure he'll show it to you when he's ready."

"I think you're right," Grace said. "We won't pressure him and he'll talk about it in his own sweet time."

The boys' bedtime came and went before their nervous energy ran out of gas, then Grace took them upstairs to bed.

It was late when we returned home but Iz got busy in the kitchen. "A cup of tea before we go to bed, Max? I still need to unwind."

We sat in the living room, our stockinged feet parked on the coffee table as we sipped our tea. "I was proud of the way my fiancée got her Irish up and put that Mob boss in his place."

She gave me a sly smile. "All in a day's work, my dear. Be warned."

"Yes, ma'am."

We were quiet for a moment and I waited for Iz to speak. "This must be such a terrible shock for the poor kid." She was squinting her eyes as she looked up at me. "It made me wonder how you coped when your mother abandoned you."

I didn't answer right away – this wasn't my favourite topic. "I didn't do well at first and I'm not proud of my behaviour back then. It must have been difficult for Frank's parents too. But they made me feel at home and I gradually became part of their family. I hope it'll be the same for Danny. It would be great if Grace were to keep him but that's a big responsibility for her family."

Isabel snuggled closer beside me, kissing my cheek then whispering in my ear, "I hope our children never experience anything as frightening as Danny has. I believe you gave him the courage to get through his scary experience, sweetheart. I think you're going to be a great dad."

My heart was pounding in my chest, swelling with love for her and I was thinking, yes, maybe she's right. Perhaps I could become the father that I'd never had. And I did seem to be on the same wave-length as Vincent and Danny and other kids I'd met … then it occurred to me that maybe I experience the childhood that I never had while I'm with these youngsters. And that felt good to me – damn good.

I inhaled several deep breaths, letting them out slowly, a new optimism now flowing in my veins as some of the unhappy memories from my youth began to loosen their grip on me. And now, with Isabel at my side, I was determined to become the best damn husband and dad in Hamilton – if only the Mob would let me.

END

ACKNOWLEDGMENTS

Once again, my sincere thanks to Cat London for her patient and incisive editorial guidance. I'm especially grateful to Julie McNeill at McNeill Design Arts for another terrific cover.

And thank you to Maureen Whyte at Seraphim Editions who started me on this path to fame and fortune. Maureen published the first three books of the Max Dexter Mystery series. However, the print publication business in Canada has become so difficult that Maureen has ceased publishing new books. I wish her well in her future endeavours.

Sadly, since the publication of *A Family Matter* in 2017, Margaret Houghton, Hamilton author and historian, has died. Her series of books on *Vanished Hamilton* remain an inspiration to me and sharp-eyed readers who knew her might see some of her wit in my recounting of Hamilton lore.

To the loyal readers of the Max Dexter Mysteries, I hope you enjoy Max's adventures in this fourth of the series. Long may he reign!

PREVIOUS BOOKS IN THE MAX DEXTER MYSTERY SERIES:

A PRIVATE MAN

"July, 1947. And hotter than hell in Hamilton."

So begins Chris Laing's intriguing novel about the exploits of Max Dexter, former RCMP officer. Max, recently discharged and limping from a serious war injury, returns to his hometown to run his own private detective agency. But he gets more than he bargained for when takes on a missing person case for a wealthy client. Soon more than the weather is making things hot for Max and his new assistant, Isabel O'Brien. They become involved with arson, art theft, murder and money laundering. The trail leads through the mansions of high society and along the gritty streets of Hamilton to a rip-roaring climax in Niagara Falls.

"There's a secret ingredient added to the polished story, character and dialogue: Laing has made the local setting a fully-fledged character ... *A Private Man* is a top-shelf winner." Don Graves in *The Hamilton Spectator*.

A Private Man was a Finalist for Best First Crime Novel, 2013 awarded by Crime Writers of Canada.

A DEADLY VENTURE

Max Dexter and his easy-on-the-eyes assistant, Isabel O'Brien, are back in the second book of this post-WWII historical mystery series set in Hamilton, Ontario. When Max's artist friend, Roger Bruce, is arrested for murdering one of his clients, Max and Isabel attempt to track down the real killer but Hamilton mobsters attempt to discourage them.

As in *A Private Man*, the city itself continues to be a vital part of the action. And readers wondering if Max and Isabel might be get together romantically, will be watching closely as the pair high-step their way through this quick-paced tale.

A Deadly Venture was the winner of The Kerry Schooley Award in 2015 presented by the Hamilton Arts Council.

A FAMILY MATTER

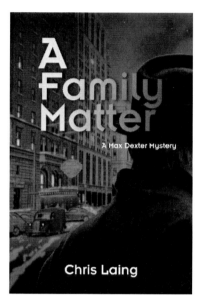

The last person I wanted to see again was my mother. But she turned up anyway"

In this, the third book in the Max Dexter mystery series, Max's mother returns to Hamilton after an absence of twenty-some years. Max is not anxious to meet with her — why should he after she'd abandoned him as a child?

To make matters worse, Max and his assistant, Isabel O'Brien, are still in the cross-hairs of crime boss, Dominic Tedesco, who's looking to even the score. But a bigger question looms. Is she involved in an internal Mob war now heating up and about to explode? Now, a week before Christmas in 1947, Max and Isabel are feeling the heat from those dark forces who don't believe in "Peace on Earth".

"Chris Laing's latest book, *A Family Matter*, is the third in his series on Hamilton private eye Max Dexter. From the first page it picks you up and drops you down into the Hamilton of 1947. With vivid writing and an encyclopaedic knowledge of what was going on in post-war Hamilton Laing transports you to a real place where you can almost taste the food and feel the grit. For anyone who likes crime fiction and local history this is the ideal read. I couldn't put it down." — Margaret Houghton, Hamilton author and historian

"1940s Hamilton obviously lives again, thanks to your writing."— Stewart Brown, former entertainment reporter for *The Hamilton Spectator* and author of *Brant Inn Memories*

ALSO AVAILABLE BY CHRIS LAING:

WEST END KID

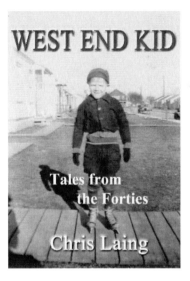

An imaginative collection of nine short stories about a group of kids growing up in Hamilton, Ontario during WWII. This collection of exciting and bittersweet stories will bring a smile to your face or maybe even a tear.

- Root for the newspaper boy who suspects one of his customers is a Nazi spy.
- Will Annie Rooney lure the boys into joining the safety guards?
- Is there a thief on the loose at the boys' summer camp?

These coming of age stories capture the spirit of the times and reflect the age-old challenges facing every generation.

"Insightful and Funny: Being an old guy, I was attracted by 'Forties' in the title. North American kids at that time could not grasp the seriousness of World War II; it just added another layer of excitement to the business of growing up. Chris Laing's detailed recall of the period is astonishing in itself. The added bonus is his ability to capture both the difficulty and the fun kids have working out their own problems and their bafflement with adult behavior. A nostalgic and rewarding read." (A review from "Haligonian" on amazon.ca)

ABOUT THE AUTHOR

Chris Laing is a native of Hamilton, Ontario. He worked in private business for 20 years before joining the Federal Public Service where he served in the Department of the Secretary of State and the National Museums of Canada in Ottawa until his retirement. Since then, he has expanded his long-time interest in detective stories from that of avid reader to writing in this genre.

For more information please visit: www.chrislaing.ca

Made in United States
North Haven, CT
17 December 2021

13077347R00145